MAFIA QUEEN

L. STEELE

1

Don't leave me, even for an hour, because then
The little drops of anguish will all run together...
-Pablo Neruda, Sonnet XVII: Love

Karma

"Michael!" I scream as his head disappears under the water, "Oh, my god, Michael!" I spring up, ready to dive into the water, but Luca catches me around my waist.

"Let me go," I yell. "Michael! No! I have to go to him."

"If you jump into the water now, you know what he's going to do to you, right? He'll not only imprison you, he's going to kill you, and then you'll never be able to see your sister again."

Summer. My breath hitches. *Summer.* I need to get out of here so I can return to her. It's what I want, right? It's why I had first stabbed Michael, then run away from him when he'd been occupied with fixing food in the kitchen. Michael... I swallow. What if he doesn't survive though? I stop struggling and Luca releases me. He focuses on steering the motorboat.

I stare back at the receding jetty as the boat pulls away. The wind whips my hair into my face and I shove it back.

"He needs help." I turn to Luca, "Please, call someone. We can't leave him alone."

He hesitates and I clutch at his sleeve, "Please Luca, please, he's your brother."

"It's too damn dangerous," he says through gritted teeth. "It'll place me squarely at the scene of the crime."

"If you don't call someone and have them help, then if he does recover, he'll never forgive you."

"He'll never forgive me anyway." Luca twists his lips, "Asshole will kill me... That is, if he does survive."

"He will survive," I say fiercely. "He has to. Please, Luca, please call somebody and have them send help. You know I am right in asking this."

He stares at me a second longer, then swears aloud. "Steer the boat, will you?" He jerks his chin toward the steering wheel. He steps back and I slide into the space in front of the steering wheel.

I grab it, and when he's sure that I have a firm grip, he releases his hold on it.

He pulls a phone out of his pocket, and presses a few buttons, before holding it to his ear. "Seb?" He snaps, "There's been an accident, at the island. Michael needs help."

He listens for a second, as the other man speaks, before interrupting, "I know because I was there, and now I am not. You'd better send someone before it's too late."

He disconnects, then tosses the phone overboard, before turning to me, "This call was a big mistake."

"It wasn't," I insist. "I don't want him to die, and neither do you."

He laughs, the sound bitter, "Asshole wouldn't die that easily. He's probably clambering onto the beach as we speak and walking toward the house."

"I hope so." I swallow as he crosses over to me and takes the wheel again. I shift to the side, sink down onto the seat next to him. "I didn't mean to...hurt him," I murmur. "I only did it out of instinct. I didn't mean for him to..." I can't say the word aloud. He's not going to die. He cannot die and yet, I can't take my gaze off of the island that's growing smaller by the second. What am I hoping to see? Michael emerging from the water and walking onto the shore? Michael standing there and watching me as I leave him? Michael with his dark gaze, his chiseled features, those massive shoulders, his wide chest... Michael with his edgy, dark scent that I will forever carry with me. *Michael. Michael. Michael.* A sob bubbles up and I don't stop the tears that run down my cheeks.

"I wish I could go back," I wrap my arms around myself. "I wish I could make sure that he's okay." I am mumbling to myself but Luca hears me.

"He has a harder head than you can imagine." He speaks in a loud enough voice that I can hear him above the sound of the breeze, "Look, I know it's unfortunate that you had to do what you did, but at least, you are free of him now."

"Am I?" I swallow, "He's going to come after me."

He has to come after me. He has to live. He has to survive what I did to him. Surely, he can't have drowned. I didn't hit him that hard, did I?

"You're right," Luca concedes, "it's the first thing he's going to do once he's back on his feet. You likely bought us a little time though."

I keep my gaze focused on the island until it recedes from sight. My heart stutters, a cold sensation stabbing at my chest. *You'll see him again. You have to...* I shake my head. What is wrong with me? I had spent the entire time I was on the island trying to get away from him. And now that I have managed to escape, I can't stop thinking about him.

This is for the best. I am leaving him behind and going to find my way back to my own life, to my home... That's what I want, right? Home... I swallow. Why does it feel like I left my home behind? That house on the island that belongs to Michael...isn't home. Not my home. It's his place. I am... His? *No, no, no.* I rub my fingers across the ring on my left hand. That...is his... The mark of his possession with which he branded me. Just as he imprinted his touch into every cell of my body, engraved his name into my soul, stamped the sensation of his thickness in between my legs. I squeeze my thighs together.

Shit, this is not the time to think about how brutally he had taken me that last time. How he had eaten me out, before positioning me on my hands and knees, then gripped my hips, holding me immobile as he had thrust into me from behind. Oh, my god, he had...taken me, owned me with the sureness of his movements. He had consumed me, imprinted himself into the most intimate parts of me. He had changed how I perceive myself... He had reached deep into the recesses of my soul and forced me to confront who I am. A woman whose tastes are extreme, someone who needs to be challenged, and subdued, someone whose spirit can only be matched by the lord of the underworld himself. A beauty who needs her beast, her master's hand upon her head as he calms her, his fingers around her neck as he chokes her, his tongue inside her soaking wet channel as he licks into her and—"Bloody hell," I swear aloud and Luca glances sideways at me.

"You okay?"

I chuckle. "What do you think? I may have murdered my husband, who I only married a few days ago, after he kidnapped me, by the way," I squeeze my fingers together, "so no, I am not okay."

I stare forward, into the wind that slaps my face. My eyes sting and a pressure knocks at the backs of my eyes. Shit, I've made a complete mess of this. Not only had I fallen for my kidnapper, aka my husband, but now I can't stop thinking that it was a mistake I managed to escape from him. What the hell am I going to do about this? I turn to Luca, "I need to call my sister as soon as possible."

"I am afraid that may not be a good idea."

"What do you mean?"

"It means if you call her, you'll only be putting her in danger."

"What danger?"

"As you said, he's going to come after you. No doubt about it... Unless..." He raises a shoulder, "Unless he didn't make it out of the water."

"He made it out of the water," I snap. "He is alive, dammit."

"Either way, it's best we lay low until we know for sure."

"Shit," I squeeze my eyes shut, "I'm so screwed if he's alive."

"And if he's dead—"

"No," I open my eyes and turn to him, "don't you dare say that."

He blows out a breath, "As you wish. My saying it or not is not going to change the reality though."

"I am aware," I mutter, as I scan the shoreline that's coming up. "Where are we going, by the way?"

"To a safe house in Bagheria."

"Bagheria?" I turn to him, "Where's that?"

"It's the town to the east of Palermo."

"Shouldn't we, maybe, try to move further away from Palermo? I assume he is well known in town and must have contacts around the city. Besides, doesn't he know about all of your safe houses?"

"Not this one." He shoots me a sideways glance, "You're no pushover, are you?"

Only when it comes to him. Oh, Michael, what have I done? If you don't make it out alive I... I'll never forgive myself. My chest hurts and I rub at the space above my left breast.

"You okay?"

I shake my head. "Not really," I mutter. A trembling seizes me and I wrap my arms around myself. If he were here, he'd fold those massive arms around me, he'd pull me into his chest, tuck my head under his chin, and rub my back... Right before turning me over his knee and spanking me for what I did.

Luca shrugs off his coat, and hands it over to me. I glance at it and shake my head. It feels wrong. I shouldn't be wearing another man's jacket. If Michael saw it, he'd kill Luca... Or maybe not. Luca is his brother, after all. Although, after this incident... Yeah, not sure how Michael will treat Luca after this... And shit, why are my thoughts back on him?

"Take it." Luca, places it around my shoulders, "You don't want to catch a cold. Michael would never forgive me if anything happened to you."

He stiffens as if realizing what he's just said. "Not that you'd want to have anything to do with him, now that you've escaped him."

Right. I stare at the shore as Luca continues to steer the boat. Half an hour later we reach a jetty that juts out from the approaching beach. As soon as we draw up next to the wooden platform, he cuts the engine again. Then walks around to the far end of the boat—the end from where I'd raised the oar and brought it down on *his* forehead.

Shit. Unable to process my feelings, with tears welling up in my eyes, I press my face into my palms and feel my body convulse. What the hell have I done? How the hell am I going to live with myself if something happened to him? My heart feels like Michael used his dagger to cut it into pieces and now part of it is missing, and he has it. My belly twists itself up in knots. I gasp for breath as I allow the tears to flow down my cheeks... Until the sobs finally subside. The boat jerks, and I glance up to find Luca's tethered the boat to the jetty. He's watching me with a look of sympathy on his face.

He bends over, holds out his hand, "We need to move fast, Karma, before one of his guys finds us."

Right. I take his hand and he helps me onto the jetty.

Two hours later, we draw up in front of his safe house on the outskirts of Bagheria. Someone had been waiting for Luca with a car at the jetty.

He'd glanced at me, and had seemed surprised. Following a flurry of conversation in Italian with much gesturing from the other guy, he'd finally seemed pacified and had left. Luca had driven us here.

I glance at the small, single-story cottage. It has white-washed walls and a fence around it. It's no more than a cabin, really. In the distance, I can see the hills, but there is nothing else around the building on either side.

I follow him inside and he scans the space, then points me to one of the bedrooms at the end of the corridor. "That's yours. Why don't you shower and see if you can find some extra clothes in there, left by some of the other guests before us?" I glance at him and he shrugs. "May as well get comfortable; not sure how long we're going to have to stay here."

I strip off my clothes and the knife—Michael's knife that I had taken with me—falls to the ground. I stare at it and tears prick my eyes again. I pick up the knife, still in its sheath, press it to my cheek. The dark, edgy scent of him instantly fills my nostrils. My chest hurts and my heart, what's left of it, feels like it's going to burst. *Oh, Mika, Mika, what have I done? Mika!* Nothing I do will ever make up for what I did to you. How am I going to live with myself after what I did? How am I going to live without you, my darling? My one and only. My...other half. My soul.

My fingers tremble, the knife slips from my hold and I manage to catch it before it hits the floor. I straighten, place it on the small table near the window, then stagger to the bathroom. By the time I shower and change, my tears have dried up somewhat. There is a hollowness in my stomach and it's not only from hunger.

That's how it is...eh? Doesn't matter that you have committed a heinous crime. Your body still needs sustenance to live, apparently. Live for what though? And for whom? A pressure builds again at the backs of my eyes and I swallow down the ball of emotion that has lodged in my throat. I walk into the kitchen to find Luca is heating up something in a saucepan.

He turns when I walk in, "It's stew, the best I could do."

"It smells of…" I walk closer, then pause next to him and peek into the contents, "It has seafood?" I frown, "I'm allergic to it."

"Ah, well." He blows out a breath, "There should be some bread in the bread basket and cheese in the refrigerator."

"That works for me." I pull out the bread and cheese, and make myself a sandwich. By the time I sit down, he's served himself a bowl of stew and poured us both coffee from the *moka* coffee maker he'd had going on the flame.

We tuck into our food, and when I am done, I lean back in the chair. "Any word on…"

He shakes his head, "I put out some feelers earlier, reached out to some old contacts who are in touch with the Cosa Nostra. They've heard nothing."

I frown, "But you dumped your phone—"

"I keep a few spare burners here."

"Right," I shuffle my feet, "so you were saying that they've heard nothing about Michael," I swallow. "Is that good or bad?"

He shakes his head, "I am not sure."

That familiar cold sensation stabs at my chest. My fingers tremble and I place my palms in my lap. "This doesn't feel right." I mutter, "Shit, if something has happened to him, I… I…" I jump up and begin to pace, "maybe I should go back and make sure he's okay. I'm his wife after all, aren't I—"

"Do you think he's going to see you in that role after everything that happened?"

My shoulders slump. "I guess not…but I wish I could do something. Why did I have to hit him that hard? Why did I have to panic? Why couldn't I have just…pushed at him or something instead? Shit, this is not good. This is so not good." I wring my hands together in front of me, "There must be something I can do?"

"The best thing you can do is stay here, until things cool off."

I pause, turn to him, "Can I call my sister?"

He shakes his head, "It would be best not to."

"Maybe I could text her and let her know I am okay, just so she doesn't worry."

"Can you put that off for a little while longer? It's best for you not to communicate with anyone."

"You think Michael and your other brothers could track us?"

"They have access to some of the best hackers, so yeah, that would be correct." He places his spoon down in his bowl and leans back. "Thanks to me, the Sovrano clan is technologically the most advanced of all of the families."

"Why did you fall out with Michael?"

"Why didn't I fall out with him?" He chuckles without humor, "From the time I was born, I've known that he was the older brother, the heir, the man who would one day be the head of the clan, the one slated to take over from the Don, when the time comes. It's always been all about him… As long as I am in his shadow, I'll never be able to come into my own."

"So, you saw me trying to leave, and seized the opportunity—" I scowl. "What were you doing at the boathouse anyway? I thought Michael asked everyone to leave."

"I don't obey my brother in everything." He smirks.

"So, you stayed on after everyone left?" I tilt my head, "Why would you do that?"

"Let's just say, I had a hunch that not everything would be fine in paradise."

"You thought I'd make a run for it?"

"I thought…that you'd try something." He rubs the back of his neck, "To be honest, I didn't think you'd get as far as you did. Michael is way too sharp, too alert. I didn't think you'd get past him." He regards me with a shrewd gaze, "But then, I don't think he realized how smart you really are."

"Is that a compliment?"

"One-hundred percent." He grins and his face lights up. I blink. Shit, this man is truly handsome, in a very classical kind of way. He has the same kind of presence as Michael. To be fair, all of the Sovrano brothers do, as do their half-brothers. But in terms of charisma, Luca is the closest to Michael. Both fill up the room in a similar way. Both have that determined set to their features, the stubborn tilt to the jaw, that sense of dominance that rolls off of them in waves and which screams that they can be very persuasive and authoritative, and that once they set their minds on something, nothing can deter them. Only he isn't Michael.

I slip back into my seat at the table, and he tilts his head. "I am guessing my brother was so taken in with you, he lowered his guard. It's why you managed to slip by him."   .

I play with the ring on my left hand. I'd tried to remove it in the shower, but of course, the stupid thing is stuck. It refuses to come off. "I think you are wrong," I murmur. "Michael never lets his guard down. Not with anyone, and certainly, not with me. It was a lucky break that I found myself alone and decided to risk running out of there."

And the main reason I'd wanted to leave was because I'd thought that I could be pregnant. How had I forgotten about that? Shit, it's too early to test if I am. Probably… I could wait for a week or more at least, right?

And what if I am pregnant and he's dead? Does that mean I would bring up my child without a father? I am keeping the kid, of course. That's assuming I am pregnant. And if I am not… Well then… I'll still be on my own, after Michael… How could I ever be satisfied with anyone else?

Shit, he's the one, isn't he? Why have I taken so long to recognize that? But this doesn't change anything… Even if I had stayed… Even though it felt like he was changing his attitude toward me… Even then, he was a man on the wrong side of the law. He kills people for a living, for hell's sake. He's not the kind of man I'd want as the father of my child, or the type of person, I'd want to stay married to… Right?

And yet… I'll never be able to forget him, or how my body had responded to him. Shit, shit, shit. I lower my chin to my chest. If only things had been different. If only he weren't in the Mafia and I had met him in more normal circumstances. If only I'd had a chance to date him like a normal person, and...

Who am I kidding? Michael would never be a 'normal' anything. That man has too much dominance, too much self-assuredness, too much confidence… Too much everything. He'll always stand apart from others. He'll always be different… And fact is, the sense of danger that clings to him only adds to his allure. The darkness in him… It's what drew me to him. The sense of menace that hovers about him… It's a turn on. The fact he wields instruments of violence like other people employ pens…is what appeals to me.

So why is it that when I thought I was pregnant, my first instinct was to escape from him? Is it because I think I can't trust him when it comes to my child? Because I don't know how he would react when he finds out? Because I know he'll want the child… And then what?

Would he forget about me completely after that? Would he want me to conform to the role of wife and mother and lose my individuality completely? Shit. What's wrong with me? A dull headache drums at the backs of my eyes and I draw in a breath. "I think I need to lie down," I murmur.

Luca glances up at me, "Everything okay?"

"Yeah." I swallow. "It's been a long day. I need to get some rest."

I am woken up by the sound of knocking on the door. "Karma," Luca calls out, "you awake?"

I clear my throat, "I am now." I glance around to find the sun's rays slanting through the open window. I reach for the lamp near the bed and turn it on.

"Can I come in?" he calls through the door.

I sit up in bed, glad I had worn all of my clothes when I'd gone to sleep. "You can come in now," I reply.

Luca enters, and his features are set.

"What happened?"

"I'm afraid it's not good news," he murmurs, as he leans a hip by the doorway.

My heart begins to thud and my throat closes. "Wh...what do you mean?"

"I managed to connect with one of my team and..."

"And...?" My voice cracks. I fold my fingers together, narrow my gaze on him, "Tell me, please, what did you find out?"

"It's Michael, he..." Luca swallows, "he didn't make it."

2

Karma

I stare at him, trying to process his words, trying to make sense of what he said. "What do you mean he didn't make it?" I throw the covers off, jump out of bed. "Who did you speak to? Maybe they are lying. He made it out of the water. Of course, he did. He had to... You, yourself, said that he's not easy to kill, that he had a hard head, remember? He has to be alive. He can't be dead."

Luca shakes his head, "I'm sorry," he murmurs, "Seb announced it at a meeting of the family. He is taking over temporarily as Capo."

"No," I shake my head, "no, no, no, it can't be true." The world tilts and my vision narrows as black spots creep into my periphery. I blindly reach behind me, find the edge of the bed, and sink back down. "Please, no. Not M...Michael." My voice breaks and tears flow down my cheeks. I cover my face in shame.

How could this have happened? How could I have killed my...own husband...the possible father of my child? The only man who's ever touched that part deep inside of me, who awoke that darkness in me... Who made me feel so alive. Who...loved me. I know he did. I saw it in his eyes right before he went under. My throat closes, my ribcage tightens and something hot stabs at my chest. Oh, Michael, Michael, what have I done? I grab my pillow and squeeze it tightly as I begin rocking.

How can I make up for this? What can I do to repent for my mistake? For having killed the man I love? My fingers tremble and a cold sensation grips me. I lift my head and glance up at Luca, "I need to go."

"Where?" He frowns.

"To Michael."

"Karma," he squats down in front of me, "Michael's gone."

"His funeral." I clear my throat, "I need to attend his funeral."

"No," he scowls, "that's impossible."

"Why?" I set my jaw. "He was the Mafia Capo. Surely, they'll have a big funeral for him so everyone can pay their respects."

"If you go, if they see you, you're dead."

"I'm dead now," I reply. "I feel like I cannot breathe, cannot live after this. I..." I hunch my shoulders, "How can I live with myself after what I've done? I...need to go see him and apologize to him. I can't go on without seeing him one last time."

"That is a seriously bad idea," he groans. "If, by some miracle, you get near the casket, they will shoot you on sight, or worse."

"I don't care." I firm my lips, "I must see him, so I can tell him..." *How sorry I am for what I did.* Not for having run away, but for having hit him with that oar. He'd been coming after me. He'd wanted to pull me... his wife away from leaving with another man. He hadn't been thinking straight when he'd jumped in the water and swum toward me. He'd lost his control, shown his weakness and I... I had taken advantage of it.

Damn it, I have to see him one last time. See his gorgeous face, kiss...his forehead, say my goodbyes... I'll never get closure for what I did, but... I can, at least, tell him how I feel. Tell him that I love him. I owe him that much, surely. "I..." I swallow, "Please, I need to go to him."

Luca rises to his feet and begins to pace, "Not only are you going to die, but you are going to get me killed with you."

"You don't have to come with me."

He snorts, "What if my brothers stop you?"

"I'll take my chances."

"Shit." He digs his fingers in his hair and pulls at it. "Seems even here, my dear *fratellone* beat me at my own game. I left the clan so I could find a way to challenge him, to show him I could wield more power than him. Just one time, I wanted to sit at the same table as him and show him I was his equal, but the bastard had to go one up on me here, too." He stops, turns to me, "And if I refuse to help you now, he'll probably never forgive me. The *stronzo* will probably come back to haunt me."

He blinks, and I swear, I can see his eyes shining with unshed tears. Guess he loved his brother in his own way. And me… How had I loved him? As a wife, his submissive, his slave…his…captive? All of the above? I bite the inside of my cheek. "So, you'll help me?"

He stares at me, then jerks his chin.

Some of the tension drains out of my muscles. "I'll probably need to get a different set of clothes."

He stares at my red-colored hair, "That's probably a good idea." He tilts his head, "We'll need to get there first thing in the morning."

"So soon?" I stiffen. Not that it would mark a difference, but I'd hoped I could get some kind of a grace period, at least a day to prepare?

"The Mafia prefer to bury their loved ones as quickly as possible. So, we need to get to the vigil before tomorrow evening."

Right. "Will you help get me the clothes I need?"

He blows out a breath, then nods.

"Thank you," I murmur

"You won't be thanking me when my brothers come after you."

I set my jaw. "We'll see about that."

3

Karma

"So, this is it?" I stare through the window of the car. In front of me are the steps to the church and next to it, and tucked a little to the side, is a small chapel, which is where the wake is being held, apparently.

Michael's wake. Mika... My husband's wake. Shit. Is this really happening? Could I have been married and widowed in such a short time? I toy with the ring on my finger, then cover it with my palm. It's the last piece of Michael I have with me and I am never going to let go of it. Unless... I press my palm to my stomach. Unless... I am carrying something else of him.

"You don't have to do this, you know." Luca's voice cuts through my thoughts. I turn to find him staring at me, a concerned look on his features.

"I do." I bite the inside of my cheek. "Thanks for bringing me here."

"I would have come in with you...but—"

"No, that's fine." I clutch at the edges of the thin black veil that covers my face. "This is something I need to do myself."

He looks as if he is about to say something, then stops himself.

"Good luck," he murmurs as I push open the door of the car and step out.

A gust of wind whips my hair about my shoulders. The veil flattens against my features and I run my suddenly damp palms down the skirt of my dress. The handbag in the crook of my arm bumps against my side. Luca had bought it for me, along with these clothes and sensible black shoes. None of which is my style... But at least, the colors are more to my liking. Not that it matters... Where I am going... There's going to be only me and my conscience...and him. The body of my dead husband.

Shit. I stumble, then right myself. I take a step forward as the car drives off, leaving me alone. I glance around the empty street, then move toward the chapel. My heart begins to thud and my pulse rate ratchets up. What am I going to do when I see his body? Will I break down completely? God, I hope not. I simply want his forgiveness, that's all. I mean, what happened wasn't entirely my fault, right? It's he who had wronged me first. If he hadn't kidnapped me...then forced me to marry him... I wouldn't have been pushed into doing what I did. I was right in wanting to escape him... It's just... I hadn't expected my actions to result in such a horrible conclusion, okay?

I square my shoulders, move toward the chapel, push open the door and step into the dimly lit interior. The door shuts behind me with a snick. I glance about the space... Take in the mourners in the pews. It's not as full as I thought it would be.

Two men stand on either side of the coffin. All in dark suits, all with their heads bowed. I recognize Seb, and next to him is the broadest of all the Sovrano brothers. The men on the other side of the coffin are the brothers who resemble each other so closely that I'd placed them to be twins the first time I saw them at my wedding. A motion to the far left draws my attention. Antonio, Michael's bodyguard stands to attention by the side door. I glance to the other side and find another of his brothers by the other exit.

My heart begins to thud. Will they stop me from seeing him? Please, God, please don't let them.

There's a man standing in front of the coffin at the end of the aisle. He bows his head, stands silently for a few seconds. As I near him, he straightens, then makes his way back to his seat.

A woman glances up as I pass, then looks away. The rest of the people face forward, their features solemn.

As I approach the coffin, the biggest of the Sovrano brothers glances up. His jaw stiffens as he watches me approach, but he makes no move to stop me. As if alerted by my presence, Seb, then the twins, turn their gaze on me. The hairs on the back of my neck rise. The tension in the air seems to ratchet up. My stomach ties itself in knots, and I feel light-headed. I force myself to put one foot in front of the other until I draw level with the first pew.

When none of the men stop me, I step up to the coffin. A dull pressure presses down on my temples, and I squeeze my eyes shut. *Oh, Michael, Michael, what have I done?* I tuck my elbows into my side, then force myself to open my eyes.

Strong features, square jaw, that hooked almost aristocratic nose, those thick eyelashes that fan against his cheekbones... The wide forehead with a bruise at his temple... The bruise that I had caused when I had hit him with the oar. I curl my fingers into fists, take in his thick hair that is combed back except for that errant strand in the center that curls over his forehead. No longer will he reach up for it and push it away. No longer will he glare at me with those beautiful blue eyes of his. A sob wells up... Oh, Mika, Mika, I am so sorry for what I did.

A trembling grips me. My legs threaten to give away and I dig my heels into the ground to steady myself. I raise the veil and push it back over my head, then touch my fingers to my lips, and press my fingers to his forehead. I lean over him. A teardrop slides down my cheek, plops on his forehead. That's when his eyelids snap open.

4

Michael

"Hello, Beauty." I bare my teeth, and her fingers tremble. Her gaze widens and color drains from her face.

"No," she shakes her head, "No, no, no."

"Yes." I allow my smile to widen, "Oh, yes, my darling wife."

"It can't be." Her voice wavers and her chin trembles. She looks like she has seen a ghost, which of course, is what I am to her now. It should be almost comical. I should enjoy just how terrified of me she seems to be, except…The throbbing pain at my temple where she had smashed the oar into me insists that she is real, and standing in front of me, arm outstretched. Tears glisten on her cheeks.

She opens and closes her mouth, grows even more pale.

She pulls back her arm and I swoop my hand out and grab her wrist. She sways; her eyes roll back in her head. Her legs seem to give way and she slumps toward the floor. *"Che cazzo!"* I growl as I sit up, then leap over the side of the coffin. I catch her before she hits the floor, then pull her into my arms as I sink to the floor. She's so fucking tiny, and weighs next to nothing. Has she lost even more weight in the last day?

The veil flutters back from her face, the paleness of her skin a stark contrast to the black of the fabric. Dark shadows circle her eyes, her cheekbones seem too prominent in her face. She seems too still, too lifeless. I hold a finger under her nostrils. The warm rush of air flutters across my skin and the tension drains out of me.

Seb approaches us. He squats down next to us, peers up and into my face, "You okay, *brother*?"

His voice is gentle, and fuck, if that doesn't annoy me. "My wife tried to kill me. Do you think I am okay?"

He hesitates and I blow out a breath. "Get them out of here," I jerk my chin toward the gathered crowd, "and the lot of you can leave too."

"But," he frowns, "Mika, you're still in pain."

My heart hurts. And I don't understand why. She hit me on my head, which has no connection with my chest. So why is it that there is a heavy sensation crowding against my ribcage?

"Go," I snap. "Keep watch for Luca. He's bound to turn up again for her."

My grip on her tightens. My own brother had deceived me. He'd helped my wife escape from me. He'd prompted my wife to hit me with the oar, then he'd sped away as I had sunk under the waves. He'd left me for dead. They both had. So why the hell had she returned? To gloat over what she'd done? It doesn't make any sense... And yet, I had counted on it.

A part of me had been confident that she would come. It's why I'd had Seb formally announce my death to my clan. Luca has a mole on my team... Someone leaked the news out to him. I'd had my suspicions... and I had been right. He'd taken the bait and believed the news. He must have told her and she'd asked him to bring her.

I'd vacillated over whether she would show up, but ultimately, I'd been sure she would, just to make sure I was dead. To ensure that she was rid of me... I'd been right. Which also means that she spent the night with my brother. Fucking, fuck. A growl rips out of me, and Seb frowns, "We need to get both of you out of here, before the Don gets wind of how you staged your own death."

"Not now," I snap.

His frown deepens, "Mika, you're not thinking straight. Let's take her and get you both home. Get you looked at by a doctor and—"

"Not-fucking-now." I glare up at him, "Leave."

"But—" He raises a hand and I cut him off.

"That's an order." I glance around to where my brothers watch me with varying expressions of concern on their faces, "All of you, out. Now."

Seb nods, then rises to his feet. He glances at the other men, who exchange glances with him, before they begin gathering up the guests and ushering everyone out the door. Finally, the door closes, leaving me alone with my errant wife. My beautiful wife who'd dared defy me. Who'd spread her legs for me then walked away from me. Who'd taken my brother's help to escape from me. Who'd left me for dead then come back to gloat in my face.

The silence deepens, intensifies... A beat, another, then her eyelids flutter. I take in her features as she opens her eyes. She gazes up at me, and for a second, there's a genuine smile on her face. As if she'd fallen asleep next to me then woken up from a dream. Then a line appears between her eyebrows as her forehead furrows. A look of pain... of helplessness... hopelessness?—taints her gaze.

"Mika..." she whispers, "oh, Mika, is it really you?"

Her green eyes hold mine. She reaches up to touch my cheek and I pull away. She swallows and her frown deepens. "You're alive," she murmurs.

"Are you surprised?" I tilt my head, "Wishing I was dead, Beauty?"

"No." She shakes her head. "No, no, no. If you were dead, I don't know how I would have survived."

"You seemed to have done quite a good job of it, considering you left with my brother."

"Luca?" She frowns.

Anger crowds in on my mind. "You dare say another man's name in front of me?"

"But, it's not like that."

She reaches for me again and I growl, "Don't fucking touch me."

She pauses, bites on her lower lip, and of course, my gaze is drawn to her mouth. Her gorgeous mouth with which she had sucked me off. Her tongue, her lips, the very teeth that she uses to chew on her food... All of it which belong to me, and she had dared turn her back on me. She'd left with another man... And not just any man, with my own brother. She had betrayed me. She had used my own blood to get back at me. My guts twist and heat flushes my skin. My vision narrows. "Did you sleep with him?"

"With who?" She scowls, "What are you talking about?"

"Enough," I roar and my voice echoes through the space. "I have had enough of your act, the way you always use your sassy attitude to disorient me. The way you stand up to me and mislead me."

"Me mislead you?" She sets her jaw, "I've always been straight-talking with you, buster. I have always told you what I wanted, have always been upfront with how I wanted to be able to choose for myself."

"And you chose to leave me for dead."

She pales.

"Tell me, did you enjoy looking into my eyes while I went under the waves and imagine that you'd never see me again? Did that gladden your heart, Karma? Did that make you happy? Did you and your lover laugh about it while he fucked you last night—?"

Her palm connects with my cheek and my face snaps back. The sound of the slap echoes back, enveloping us in a cocoon of rage before it fades away.

She gulps, then covers her mouth with her palm. "I'm sorry," she whispers, "so sorry. I didn't mean that."

"I don't believe you."

"Please, Mika, please believe me when I say that Luca didn't touch me. I left with him, only because he happened to be there and I wanted to escape. He was just a means to get out of there. That's all."

"And you hitting me and leaving me for dead, are you sorry about that too?"

"More than you can imagine." She tries to sit up and I release her. She tips up her chin, gazes into my face, "You have no idea how much I hated myself. How I couldn't believe I'd done that. How I hoped that you would survive. How I prayed that you would be alive."

"Seems your prayers were answered."

"And I am so grateful," she swallows and a tear runs down her cheek. And my heart stutters; it fucking stutters. What the fuck? The woman is barely back for a few minutes, and already, I am softening. Already, I can't wait to take her home, to my bed, to make love to her, and ensure she never leaves me again... And... I am setting myself up for a fall again. The next time my back is turned, what guarantee do I have that she won't do the same thing? How do I know that she won't murder me in my sleep? Why does the thought of clashing with her send all of my senses into overdrive? Adrenaline laces my veins. My groin hardens.

"Turn over," I growl.

She blinks, "Wh…what?"

"On your hands and knees; turn over."

5

Karma

Anger rolls off him in waves, and the hair on the back of my neck rises. I stare up into his blue eyes and shiver. There is no trace of the man who had fucked me... Or of the man who had married me... Who had made pancakes for breakfast for me. This man is closed up and hurting. He is raging at me... At the world. He is wounded, and not just from the physical hurt I had caused him. It's the fact that I had run away from him. That I had taken the little bit of empathy he had begun to show me, and turned it against him. I had left him...had insulted him, had ground his ego underfoot as I had run away from him... With the help of his brother, who had also betrayed him. It probably convicts his brother doubly in his eyes.

I chew the inside of my cheek, "I... I know you are angry with me Mika, but —"

"You know nothing." His voice is low, so hard... So harsh that a shiver runs down my spine. He is shutting down, taking any emotions that he may have once shown me and shoving them so deep down that I might never reach him again. My heart begins to thud in my chest and my pulse rate spikes.

"Mika, please listen to me."

"You may call me Michael," he commands as he takes in my features. Those blue eyes are cold fire, like ice-chips, that glow with the reflection of the northern lights.

A cold sensation coils in my chest. I have to reach him. I can't let him build up these walls between us again. If he does, I'll never be able to get through to him.

"Mika… I mean, Michael," I tip up my chin, "I have something for you." I reach for my bag and he grabs my wrist.

"Don't fucking touch that."

"I just want to return something that I took from you."

"Oh?"

I nod, "If you'll only let me open my handbag."

He releases me, only to snatch my bag from me.

Jerk.

He opens the handbag, pulls out the knife, then throws the bag aside.

"Did you think you could stab me again?"

"No, Michael. It's not that; its—"

"Shut the fuck up," he growls. "I don't believe a word you say. Do you know how much this knife means to me? Is that why you took it?"

"Michael, please. Please, let me explain."

He laughs, "If you think you can tell me what to do, you have another think coming."

"Oh, for heaven's sake!" I curl my fingers into fists, "Will you, for one second, stop posturing and let me explain, you macho asshole?"

He stills, then looks me up and down, "You, clearly, have no attachment to your life. It's why you marched in here, and with my knife on you."

"That's what I am trying to explain to you." I swallow, "I came because—"

"Shut up," he snaps, "just shut the fuck up. I have had enough of your tricks, you pathetic excuse for a woman."

I pale, "Thought I was your Beauty."

"I was, clearly, mistaken."

"I am not, though."

He frowns, "The fuck do you mean?"

"There's a reason I returned, and with your knife." I swallow, "I want you to use it on me."

He sneers. "How many lies can you tell? It's a record, even for you."

"It's not a lie," I say through gritted teeth. "Seriously, haven't you been listening to a word I am saying?

"No more tricks," he growls, "turn around. On your hands and knees, or I'll make you do it."

"I'll do it… Just… I want you to use your knife and—"

He grips my shoulder, applies enough pressure so I am forced to turn around. I push up on my hand and knees, then flinch when he taps the outside of my thigh.

"Spread your legs," he says in a hard voice, and fuck me, but my knees go weak. Moisture beads my core and my pussy clenches. I slide my legs apart, or as much as the skirt of my dress will allow.

I hear the sound of him moving, the scrape of metal on metal. I turn, glance at him over my shoulder, in time to see the glint of light off the blade. He swoops down. I flinch, then cry out when I feel him slice through the skirt of my dress. Cool air assails the heated flesh of my thighs.

"Wider," he growls. "Part your thighs."

I obey, slide my legs apart, even as my core dampens further. What the hell is wrong with me? Why do I find his rough handling of me, the thought of him taking me right here in this church… Which is, technically, a blasphemy… Why do I find that so much of a turn on?

I sense him move a second before the blade nicks my skin. I whimper, feel the draft on my pussy lips and know he's cut through my panties.

Silence descends and I can feel the blood pumping in my ears. My heart beat ratchets up further, even as a sinking sensation crowds in on my chest. My belly twists and more moisture slides down my inner thigh.

I hear the jingle of his belt, the rasp of his zipper being lowered, and all of my nerve endings seem to catch fire. I push up my butt, knowing he'll spot the small movement…but I don't care. I am horny for him. I want to feel his thick, fat cock inside me. I want him to take me, to fuck me, to prove to me that he is alive. To show me that I am still worthy of him. Bloody hell. I squeeze my eyes shut. Why am I so ready to degrade myself like this? I lower my chin… Wait… Wait as he grips my hip.

I sense him move closer, the heat of him enveloping me, holding me in a space where there is only me and him.

"Stay still," he commands as his hand moves.

I glance over my shoulder in time to watch him slice through the dress at my hip. He rips the fabric apart, and cool air strikes my hip, a second before a lick of pain slices through me. I huff, crane my neck, to find his hand moving. What the hell? The breath rushes out of me. He's carving something on my hip. Another tingle of pain crawls up my spine.

"Michael," I groan, "what are you doing?"

He doesn't answer, continues to cut into the skin over my left hip. More pain sears through me and I bite down on my lower lip. Whatever he is doing… I deserve it. More than deserve it. At least, it shows that he heard me. At least, this means he cares about me enough that he is marking me.

He digs the knife deeper than the previous times and I stop the cry that bubbles up my throat. I taste blood and realize I have bitten down on my tongue. I swallow down the urge to sob, tilt my chin up. I can do this. I can get through this. If it means, in the end, Michael will forgive me… Can he forgive me? Will he forgive me?

He wipes the blade on my sleeve, and I turn again in time to see him slide it into the sheath.

I draw in a breath, only to cry out when fire slices through me. I dart my gaze to where he scoops up the blood from my freshly cut skin, then he teases my backhole with it.

Fear grips me. "Michael, please," I swallow, "please don't."

He glances up at me, "Are you saying no?" His voice is cold, as remote as his gaze. His shoulders are bunched and his chest planes seem hard enough that if I touched him, I am sure I'd come away hurt… And bleeding… More than I am now.

"Well?" He raises an eyebrow, "Say the word and I'll back off."

I swallow, then jerk my chin.

"What was that? I didn't hear you?"

"I…" I swallow down the ball of emotion that threatens to clog my throat. "Yes," I reply and am glad my voice doesn't waver. "Yes. I say yes."

He instantly slides his finger inside my puckered hole and a groan spills from my lips. I feel myself tense around the intrusion, and draw in a deep breath. In, out, in. I force my muscles to relax as he moves his finger in and out of me. He adds another finger and I stiffen. It's already too much, too soon. Shit, how am I going to take all of him inside. He pulls out of me completely, then slides both fingers back in.

"Open for me," he commands and the sound off his voice shivers over my skin. My pussy clenches and warmth sears my skin. He brings the fingers of his other hand to my pussy, then slips them inside my soaking channel. He scoops up the moisture, drags it up to my backhole, smears it around the entrance. He adds a third finger, and I throw my head back.

"Omigod, omigod," I chant as he thrusts the three fingers in and out of me. In and out. He pulls them out, then a blunt something nudges at my back entrance. "No, not yet, please, Michael," I burst out, and he pauses.

"Do you want me to stop?" His voice is remote, so standoffish, almost bored.

I stiffen, turn to stare at him over my shoulder. He holds my gaze as his features take on an impenetrable look. I have come this far. I can do this. If this is the only way to get through this, then I am going to let him fuck me in the arse. I wince, then steel myself. Tip up my chin, and shake my head. "No," I say in a firm voice, "I want you to take my arse. I want you to bury your thick, hard cock inside my—"

He pumps his hips and breaches my backhole.

Oh, bloody hell. I dig the heels of my palms into the ground, grit my teeth against the strangeness of the sensation. I won't lie, it's painful, and weird…and feels unnatural… It feels like… I have something up my arse… Which I do. I swallow down the stupid giggle that bubbles up. Jeez, that's what comes of having a stupid sense of humor. It takes me by surprise at the most inconvenient of times. He grips my hips, and I sense him stay still as he allows me to adjust to his size.

Then he reaches around and cups my breast. He tweaks my nipple with such ferocity that a groan spills from me. The trembling starts at my toes, creeps up my legs and what the hell? I can't already be coming. Not so soon. He releases my nipple, only to slide his hand down to my clit. He plays with my piercing and my pussy instantly clenches. Jesus, God. I had no idea, that I could respond with such intensity when my piercing was tugged. A warmth builds in my core. I draw in a breath and that's when he slips inside me further. So full. So… Packed… How do I even describe the sensation? A tingling sweeps up my spine as he pulls out of me. He reaches down to play with my pussy lips at the same time that he thrusts forward.

A burning sensation coils deep inside and I yell out as he hits a spot deep inside me. My eyes roll back in my head and oh, my god… What the—what is that? How is it that this is even more intense than the time he fucked me before? My knees protest and pain shivers up my thighs, meets that gnawing, yearning, sensation that coils in my core. He pulls out, then begins to fuck me in earnest. He thrusts into me and I shudder. He pulls out once more, then lunges forward, impales me with such force that my entire body bucks.

"Michael," I groan, "Oh, my god, Michael."

"That's it," he says in a hard voice, "you scream my name, every time you think of coming, you get me?"

I nod.

He thrust into me again, hitting that spot deep inside me again and sparks go off behind my eyes.

"Michael," I whine, "Please, Michael, please."

He propels himself forward with such force that I almost fall over. It's only his grip on my backside that holds me up. A burning sensation radiates out from where he cut into me and heat sears out from where his cock, once more, hits that secret space in my core. The feel of his big hands on me as he impales me, yet again, makes me feel like I am a puppet being moved around in a fashion designed to give him the most pleasure, even as I surge toward my climax.

With each thrust, my breasts jiggle, my muscles coil, and that tension at the base of my spine tightens, hardens into a knot. The trembling grows more intense, sweeping up my thighs, up my back. That's when he pulls out of me.

What the—?

I glance over to find he's already on his feet. He tucks himself inside, zips himself up, and tightens his belt.

"What are you doing?"

"Leaving." He saunters past me and I stare at that tight behind of his. Those powerful thighs, clad in a custom-made suit, those shoes made of the finest leather… H-o-l-d on. "What the hell?" I yell, "Why did you stop?"

"Because I can?" He snaps his fingers in the air, "With me."

I stare, "What do you mean, *with me*?"

He pauses, then turns to rake his gaze over me, "On your feet; walk toward me. You do understand English, don't you?"

Asshole. That prick… That complete, wanker. Here I am, getting all emotional, ready to do anything for him… Hell, I had done everything for him. I let him take me in the arse, in the middle of the goddam church, and this is what he does? He...fucking pulls out before I can come. I scramble up to my feet, aware of the dampness between my thighs, of the sorry state of my dress. I stomp after him as he walks out of the church. There are two cars parked in front of the church.

As we approach them, Seb walks over to Michael, followed by his other brothers.

"Did you get him?" Michael asks.

Seb shakes his head. "He hasn't shown up, not that I blame him. He'd have known that you would shoot him, if he did."

They don't mention him by name, but they have to be talking about Luca.

"Or worse, you could ask him, why he did what he did," I burst out.

Both men turn to me. Seb glances at me, then averts his gaze. I look down at myself and heat flushes my cheeks. The skirt of my dress is in tatters. The bodice is not torn, but it's clear from the creases on it, not to mention how my veil is half off my head, what Michael and I had been up to. And I don't even have an orgasm to show for it, damn it.

Michael... He simply takes in my features, before he turns back to Seb, "Take her home."

"Xander, Christian," he nods toward the twins, "follow me. Massimo," he jerks his chin toward the biggest of his brothers, "I'll meet you at Venom. You too, Adrian."

The remaining brother nods.

Michael walks off in the direction of the Maserati parked on the road.

"Wait!" I call out, "What do you mean *take me home*? Where are you going?"

He ignores me as he opens the door to the Maserati. Anger flushes my skin and I march over to him, "You'd allow someone else to take your wife home?"

He slides into the driver's seat, then glances up at me, "You left me, Beauty, and now you expect me to treat you as my wife?"

"Yes," I snap.

He chuckles. "Your innocence knows no bounds, *amore mio*."

"I am not innocent."

"And I don't see you as my wife anymore."

"What then?" I scowl. "What do you see me as?"

"My whore."

6

Michael

I lean back in the chair in my office at Venom. By rights, I should be out there in the room that my crew and I use whenever I am here. But that hit to the head did a number on me. Because I refuse to take the painkillers, the pain is a constant heaviness behind my eyes. And the last thing I want to face is the constant throb of the music that pulses through the nightclub. I bring the glass of whiskey to my lips, then hesitate. I am taking antibiotics… And the doctor had warned me not to mix alcohol with it… But fuck that. You only live once… And right now, I need something to take refuge in. Considering I just disowned my darling wife…

I had called her my whore… And that look of absolute shock, and confusion…and sadness on her face… *Merda*, it had almost gutted me. I tighten my grip around my glass, then bring it to my mouth and throw back the contents. The whiskey burns a path down my throat. It hits my stomach and heat explodes in my gut. Too bad it doesn't fill the emptiness that tears at my insides. I place the glass on the table with a thump, just as the door to my office opens. The throbbing of the music instantly fills the space. Seb walks in, followed by Massimo, then Adrian, Christian and Xander. The door shuts, cutting of the music once more.

Porca miseria! "What the hell are you *stronzi* doing here?"

Massimo bypasses Seb and walks over to the bar on the far side of the room. He grabs five glasses, then stalks over to me. He places the glasses on my desk, and fills them up, including mine, before placing the now empty bottle on the surface. "*Salute, fratellone,*" he clinks his glass with mine. Christian and Xander snatch up a glass each. Only Seb folds his arms across his chest as he glowers down at me.

"What?" I frown, "The fuck you looking at me like that?"

"Feeling guilty, yet?" His gaze intensifies.

"Why should I feel guilty?" I take another sip of my whiskey, then survey the contents of my glass, "If this is about her—"

"Of course, it's about her," Seb growls. "The state in which you left her... You should be ashamed of yourself."

I chuckle, "And you are...what? An expert in relationships?"

"More than you, for sure." He rocks forward on the balls of his feet, "I understand you are upset with her. I know you can't get over the fact that she injured you and ran—"

"Injured me and left me for dead."

"You weren't even close to dying." He mutters, "You have too thick a head for that."

The wound at my temple pulses as if in agreement. The headache behind my eyes increases in intensity. "She spent the night alone with Luca," I snap.

"She'd never be unfaithful to you," Xander insists.

"No, she'd only leave with another man." I fold my fingers at my side.

"You need to be more broadminded in your outlook, *fratellone,*" he chides. "Luca would never betray you."

"And yet he did."

Xander grimaces, "Have you asked her if anything happened with Luca?"

I glare at him.

"So, you are just drawing conclusions based on circumstantial evidence?"

"Are you saying I should forget what she did to me?" I retort.

"I am saying that you should treat her with a little more sensitivity."

"Wait until you meet a woman who gets under your skin, and then have her try to kill you and walk away from you, then we'll see how you react."

"You admit that she's gotten under your skin?" Massimo smirks. "Also, are you sure she tried to kill you?"

"I admit to no such thing." I scowl, "I only meant that as a figure of speech, and," I roll my shoulders, "as to the answer to your second question, the intent in her eyes when she took the oar to my head was very much about keeping me away from her."

"Maybe she panicked? Maybe the oar slipped from her hands?" Seb strokes his chin, "Have you considered that?"

"She hit me on the head. Twice." I tip up my chin at him. "Trust me when I say that the second time it was clearly with an intent to hurt."

"Maybe she was simply trying to hold you off. After all, you did kidnap her and force her to marry you."

After which, I had made love to her. Damn it, those couple of days when it had been just the two of us on the island, when we had consummated the wedding… When I had fucked her and poured my heart, my soul…my cum into her. When I had made her mine, and…she…she had walked away from me.

"*Vaffanculo!*" Christian smirks. "The Capo has tied himself up in the proverbial knots."

I glower at the most irritating of all my brothers. Christian has the face of a model and the IQ of a genius. It's one of the reasons he's in charge of my finances. The man keeps all of the figures in his head, never gets his numbers wrong. He's also blessed with eidetic memory, which means he has a nearly perfect photographic memory of most things he sees. Which he often uses to his advantage. Which means he's normally one step ahead of most people. Just not me… Except this time, he, clearly, is.

I reach for the bottle of liquor, then frown. "You guys finished my booze."

"You're on antibiotics, aren't you?" Christian scowls at me, "Should you even be drinking?"

"Mind your own damn business, *fratellino*," I growl.

He raises an eyebrow, "Clearly, fighting with the wife has not improved your disposition." He chuckles.

"Hey," I glance around at their faces, "thought you guys were on my side."

"We are," Adrian murmurs. "It's why we are looking out for you, *fratellastro*."

"Seems more like an intervention," I growl.

"What if it is?" Seb drawls, "It's not every day that our Capo goes a little *pazzo*." He smirks, "I wouldn't miss this chance for anything."

"Fuck off." I snap, and Seb chuckles.

"Seems you're angry enough to use English swear words instead of your favorite Italian ones."

I glare at him and he merely laughs. "*Gesù Cristo*," he drawls. "This entire incident is affecting you more than expected, huh?"

I take in the expression on the faces of all the guys... There's concern and worry, and yeah...love, too. Fuck, I must be completely losing it if I am actually picking up on the emotions from them. Not that I've doubted for one second that my brothers and stepbrothers love me... Okay, so maybe with Seb, I've always been sure that he wouldn't hesitate to betray me. Seems I was wrong. Seems I should have been more worried about my wife...and my own brother. Luca... Damn it, how could Luca do this to me?

"You are thinking about him, aren't you?" Xander's voice interrupts my thoughts. Of course, my youngest sibling picks up on my disquiet. He always has been the most empathetic, the most instinctive of all of us.

I glance toward him, then nod.

"It's okay to share your concerns with us, big brother." His lips curve, "We are family, after all. It's what we do. We talk, we air our worries, we support each other."

"That's what I thought about Luca, then see what he did."

Silence descends, then Seb straightens to his full height. "Take that back," he growls. "Everyone in this room is here because they are concerned about you."

"I don't fucking need it," I snap. "Speaking of, I am tired of this emo shit. Why the hell don't you guys get the hell out of here?"

No one moves. They stare at me, with varying degrees of sympathy. *Merda*, that's all I need, my own family looking on as I fall apart in front of them. To think, I had sworn never to appear weak in front of them. I stare down into the depths of my empty glass, "*Che cazzo*, I need a refill."

Xander steps over to the bar. He leans over, grabs a new bottle, then walks back to my desk. He opens the bottle, tops me up, then places the bottle within reach.

I toss back the liquor and it burns its way down my throat. My stomach protests; my head spins. Shit, maybe I'm weaker than I thought. Guess that blow to the head really has affected me more than I realized.

Xander leans forward on the balls of his feet, "You're hurting, *fratellone*. It's understandable. Losing both your wife and your most trusted confidant and friend in one go, it's not easy. Hell, it would have felled a lesser man."

"But not me," I declare.

"Not you," he agrees, his expression filled with understanding. Shit, that's all I need: Xander's particular brand of empathy that would most definitely prompt me to open up about my fears, my anger, my utter disappointment at having been cast aside... Like I don't mean anything to either of them.

Just like my father has only ever needed me to the extent that he needs an heir, someone to carry on his legacy. He's never seen me as anything else. Not his son, not a child who needed someone to look up to. He had been my hero and he had destroyed me. Abused me until I had begun to look at the world with suspicion, with mistrust. Something that I have never gotten over. No wonder her turning her back on me had sent me into such a spiral. And now, I am psychoanalyzing myself. Shit, enough of this emo shit.

I set down my glass, then rise to my feet, "If you all think I am going to sit around and commiserate about the loss of my wife and brother, you are mistaken."

"They are lost," Xander frowns, "but not in the way you are making it out to be. They just need to be guided back home. You need to only speak to them, Mika. Open your heart to your wife; talk to her. Reach out to Luca; forgive him; talk to him about how the two of you can work together and —"

"Enough," I snap. "You're the youngest, Xander, and in many ways, the most thoughtful of all us. You mean well. It's why I have tolerated your reactions thus far. But don't think you can tell me what I should feel toward what happened. They both betrayed me, and shall be suitably punished."

"But —"

I raise my hand. "I am leaving, now, and I expect the lot of you to track down Luca, and bring him to me." I turn to Seb, "You have ten days."

7

Karma

I raise my face to the shower. The hot water pours over me, down my back. My side twinges. It's where he etched something into my skin. To be honest it hadn't hurt too much—not then, not now... Probably because I have a high pain threshold. Also, because he hadn't pressed down too hard. It's more like he had scratched the surface of the skin enough to draw blood. Bet that had made him happy. He probably wanted to see me bleed. After all, I, too, had drawn blood when I had smashed the oar into the side of his head. I wince. Jesus, we really are all wrong for each other. The way we are hell bent on causing each other pain... It's just plain unhealthy.

I'd tried peeking in the mirror earlier but hadn't been able to make out what he'd etched into my skin. What could that alphahole have written there? The man who had pretended to be dead just so, what...? So he could surprise me with that crazy back-from-the-dead enactment in church? Jesus Christ, the man has a macabre sense of humor. That particular scene was like something out of a horror flick... Or some gangster flick I saw with Summer, who's name I can't quite remember, in which the guy rises from the coffin and proceeds to gun down everything in sight.

Not that Mika had had a gun on him. He didn't need it. Not as long as he had his knife. The knife I returned to him; the one which, clearly, has sentimental value for him, even though he hasn't mentioned anything about it to me. The man has more secrets than the Mafia. Oh, wait, he *is* the Mafia. I shake my head. Seriously, I am losing it.

Seb had driven me here to Michael's house, making sure to keep his gaze averted most of the way. He'd paused only long enough to guide me up the steps of the house and to what looked like a spare bedroom. He'd told me someone would be along shortly with clean clothes for me. Before leaving, he'd also warned me that I shouldn't try to escape because the place is guarded.

Question is, do I want to escape? Frankly, right now I am not sure about anything. I had had my chance to be rid of him, and I had come back. I pause in the act of massaging the shampoo into my hair. If I had stayed on with Luca, it was only a matter of time before I could have gone home. But I hadn't. I'd insisted on returning for Michael's fake funeral. Had I wanted to make sure that he was really dead? Had I wanted to satisfy myself that he was truly gone? Or had my subconscious known that he was alive? That he'd grab me, and make me his prisoner again? Is that what I wanted? To be reunited with my husband?

I lower my hand, stare at the ring on my left ring finger… The ring I have grown attached to, the one that I am not in any hurry to remove. The one I consider mine. Just as he is. All mine. My capo. My captor. My husband. Shit, I really am a goner. I am half-way into falling for him… Or maybe, I am already in love…or at least, in lust with him. It had taken almost killing him to figure that out. What does that say about me, huh? Guess you have to lose something to find out how much it means to you, eh?

I rinse off my hair, shut off the water, then dry and wrap a terrycloth robe around myself. I step out and glance about the bedroom. It's smaller than the room I'd had at the villa on the island, but the view is still breathtaking. I walk to the window, glance at the sea that stretches out in front of me. Clearly, the Capo ensures that all of his homes come equipped with the most spectacular scenery.

As soon as I had stepped into this house, I'd known that this was the alphahole Capo's place. It had to be because his scent had wrapped itself around me like that of a security blanket. I wrap my arms about myself. It's crazy that, despite how horrible he had been to me at the chapel, I still...trust him? Or maybe trust is too strong a word... Let's just say that I still sense the connection I have with him. The attraction I feel for him... That mindless lust that I seem to succumb to every time I am near him. And he feels the same. I know it; I can feel it. Can sense it. Had seen the lust in his gaze when he had told me to turn around and drop to my hands and knees. Had heard the heaviness of his tone when he'd instructed me to part my legs for him.

My core clenches. My nipples bead. Shit, all I have to do is think of him and I am already dripping. Also, because that jerk had denied me my orgasm. Honestly, how dare he? If he thinks he can continue to do that to me... Well... No way, am I standing for it. He has to come to me at some point. Unless... he's fucking someone else? I curl my fingers into fists.

Still, that little encounter in the chapel had confirmed that he wants me. So why had he not escorted me back? Why had he left it to Seb to do so? The Michael I have come to know is so possessive, so primal in his ownership that, no way, would he have allowed anyone else to come near me, let alone hand me over to another man's care, even if it had been only for a little while. I hunch my shoulders, stare at the horizon...

Unless...what I had done to him, had really broken down the trust —tremulous as it had been—between us completely. Unless he really doesn't consider me as his wife anymore. No, not possible. He's not someone who would let go of his possessions. And really, that's what I am. That's what I want to be... His property. His plaything. His.

There's a knock on the door, and I jerk my head around.

A familiar face peeks through the gap between the door and the wall.

"Cassandra?" I exclaim, "OMG!" I pivot, walk over to her as she steps inside the room. I throw my arms around her. "Am I glad to see you, or what?" Okay, maybe I am overdoing the welcome a little bit, but seriously, I am just happy to see a familiar and friendly face. So what, if it's the alphahole's housekeeper?

She steps back, and that's when I notice that she's carrying clothes, and what looks like a first-aid kit in her arms.

"Are those for me?"

She nods, "The Capo instructed me to tend to your wounds."

"Did he?"

She nods, "If you take off your bathrobe, I can attend to them."

I hesitate and she holds out the clothes, "Perhaps you'd be more comfortable wearing a fresh set of clothes first?"

"Whose clothes are they?" I murmur. She opens her mouth to answer and I hold up my hand. "You know what? It doesn't matter. Either it's clothes from someone who's left them behind, or else, he'll have some dumbass explanation of how he ordered them for me or something. Either way, they aren't clothes that I stitched, so it's all the same."

She hands over the clothes, as well as underwear, complete with tags. So, he bought me fresh underwear, huh? Guess I should be grateful, but honestly, it's the least he can do for me. Besides, the thought of him buying lingerie for me feels... Intimate and somehow, right. Okay, maybe a little bit creepy, but hell, he is my husband, he knows my size, and yeah, I definitely need clean underwear right now, so I'll take it.

I accept the clothes from her, murmur my thanks, then walk back into the bathroom to change. Not that I am a prude or anything... But it feels weird just drooping my bathrobe in front of her, you know? Apparently, I have no such qualms when it comes to the Capo. Heat flushes my cheeks. Need to stop thinking about him, seriously. And considering he sent Cassandra to tend to me, he can't be all that angry with me, right?

I pull on the jeans and the T-shirt. It's all in my size, and thankfully, neither is pink in color. Or beige. Or cream. Not even the underwear, which is all black. Hallelujah. I pull on the socks, then walk out into the bedroom, where she's waiting.

"Okay, so while you are applying antiseptic to it, or whatever, can you tell me what it is?" I turn my back to her and pull up my T-shirt.

A gasp fills the air. "What the—!"

I stare at her over my shoulder, "What's wrong?" I frown at her features. She's definitely gone pale.

"What is it?" I ask again as she stares at whatever it is that he drew there.

"It's," she swallows, "it's nothing."

"It's something." I scowl, "Go on, you can tell me."

"No really, it's just, uh, a scratch."

"It didn't seem like a scratch when he drew it onto my skin with his knife."

She walks over to the bed, "Why don't you lie down on your front so I can bandage it?"

"Not before you tell me what it says."

"No," she shakes her head. "Really, Karma, you should let it go."

"You do realize that refusing to tell me what he drew on me is only making me even more determined to find out what it is, right?"

I march back inside the bathroom, turn my back to the mirror, then lift my T-shirt, twist around and try to make out what the hell he carved into my skin. I catch sight of the edge of what looks like a letter. Huh, did he write something on me? What could it be? His name, maybe? Perhaps a declaration of his love?

My heart begins to thud in my chest. Maybe he'd done it and then he'd been upset about it, and that's why he had pushed me away. My capo hates being vulnerable. It's probably why he had asked Seb to drive me here. He probably needed some time to come to terms with having bared his soul to me. That's why he had turned away from me and driven away. Yeah, that's what it is. But why would Cassandra gasp like that?

I arch my neck, trying to sneak a peek. Oh, bloody hell, can't see a thing yet. My spine protests and my side hurts. I turn back, glare toward where she is hovering at the doorway to the bathroom. "Come, on, Cassandra," I whine, "you have to tell me what it is."

"I can't."

"If you don't, I won't let you clean the wound and bandage it, and then the Capo will be angry with you."

Her shoulders slump. "Please, Karma," she says in a low voice, "you are not going to like it."

"Oh, please," I swipe my hair over my shoulder, "I am a big girl; I can take it. Besides, I have an inkling what it could be."

"You do?"

I nod, can't stop myself from smiling. "Sure, he's my husband, remember? We already had a fond reunion," I smirk, "earlier at the chapel. Trust me when I say that it won't be a surprise for me."

She hesitates.

"Come on, please, Cassandra, please," I beg.

She blows out a breath, then walks over with the first-aid kit that she places on the counter near the sink.

She begins to roll up the back of my T-shirt and I turn my head, "Well?" I scowl, "Are you going to tell me, or what?"

"Whore," she mumbles.

"Excuse me?"

"Whore." She grimaces. "He wrote, whore."

8

Karma

"How dare he!" I pace back-forth-back across the floor of my bedroom. How could he do that? After Cassandra had told me what he had scrawled across my lower back I hadn't been able to believe it. She had finally procured another mirror from somewhere in the house and had held it behind me so I could see in the mirror over the sink exactly what he had scrawled on me.

Asshole! What a fucking bastard! How the fuck could he do this? "Aargh!" Anger spikes my veins. Adrenaline laces my blood. I glance around the room, looking for something to break, but can't see anything handy. Damn him. Bet he purposely put me in this room because there's nothing to vent my anger on. I need to do something... Anything...to give vent to this frustration inside of me.

Why the hell did he do this? Is he that angry with me? Not that I don't blame him. Guess I'd be very cheesed off if someone had smashed an oar into my head, and then left me to drown... But he'd pushed me to it.

He kidnapped me first. Surely, I was justified in doing anything and everything to get away from him? I hunch my shoulders... Yeah...

No... I don't believe that rationale myself. I mean, when I had thought that I had lost him, I had pretty much fallen apart. So yeah, facts speak for themselves.

I do regret what I did. Nothing justifies what I did to him... Only, he had survived... Thankfully. So, while I understand that he is pissed off at me....

Seriously though, I still can't condone what he scrawled into my skin. Asshole had marked me...in more ways than one. And I'd thought he tattooed his name onto my body...or professed his love for me? Ha! I pivot and begin to pace again. At least, he'd sent Cassandra to take care of me, so that has to count for something, I suppose. More likely, he wanted to be sure that I don't fall prey to an infection and die. If I did, he won't have anyone to torture. No doubt, that's the only reason he had her clean the scarred skin and bandage it.

That had been two days ago. Since then, the only person I have seen is Cassandra. When I'd asked her where Michael was, she'd said that she didn't know. She'd brought my meals to my room. After the first two, I had insisted on eating at the breakfast counter in the kitchen, and she hadn't dissuaded me. I'd eaten dinner on my own earlier—Cassandra had left, saying she had to run some errands—then I had come up to my room...stared out of the stupid window, gone for a walk around the terrace until it had grown a little too chilly.

I had walked around the huge house... Even peeked into the asshole's bedroom which, holy shit...has a bed which is even bigger than the one at the villa. The bedspread is as blue as his eyes, and the wooden headboard seems to be hand-carved. The entire bed stands on a platform and dominates the room. Other than that, there's a door leading off to a closet, another door that leads to the ensuite, thick carpet on the floor, also blue, a table and two chairs by the window, another table and chair at the far end of the room with a bank of screens that indicates he worked from there.

The scent of him had been so strong and I had filled my lungs with him. Pure, one-hundred percent Capo. My body had instantly switched on—nipples pointed, skin flushed, blood rushing to my cunt, which I admit, is still wet. I had come back to my bedroom, but haven't been able to go to sleep.

Where the hell is he? Why hasn't he returned? Who is he with? Some whore... No wait, that's me, apparently. So, who is he with? Someone else? Someone he is fucking right now, no doubt, trying to get rid of the touch of my skin on his, trying to remove any trace of my scent on him, trying to bury his cock in someone else's pussy, eh? Asshole that he is.

I spin around, stomp to the door, then march down to the library I saw earlier. Maybe I can read some books. That will take my mind off of where my bastard of a husband is.

I grab a book, some stupid strategy book — *Sun Tzu and the Art of War.* Since when did the Capo read books about war? Though, come to think of it, you could apply the same strategies to Mafia business, I suppose.

I manage to read a few chapters, when the sound of the front door opening reaches me. I hear footsteps approach, then move away. I jump up, run to the door of the study, but can't see anyone. I walk out of the room, down the corridor, peek into the massive living room, which can seat fifty, maybe? Does he use it for his mafia meetings or something? What do they do during that time? Hopefully, not just sit around and shoot at each other. Ugh, I really am going by stereotypes here, huh?

I pivot, walk toward the kitchen, peeking around the doorway to find him standing at the open refrigerator. As I watch, he pulls out a bottle of beer, shuts the refrigerator door, then snaps off the cap and tosses it in the direction of the bin. It misses, hits the floor and rolls away. I step inside the kitchen and realize I am wearing sleep shorts and a T-shirt, along with a thick pair of socks. It's from the pile of clothes that Cassandra had gotten. Huh, not quite the outfit I had in mind for when I'd see him again. Not that I have anything else to wear, anyway. I pad into the kitchen, walk around the island and toward the fallen cap of the beer bottle. I pick it up and he swings around. I straighten, flinch when I stare straight down the barrel of a gun.

"Jeez," I murmur, "it's only me."

Okay, so I had come to chew him out, to rage at him, to maybe slap him, and ask him what he meant by what he did. But now that I am in his presence, surrounded by his overwhelming masculinity, that brooding heat in his eyes as he looks me up and down with no change in expression on his face, and that gun. OMG... There's something about Michael holding a weapon that's so damn sexy. Jeez, it's Summer's fault. I've been watching too many movies with her. That's why I can't do anything but gape as he slides his gun back into his underarm holster.

He tilts the bottle of beer back, chugs down half of it. The tendons of his throat move as he swallows, and I swear, my toes curl. This man, he's a walking, talking orgasm-a-minute, and no, I am not kidding, honest.

He's wearing another suit… Similar to the one he'd been wearing at the chapel, but without a tie. So, he must have changed somewhere else. At his mistress' place maybe? I grimace.

His chin sports a five o'clock shadow… Which would feel scratchy to the touch if he dragged it across the skin of my inner thigh… OMG, bet I'd come just from the friction. My scalp itches. My skin feels too tight for my body. The tanned skin of his neck looks so damn inviting. My fingers tingle and my toes curl. I bite down on my lower lip, watch as he lowers the bottle. The white bandage at his temple stands out against his skin.

"Does it hurt?" I jerk my chin toward his forehead, "It looks like it's healing nicely."

He doesn't answer, simply swallows down the rest of his beer before placing the bottle on the island. Then he pivots and leaves the kitchen. *What the hell?* I follow him up the stairs, and into his bedroom. I stand at the threshold, watch as he takes his jacket off and throws it on the bench at the foot of the bed. He sits to remove his socks and shoes, then reaches for his cufflinks, tries to unhook one.

I walk over to him, "Here let me do that."

I undo the cufflink, pull it off, then turn to the sleeve on his other arm. "Who even wears cufflinks nowadays?" I laugh lightly, "It's quite old-fashioned, actually. But then, you are Mafia. Keep forgetting you guys are still stuck in the sixties." He glowers at me. "Okay, seventies."

He frowns.

"Fine, eighties…"

The furrow in between his eyebrows deepens.

"All right, nineties, okay? Happy now?"

He snorts.

I unhook the cufflink on his other sleeve, and he stands up and steps around me. I turn as my eyes follow him. He begins to undo his shirt, baring more of that glowing tanned gorgeous expanse of his chest. My throat closes and my nipples pebble. He shrugs off his shirt, tosses it on the bench, then rolls his shoulders. I take in the sculpted pecs, the trim waist, the trail of hair disappearing into the waistband of his pants. He reaches for his belt and I swallow. He unfastens the buckle, lowers his zipper. The metallic rasp shivers across my skin. My nerve-endings pop. He shoves down his pants and his boxers in one smooth move, then steps out of them. His full, thick, hard cock stands at attention. A vein runs up the backside, leading to the engorged, angry, purple head.

I salivate, then gulp. Moisture beads my core. My palms begin to sweat and the cufflinks slide from my grasp. "Whoa!" I tighten my grasp on them. When I look up, the full blast of those icy blue eyes of his greets me.

The hair on the nape of my neck rises. Shit, what am I doing? Why had I walked in here? Oh yeah, it was to confront him about what he'd done to me. "How dare you—" I swallow the rest of the words as he wraps his thick fingers around his much thicker, much broader cock. He pumps his shaft once, twice, thrice…and I swear, his dick swells further. A bead of precum oozes from the tip. I step forward, sink to my knees and open my mouth.

9

Michael

What in the name of the *Santa Madre Maria* is she doing? I glare down at where she's positioned on her knees, her fingers still clasped around my cufflinks and linked together in front of her. Her mouth is open in that perfect 'O' that invites me to stuff my cock between her lips. To bury my fingers in her hair, hold her in place as I fuck her mouth, and shoot my load down her throat. She holds my gaze, those green eyes beseeching, pupils dilated enough, breathing ragged enough to indicate that she's turned on.

If I bent down and sank my fingers in her pussy, no doubt, she'd be dripping. Her cunt ready and open and willing to take my cock. She'd tighten her inner walls around my length, milk me, and not let go until I had come inside her, until I had impaled her and fucked her so hard that she'd feel me in her throat. Her chest rises and falls, nipples pebbled against the tiny T-shirt that stretches across her chest. Fuck me.

I begin to jerk off in earnest. Squeezing my cock from base to crown, again and again. In seconds, the tightness at the base of my spine curls in on itself, tighter, higher, until it snaps. The orgasm slams into me with the force of a thirteen-millimeter bullet. My balls draw up and I come, shooting my cum across her face, in her mouth, across her hair, her breasts.

She licks off the white ropy strands without breaking the connection of our gaze. And fuck me, but this woman... She is going to be the death of me... Correction, she had been the death of me... She has tried to kill me, not once, but twice, so far. Will she be lucky the third time? Why do I keep coming back to her?

I had managed to stay away for two full days. Two days in which I had thrown myself into work with a ferocity that had taken my brothers by surprise. Two days in which I had taken meetings separately with the Bratva and the Kane Company, had negotiated deals with both of them which would secure the future of my clan within the Cosa Nostra and cement my bid to be the next Don. Two days in which I had learned that it wasn't the Kane Company which had sent the four unarmed men who had tried to kill me a few months ago. Two days in which I had not stopped thinking about her. In which I had tried to fuck a woman in my apartment above Venom—which is where I had stayed the last two nights. I hadn't been able to get it up then. Couldn't bear the thought of any other woman touching me either. But one glance at her, one sniff of her scent and I had gone rock hard.

Fuck. What the hell is Beauty doing to me? My wife, my would-be-murderer, what kind of magic has she woven around me that I seem to find my way back to her, whether I want to or not?

"Michael," she murmurs, "you okay?"

I lower my hand to my side, brush past her. I head for the ensuite and her footsteps follow me.

"What the fuck?" she yells. "What's wrong with you?"

Something hits me on the back and I freeze. I turn to find the cufflinks on the floor between us. I glance up at her, and the color fades from her cheeks.

She squares her shoulders. "I am not going to apologize for that." She looks down at the cufflinks, then shifts her gaze to me and firms her lips. "You deserved it, the way you've been acting."

I look her up and down and she shuffles her feet. I turn, take a step forward, and she skitters back. Another step and she props her hands on her hips.

"You... " she clears her throat, "you don't scare me."

I bare my teeth, snap at her and she squeaks.

"What the hell?" She jumps back a few more steps, putting distance between us.

"You're the one who carved…that…that horrible word on my back. How could you do it, Michael, how could you?"

"Because it's true."

"What are you talking about?" She gulps, "I am your wife, Michael. Your wife."

"You didn't think about that when you left me for dead?"

"And I've already apologized to you for it."

"You think you can say sorry and it wipes away everything you did, Beauty?" I glare at her, and she pales. My cum drips from her chin, trickles down the valley between her breasts and my dick begins to harden again. Fuck, but as long as I am in her presence, I can't stop myself from wanting to be inside of her again.

"I really am sorry, Michael."

"Not as sorry as I am for having married you."

She inhales sharply, "You don't mean it."

"Don't I?" I growl, "You left with Luca. You spent the night with him."

She frowns. "I spent the night in a safehouse with him."

"Under the same roof as him."

"Yes, but not in the same room," she frowns. "We slept in different rooms."

I set my jaw.

"Is that why you are so pissed at me? You think I slept with him?"

I grit my teeth so hard, pain shoots up the side of my face.

"Nothing happened, Michael." She takes a step forward.

I hold up my hand, " I am not interested in your pathetic excuses."

"I wouldn't do that to you, Michael. You must know that."

I glance away, then back at her.

"It's because, to the outside world, it seems like I slept with him. That's what's got you so riled up, isn't it?"

I curl my fingers into fists at my sides.

"OMG," she gasps, "that's what it is. I mean, you guys are old-fashioned enough that you think you've lost face because I spent the night in the same house as another man."

Heat flushes the back of my neck. Damn her, for guessing that. She's way more perceptive than I gave her credit for.

"I swear, nothing happened between us, Michael." Her features soften. "As for having embarrassed you? I really am sorry about that." She tips up her chin, "How can I make it up to you?"

"You don't want to know."

"Try me." She sets her jaw, "I almost lost you, Michael. You have no idea how relieved I am to find that you are still alive. Let me make amends for what I did. I'll do anything to show you how sorry I am."

"Are you sure?" I fold my arms across my chest and her gaze flits over my biceps. Her lips part, and it's as if she can't stop herself from glancing down at my crotch.

"My face is up here," I drawl.

She flushes, jerks her chin up, "Yeah, yeah I know." She juts out her lower lip, "So what do you say? I'll do anything you want, and in return, you'll forgive me?"

I laugh. This woman… She has too much gumption. Does she actually think that she can manipulate me like this?

"Anything, huh?" I drum my fingers on my chest. "You sure about that?"

She shakes her head, "No, I am not." She swallows, "But I am not going to back down from your challenge, Michael. I need you to believe in me and if this is the only way to do it, then so be it."

I lower my arms to my sides, walk over to her. She flinches, then releases a breath when I pass her. I circle her, coming back to stop in front of her. "So," I drawl, "you think you have the guts to stand up to me, huh? You think I can't punish you the way I do my men."

"Oh, I know you can, and that you will. In fact," she draws herself up to her full height, "I am counting on it."

"You can't take what I have in mind, *Bellezza*."

"Oh?" She tilts her head, "Try me, Capo."

Sant'Iddio! I bunch my fingers into fists. She only has to call me by my title and my entire body strains to cover hers. To throw her down and bury myself inside of her and— I shake my head. "Shut up," I growl. "From now on, you won't speak. Not until I give you permission."

"But—"

I raise an eyebrow and color suffuses her features. "Do you wanna play or do you wanna play?"

She opens her mouth and I shake my head.

She raises her hand and gestures.

"Sorry?" I smirk, "Not sure what you are telling me."

Her green eyes blaze with a combination of anger and frustration, and fuck, if I don't want to subsume that fire inside of me, to have her spirit consume me, even as I draw on the darkness inside of her. But first, I need to find out if she can actually deliver on her word.

"Take off your clothes."

She tosses her head, then grips the bottom of her T-shirt. She tugs it up and over her head, drops it to the floor.

Her breasts, enclosed in her lacy black bra, spill out over the top. Her nipples are outlined against the sheer fabric of her lingerie...that I had bought for her. She's wearing clothes that I had picked out for her, personally. Call it a moment of weakness, but I hadn't been able to resist shutting down yet another shop in Palermo while I had searched through the lingerie on offer and chosen exactly what I wanted her to wear.

Maybe it's the blow to the head that changed my view of the world... Maybe it's that I had known that she would come back to me... Either way, my brothers had thought I was crazy to drag myself out of bed, when I had barely begun to heal, to pick out the clothes for her. But then I had been vindicated, hadn't I? She had turned up at my fake funeral and she had been shocked to see me come to life. The amazement and then the relief in her eyes when she had realized that I was alive... She couldn't hide that.

Her waist is so tiny I can span it with the width of my hands. She seems so strong, this woman, so full of spunk, so always ready to stand up to me, that I forget how fragile she really is.

And she tried to kill you.

But had she meant it? Had she been acting out of instinct...because she was as afraid of what was between us as I am? And now what? I am making excuses for her?

Che cazzo! I am making excuses for her behavior! What the hell is wrong with me? Why is it that every time I am with her, I lose all sense of myself? That I can't stop myself from wanting to wrap my fingers around her throat and pulling her close, and kissing those gorgeous lips as I play with her breasts while I thrust my hips forward so my cock nestles in its real home...between her fleshy thighs? Thighs I can't stop myself from squeezing, and leaving my mark over her creamy skin.

She licks her lips and all thought empties from my head.

"Take off the rest of your clothes." My voice cracks, goddamn it, and I clear my throat. "Do it, Beauty, now!"

She swipes her hair over her shoulder, then reaches for the waist-band of her shorts. She shoves them down, then kicks them aside along with her socks. Straightens to stand in her bra and panties. Color blooms on her cheeks. How sweet. After everything I've done to her, after how she's come apart under my fingers, she still blushes when she stands almost naked in front of me. I jerk my chin and she bites down her lower lip, and fuck me, but my dick instantly twitches. My balls harden.

I close my fingers at my sides, glare at her. "Take it all off," I snap.

She stiffens. then pulls her shoulders back. Without taking her gaze off of mine, she reaches behind to unhook her bra, then tosses it at me.

I snatch up the piece of fabric and she makes a noise deep in her throat. I stare down at her panties and her flush deepens.

"Do it, Beauty," I growl.

She tips up her chin, hooks her fingers in the waistband of her panties, and shoves them down her legs. She throws them at me. I catch them with my other hand, bring them up to my nose and inhale. The scent of Beauty fills my senses. A pulse flares to life at my temples, behind my eyelids, even in my fucking balls. Fucking fuck, this woman is doing me in.

"You are an animal," she scowls, "you know that?"

"No talking," I growl as I toss her underclothes aside, then stalk over to her. "Also that wasn't me being an animal; but this is."

10

Karma

He prowls toward me and I stumble back. He closes the distance between us even as I try to evade him. Which is stupid. I mean, I am the one who initiated this bizarre scenario, and here I am, trying to escape him. Why is it that since I've met him, all I've seemed to do is run from him as he's tried to chase me? There is something wrong with this situation... Something I intend to rectify. I've had enough of always being on the defensive. Enough of always being the one who is trying to get away from him. Why should I be afraid of him? What can he do that he hasn't already done thus far, huh? I do not fear him; I do not. My back hits the wall of the bedroom and I squeak. Jesus, so much for my pep talk.

He pauses in front of me, and my heart hammers in my chest.

One side of his lips kicks up in that smirk I hate...and love...and can't resist. My pussy spasms. Argh, stupid cunt, that's my pussy, not me. Okay, also me, for having put myself at his mercy.

A plume of heat seems to spool off of him and crash into my chest. I gasp. My throat dries. The strength of his dominance is a tangible presence that pushes down on my shoulders and pins me in place. I want to shove at him, raise my knee and bury it in his groin, kick him in the shin and try to escape him, but my arms and legs seem to be frozen in place. My fingers tremble and my toes curl as he leans in close enough for his eyelashes to tangle with mine.

He peers into my face. Those blue eyes of his are ablaze with a fire that seems to come from somewhere deep inside. I've never seen him this...turned on. This...consumed with an emotion that I can't quite place. Does he want revenge? Does he want to punish me, perhaps? Maybe he wants retribution for what I did to him. For heaven's sake, I practically killed the man. It's a wonder he hasn't tried to do the same to me yet—he grabs me by my throat and I gasp.

Oh, hell, maybe I should watch my thoughts? Maybe, that's what he meant when he said I couldn't take what he has in mind. My breath catches, my heartbeat ratchets up, and my pulse rate spikes, even as moisture pools between my legs. Shit, shit, shit. Clearly, my body is all mixed up with the signals it's getting. I am supposed to want to take flight or fight...not... Fuck. Not get turned on. Not wrap my fingers about his thick wrist as he hauls me to him and slams his lips to mine. Not open my mouth and allow him to thrust his tongue inside, tangle with mine, swirl it over my teeth, before he sucks on me as if he wants to consume every last morsel of pleasure that I can offer him.

He growls deep in his chest as he increases the pressure around my throat, even as he plants a massive thigh between my legs and cups my bottom with his free hand as he hitches me up and pulls me even closer to him. The thick length between his legs pushes into my melting core, as he begins to move me up and down the column of his thigh. The ridge of his cock grinds against my pussy as he continues to kiss me, even as he maintains his grasp around my throat.

The trembling starts from somewhere deep inside as he intensifies the action of making me ride his thigh. A moan slips from my lips and he swallows it, snarls low in his throat as if in answer. A primal mating of man and woman, of Beast and Beauty, of a husband and...his whore?

I blink. My muscles stiffen. Every part of me protests that I can't just allow him to do whatever it is that he has in mind. Yeah, so I started it, but it's a woman's prerogative to change her mind, right?

I slap at his shoulder and he only tilts his head. His gaze intensifies as he deepens the kiss until it feels like he's literally sticking his tongue down my throat. I grip his shoulders, try to push him away, but it's like trying to shove at a brick wall. I dig my fingers into his biceps...and that strength of his shimmers, coils, thrums under my fingertips. Oh, hell. I stare into his face, try to pull away, and his grip around my throat tightens. Spots of black flicker at the edges of my vision as he pulls me into him with such force that my breasts are crushed against his massive chest, and his cock stabs against my pussy lips as if seeking entry. *Not yet... No fucking way. Not until I decide I am ready to spread my legs for you, buster.*

I bite down on his tongue with enough pressure that the salty taste of blood fills my mouth. His gaze widens, he tears his mouth from mine and blood drips from the corner of his mouth. The blue of his eyes darkens to nearly black as he bares his teeth. His chest planes flex and his shoulders seem to grow bigger in size, as he slides his hand up my throat so I am forced to tip my chin up.

"Want to play dirty, is that it, Beauty?"

No, you asshole, I want you to tell me what's going on in that dark as Hades mind of yours.

I would open my mouth to answer him, but the jerk still has his fingers wrapped around my throat. Not to mention, he told me that I can't speak until he gives me permission, and annoyingly, my body, at least, seems to respond to his suggestions. Shit. I struggle against him and that shark-like grin of his widens. I swallow and fear skitters up my backside.

"I'd hoped to save this for later, but guess I don't have a choice, eh?"

I scowl at him. What the hell is he talking about? He licks his lips, sucking down the blood that smears his mouth, the blood that I had spilt. Again.

Honestly, I am not a person with violent tendencies. I mean, I fight for what I believe in, but that's only fair, right? You need to stand up for yourself, after all.

I release my grip on his shoulder, only to wrap my fingers around his wrist. I stare at him and he holds my gaze. Without breaking the connection, without letting go of his hold around my throat, he pulls back so I slip off his thigh. He loosens his chokehold just enough to spin me around, so I am pushed up against the wall. He pushes his body into mine and my entire body trembles. Heat from his frame envelops me, as he places his cheek next to mine, "From the moment I saw you, I knew you were trouble. I just didn't realize just how much I'd enjoy also being challenged by you."

I grit my teeth, push my cheek into the cool surface of the wall, as I stare at him from the corner of my eye. "You don't have to say a word, Beauty. I know what you need."

Do you, asshole? Do you have any idea how it feels like you are infiltrating my body, my soul, every part of my mind, my heart? Shit... Do you understand how threatening it is to feel so consumed by your presence, to be overwhelmed by your dominance, to want to surrender and yet not giving in? For something inside me insists that if I do... I'll lose your respect. And that... That is what I crave more than anything. To be your equal. Do you see that? Can you sense how I want to be able to meet you on your level?

He lowers his head and bites down on where my neck meets my shoulder. My pussy instantly clenches even as I throw my head back. A scream boils up, but his hold on my throat stops any noise from escaping. He slides his fingers between me and the wall, and strums my pussy lips. He raises his head, sucks on the skin that he'd just bitten, and a thrill chases down my spine. More moisture laces my core and he scoops it up, steps back, only to bring his hand up and around to slide it between my butt cheeks. I sense his intent a second before he probes my back hole.

I slap my palm against the wall as he slides his finger inside my back channel. I struggle against him, and he brings his mouth near my ear, "Shh, Beauty, trust me."

My heart beat ratchets up. I close my eyelids and a tear squeezes out from the corner of my eye. He licks it up and my heart stutters. Of everything he's done to me, that feels the most intimate. And why the hell am I crying? I never cry.

Not when my father left us. Not when I found out I had a heart condition. Not when I found out that Summer was getting married, that I was going to be alone... Not that Summer would ever forsake me or anything, it's just ... You know what I mean, right? I hadn't even cried when this bastard had kidnapped me...

So why am I feeling so overwhelmed when he licks the shell of my ear, then sucks on my ear lobe as he plants his leg between mine, forcing me to widen my stance? As he adds a second finger to the first and pushes his digits inside my backchannel. I stiffen, clench down on his fingers, and he groans. The sound is so hot, so male, so dominant that my nipples harden. My breasts seem to swell as he curves his fingers inside of me. A groan trembles up my throat. He leans in, kisses the corner of my mouth as he pulls his fingers out of me, only to replace it with something bigger, more blunt. Something that feels awfully like the crown of his monster cock.

I swallow and my throat moves against his fingers. "F-u-c-k," he growls, "do you have any idea how erotic it is to feel you swallow?"

He nudges my back opening and I wriggle against him. He wraps his fingers around my hip, holds me in place as he whispers in my ear, "Do you want me to stop, Beauty? All you have to do is tap out."

A-n-d, there it is. Him telling me to give up. To admit that I can't take what he throws at me. If I ask him to release me now, he will… and…then… I'll know I am not as strong as I think I am. But him taking my arse… Isn't that a test of my strength of character, too? I mean, it does test my arsehole. *An alphahole testing my arsehole.* I snicker, and he licks my cheek.

"I take it that means you are fine to continue?"

I scowl at him, and he kisses the tip of my nose. "Nod, baby," he whispers, "tell me you are going to keep pace with me all the way."

Shit, I am a glutton for punishment, and clearly, my inability to turn down a challenge is going to land me in a lot of pain. Fine, whatever, nothing I can't bear. I nod, and his entire body seems to harden. He kisses me on the mouth, then leans back, and propels his hips forward.

His length breaches my backchannel and a flash of pain slices through me. I squeeze my eyes shut as my muscles tense, as I push my palms into the wall, flatten my forehead against the flat surface. He pauses, allowing me to adjust to his size—as if that's going to happen anytime soon. I sense the tension radiating off of him as he stays where he is, as his cock throbs inside of me. The pain ebbs away, and a shimmer of lust licks my veins. My pussy throbs and my toes curl as he rubs his thumb across the front of my throat. A shiver crawls up my spine and all of my pores seem to pop as he leans in and kisses my cheek.

"I am going to fuck you now."

11

―――――

Karma

What the hell! What does he mean by that? I open my mouth to ask, then gasp when he pulls out of me. He pushes forward again, and this time, sinks his cock deeper inside of me. Oh, hell. Oh, bloody hell. He's filling me up, cramming himself into me, throbbing inside of me... It's so real, so vital, so full of the kind of energy that had attracted me to him in the first place. A groan trembles up my throat as he pauses again, allowing me, once more, to accommodate him. Once more, the pain fades away and a trembling starts up somewhere deep inside. Moisture beads my core, slides down my inner thigh. I glance up at him, find his attention is focused on my face as he begins to move. He pulls out, then thrusts forward and impales me with enough pressure that my entire body jerks. He retreats, then lunges forward, buries himself inside to the hilt, and hits that spot deep inside of me.

OMG! OMG! My eyes roll back in my head as he begins to slam into me in earnest. That's my Capo for you. He always fucks like he's throwing the weight of his entire body behind his action, like his very life depends on just how deeply he can ram into me, like his soul is urging him on to possess me, own me, break me. He thrusts forward, once more hitting that spot deep inside, and my belly spasms. My pussy clenches as I push my breasts into the wall, jut out my butt, trying to take him in even deeper.

"*Dio santo,*" he growls as he begins to slam into me with even greater intensity. In and out of me, in and out, he crams his entire length inside me once more and I sense his body go rigid.

My climax threatens, lapping at the edge of my consciousness, and that's when he releases his hold around my neck. The orgasm roars forward just as he pulls out of me, only to retreat. *What the hell?*

I open my mouth to protest, and that's when he turns me around to face him. He drops to his knees in front of me, then buries his head between my legs. *What the —!* I glance down just as he swipes his tongue from my arse crack all the way up to my clit. *Oh, my god!* I throw my head back and pant as he licks around my pussy lips, then curls his tongue around the nub of my clit. I dig my fingers into his hair and tug as he swipes his tongue in between my lower lips, then bites down on my clit. I cry out, feel him smile against my core, right before he plants his shoulders between my thighs, forcing them apart further, then thrusts his tongue inside my sopping wet channel. In and out, in and out, he sucks on me, slurps up the moisture that leaks from me. He laps his tongue inside my core and a moan spills from my lips. He squeezes my arse cheeks as he yanks me even closer until I am riding his face. Until my thighs clench around his ears, until I slam my head back against the wall, as I writhe to get away from him, even as I pull on his hair, trying to urge him closer, closer to my weeping center. *OMG. OMG. I am going to —*

He pulls out of me. He releases his hold on my thighs, and I stagger back against the wall. I open my eyes—uh, when had I shut them?—to find that he's walking away from me. The planes of his back ripple, the muscles of his tight arse flex as he strides away from me.

"What the fuck?" I yell, "You come right back here and finish what you started, you son of a—"

"Don't insult my mother," he warns as he raises one finger above his head, "Also, I don't recall giving you permission to speak, *Bellezza.*"

"Fuck that." I stomp over to him as he enters the bathroom. "What the hell are you playing at, you imbecile, you dithering wanker, you… you…*stronzo.*"

He laughs, the jackalope actually laughs as he prowls over to the spacious shower enclosure and steps inside.

I walk over, yank open the door to the shower as he flicks on the water. The spray pours over him, ripples down his back, down those powerful thighs and all thought spills from my head. Jesus Christ, to see him naked and with the water cascading over him... It's like my favorite wet dream. Well, he is wet, and so am I... I slip my fingers inside my empty channel. I weave my fingers in and out of myself as he turns. His gaze roams over me, then intensifies as he realizes what I am doing.

He tilts his head as I return the gesture, rake my gaze over that gorgeous torso, those to-die-for abs, the V-shaped muscular grooves on the abdominal muscles alongside his hips, which, holy Mother of God, is absolutely perfect, to that fat cock of his, now turgid and standing to attention, with his swollen balls nestled between his legs. Oh wow, this is like my personal pin-up to jerk off to, and trust me, I am going to make the most of it. I grip the edge of the shower door as I thrust a second finger, then a third inside of myself. Damn it, it's still not enough to fill me up, and the asshole knows it.

He bares his teeth as he grabs the shampoo, pours out some of the liquid in his palm and begins to wash his hair. His biceps bulge, the tendons of his forearms tauten as he digs his fingers into his hair. He lowers his gaze to my crotch where I still continue to finger fuck myself. I grind the heel of my palm into my clit and goosebumps rise on my skin.

He leans his head back, so the shower begins to wash away the soapy suds as my core clenches. My backchannel which is still sore from his earlier ministrations protests at the lack of intrusion. What the hell? If his plan is to train me to seek out his touch, then he's doing a damn good job of it. Something I intend to put an end to right now. I manage to fit a fourth finger inside myself, when the climax threatens again. This time I am going to come, I am not going to follow the dictate of any dumbass Capo. So what, if he hasn't given me the permission to come yet. The vibrations shiver up my thighs, to my core, continue upwards, and that's when he switches off the shower.

"Stop," he commands.

My fingers tremble.

"Now, Beauty." He lowers his voice to a hush, and my nerve endings pop. Only when I tuck my elbow into my side, do I realize that I have lowered my arm.

He walks toward me, comes to a stop in front of me. The heat of his body, and the steam from the shower envelops me.

"Why?" I demand, "Explain why you wrote whore."

He merely smiles, then goes to brush past me. I grab his wrist, "Answer me," I snap. "Goddammit, Michael, why did you do that?"

He turns, grabs my throat with his free arm, pushes me up against the frame of the shower door. "Because you are," he growls as he thrusts his face into mine. "You are my whore. Mine to do with as I want. Mine to own. Mine, Beauty. Only mine. Don't forget that."

12

Michael

I pace the length of the conference room in my office above Venom. How dare she question me about my actions? What right does she have to make me feel sorry about what I did? I will not regret it. She deserves it. She is mine to do with as I want, after all. I will do what I want to her, and she'll damn well take it.

After that scene last night Beauty, had returned to my room, picked up her clothes, then stomped out. I had almost called out to her and told her to stay, but thankfully, for once, my brain had won the war over my dick... Okay, not really. My cock had wept to see her go, and I hadn't stopped myself from watching the sway of her butt, or the flow of her hair down her back as she had marched out without a word.

I had gotten dressed, then decided to get the hell out of there. I hadn't wanted to spend the night in my own house. If I had, nothing would have prevented me from going to her room, throwing her down on the bed, and rutting into her... That's the only word for the intensity with which I want to fuck her. Only, I can't, because of some stupid notion that I won't allow her to come. Nor myself, for reasons I cannot begin to articulate.

F-u-c-k! I grab my hair and tug, and the wound at my temple protests. The wound that *she* inflicted on me. The almost healed one on my chest itches and I curl my fingers at my side to stop myself from worrying it. I had spent the night in the apartment adjacent to my office, which I have used in the past when work was so intense that I didn't have the time to make it back home.

Not that it helped my disposition, to be honest… Or my shaft, which still tents my pants. I glare at my crotch. *Get a fucking life, you complete cock.* I frown. *Great, now I am talking to my dick.* Something I would never have done in the past. But then, I never had her to contend with in the past either. This is what she does to me. Ties me up in knots, then twists, just to ensure that I realize how much of a mess my life has become since I chanced upon her.

The door to my office opens and Sebastian saunters in.

"Whatever happened to knocking?" I scowl.

"Whatever happened to your demeanor?" He smirks. "Not that you'd ever be caught dead in a good mood, but this," he looks me up and down, "your frame of mind leaves much to be desired, brother."

"What-fucking-ever," I grunt.

He laughs, "Very eloquent of you, Mika. I take it things are not going well on the home front?"

You can say that again. Clearly, I have backed myself up into a corner, where I won't let myself come and I will not allow her to come either. The result is that not only am I sporting a raging erection since I walked out of my house but I also have no way of alleviating it. No way, am I going to back down from my position of not allowing her to orgasm. But why is it that I am unable to satisfy myself either? Is it out of some sense of solidarity with her? Which, considering I am the one who decided to leave her unsatisfied—is poetic justice. Or is it because I want to punish myself…?

Not that I regret one bit that I took her in the first place. Or that I forced her to marry me. Or that I marked her in a way that I knew would upset her. Make her feel a little bit of what I had gone through when I had realized that she had left me.

Only she returned.

After you pretended you were dead.

And then you had to go screw it up again. Why the hell can't I forgive her for what she did? Why can't I be more normal with her? And that would bore her. My Beauty has a soul as dark as mine, her tastes as perverted as mine. Her need for the extremes that turn me on were clear to me from the first time I looked into her eyes. It had thrilled me as much as it had frightened me.

And in a way, I have been running from facing those thoughts ever since. It had stopped me from sharing all of myself with her... For if I do that, there will be no turning back. I'll be lost to her. I'll be vulnerable in a way that I have never been before. Hell, I am already vulnerable to her. If anything were to happen to her... If I lost her again, I wouldn't be able to take it. It's something I need to figure out how to manage... Just as I need to come up with a solution for the problems that have been plaguing the Cosa Nostra.

"Michael?" Seb frowns, "I asked you a question."

I glance at him. "I heard you," I growl, "doesn't mean I have to answer you."

"But you have to answer to us." The door opens wider to admit Massimo, followed by Christian and Xander. Adrian brings up the rear, as Antonio shuts the door behind him.

"*Figlio di puttana.*" The day hasn't even started and I wish it were over already. Since when had I become so disinterested in work? The one solace that has kept me going all these years, the only focus of my life so far, the one thing that I value more than anything else, the key to underwriting my future... That's what my role as Capo has been to me so far... And now...? I am not so sure.

I stalk toward the bar, grab a fresh bottle of Macallan. I twist open the top, pour out a generous amount in a glass, then toss it back. The liquid burns its way down my gullet, and I slam the glass back on the counter.

"Replacing coffee with whiskey, are we?" Massimo drawls. "Didn't take you for a quitter, *fratellone.*"

"Quitter?" I pivot and level a glare at him. "What do you mean?"

"You're here weeping into your whiskey, while she is there weeping into her pillow, no doubt."

"Weeping?" I scowl. "Who's weeping? Not me, and certainly not her. I promise you, she's undoubtedly figuring out yet another way to bring me down."

"Have you spoken to her yet?" Xander walks over to the coffee station in the corner of the office. He tops up the coffee beans in the machine before switching on the grinder. Once the coffee is ground he taps the handle, tamps down on the coffee powder, before scraping off the excess coffee. He inserts the handle in the brew head and proceeds to extract the espresso. He places the cup on a saucer, then reaches into the jar next to it to and takes out a biscotti that he places on the saucer. He tops off a glass with water, then places it all on a tray. He turns and walks over to the couch, "Sit, *fratellone*," He gestures to the settee.

I walk over, seat myself, and he places the tray in front of me.

"Drink." He stabs a finger at the espresso, and I arch an eyebrow at him.

"No one tells me what to do, not even my favorite brother," I murmur.

He laughs, "At least, you admit that I am your favorite."

"*Che cazzo!*" Christian frowns. "Just because *stronzo* here is the most creative of the lot of us—"

"Also, the most handsome," Xander chuckles.

"If you like the cookie cutter definition of handsome." Christian counters. "I have the rugged good looks, don't forget that."

"And I have—"

"A talent for brewing espresso that tastes better than what I make, and that," I nod in Xander's direction, "is not praise I give lightly."

I take a sip of the espresso and the dark complex notes of coffee laced with chocolate and cinnamon fills my senses. I take another sip, and my sinuses seem to clear. Another and my brain cells finally seem to start firing. I place the espresso cup back in the saucer, dip the biscotti in the coffee and crunch down on it. "These are good." I scowl at the baked item, "Different from what I normally have, but really *eccezionale*."

"New supplier," Massimo, who is also in charge of procurement, offers. "They are homemade, and sold only through our coffee shops."

Yep, we also run a coffee shop chain. One of our many businesses through which I launder the not-so-legit money. The coffee shop chain is one of the more successful ones.

I crunch down the rest of the biscotti, then drain the last of my espresso. My muscles relax, and whether it's the effect of the baked good or the coffee… Or perhaps, a combination of both, I don't know, but I feel almost human.

"So, what are you guys doing here?" I glance between them, "Don't you have enough work to take care of? Do I need to rebalance the systems and make sure you all get more to do?"

"Whoa!" Massimo blinks. "You don't remember?"

"Remember what?"

"You, *fratellone*, who never forgets a work gig. You don't remember why we are here?"

I blink around at them, "I still remember all my work appointments —"

"Except why we are here?" Christian smirks.

"You guys going to spill it, or what?"

"May I?" Seb glances at the rest of the guys, who nod.

"Go right ahead," Massimo acquiesces. "Enlighten *fratellone*, here, about what has slipped his mind completely."

"Enough with the fucking drama." I scowl. "The hell are you guys trying to imply?"

"That you are right." Seb tilts his head.

"I am?"

"You bet." Seb's grin widens, "You don't remember there being a meeting this early in the morning because it wasn't planned."

"It wasn't?"

He shakes his head, "However you did miss a meeting."

"I did?"

"Last night." Adrian adds.

"The fuck you mean?"

"Last night, we had a meeting scheduled with the Russians, which you didn't turn up for," Seb informs me.

"I didn't?" Shit, I am repeating myself, but clearly, these guys are fucking around with me. "Get out of here," I murmur. "You guys could do better if you wanted to play a trick, which by the way, is something so juvenile I'd have expected it of the twins."

"Hey," Both Christian and Xander protest, for once, sounding exactly like the twins they are.

I continue, "It's not something I'd expect the possible future Capo to be after me to say."

Seb blinks, then laughs, "Now, you're the one yanking my chain, *brother*."

"Am I?" I allow my lips to tilt up. "You stepped in when I was out of commission."

He opens his mouth and I raise my hand, "I know it was only for a couple of hours, but you stepped in, took up the reins like you were born for it. And given Luca is, clearly, not the person we thought him to be —" I raise my shoulder, "I can't think of anyone better succeeding to become Capo after me."

"But," Seb frowns, "I am the bastard child—"

"Who was more loyal to me than my own blood brother." I rise to my feet, walk over and grip his shoulder, "I confess, I doubted your loyalties to me, but you came through for me when it most mattered, Seb."

He opens and shuts his mouth, then shakes his head, "But the rules of the Cosa Nostra—"

"I *am* the Cosa Nostra," I draw myself to my full height, "and as soon as I am Don, I will ensure that these archaic rules are overturned. We need to move with the times if we hope to survive in a fast-changing world."

"And her?" Xander's voice has me glancing at him over my shoulder.

"What about her?" I scowl.

"You want to modernize the Cosa Nostra, but what about your views toward women?"

"What about them?" I draw myself up to my full height, "What are you trying to tell me, *fratellino*?

"That you need to treat her more as your peer and less as your possession."

Silence descends on the gathering. Adrian shifts his weight from foot to foot. Seb glances between us, turns to me, opens his mouth as if to speak, then seems to change his mind. Massimo tenses, and Christian… He's the only one who doesn't seem bothered. He watches his twin with something akin to admiration on his face but he stays silent. Thank fuck.

Bad enough, one brother is trying to tell me something which my subconscious, perhaps, even recognizes as the truth…but fuck that. No one tells me what to do. Not her…and definitely not, my youngest sibling… So what, if he's always been the conscience among the group? Only I decide how I manage my wife, and no one else.

"You advising me on how to run my domestic life?" My voice is soft, yet it seems to echo back from the walls of the room.

"Of course, not." Xander's lips quirk, "All I am saying is that you might want to do the one thing that most couples don't seem to master even after years together, which is tell her the truth."

"Thus says the man who hasn't been able to come out and share his truest feelings for the woman he's spent most of his life loving from afar."

Xander pales. His features take on a stricken look. He glances away, and when he looks back at me, his features are once more composed into that angelic face that all of us associate with him. "You're right." He lowers his chin, "I have never managed to tell her how I feel, probably because I suffer from the same issues as you when it comes to women. Apparently, our father's treatment of our mother screwed all of us over enough that, when it comes to the opposite sex, we have only one use for them."

I stare at him. "Now, that is not what I was expecting from you, I confess. You surprise me often, little brother, with your insight into human nature."

"Not as much as you surprise me with your empathy."

"Me? Empathetic?" I laugh, "Surely, you are talking about someone else?"

"If you weren't, you would have killed her as soon as she showed up in that chapel—which you didn't."

"Thought you said you didn't like how I treated her."

"I wouldn't dare butt into a relationship between a Capo and his wife, but when it comes to my brother and his soulmate…"

"Whoa, hold on." I raise my hand, "Who said anything about a soulmate?"

"It's not what you say as much as your gestures that indicate that you love her."

"No, let's not get ahead of ourselves." I smirk, "All this emo shit is not in my vocabulary."

"Maybe it's time you made it. Maybe it's time you actually shared what's going on in your mind, in your heart, how your soul feels about her. I—"

Seb's phone pings just then. He glances at it, then back at us. "Don't mean to cut in on this touching family scene," he drawls, "but the Russians are here for the meeting."

"Why the fuck are they here for a meeting?"

"As I told you," Seb chides, "you didn't make it to the meeting with them last night."

"A meeting in which the rest of us covered for you, by the way," Massimo adds.

"But, of course, they need to meet the Capo to confirm the deal we struck is legit." Christian raises a shoulder.

"*Merda.*" I rake my fingers through my hair. "How the hell did I miss that meeting?" I walk toward where my jacket is hanging over the back of a chair. I slide my hand in the pocket, pull out my phone, which is dead. "*Porca miseria,*" I growl. My phone had run out of battery at the office, and I hadn't bothered to plug it in when I got home…because I had been otherwise distracted. Nor had I once checked it throughout the night, thanks to my infatuation with one feisty woman who had, clearly, pushed herself to the forefront of my mind. I have never once not made it to a meeting on time in all the years since I joined the Cosa Nostra. Apparently, there is a first time for everything. Apparently, my brain is going to shit because I can't even remember to charge my phone anymore.

"Fucking fuck." I slip the phone back in my pocket, then turn to Seb, "Let's get the Russians in here and get this over with."

13

Karma

He left me. Yet again, he hadn't let me come. Well, neither had he come, to be fair, and then, he'd left. I know because, after I'd gone to my room and showered, I had marched out and back to his room, which had been empty.

I had walked down the stairs, headed to the living room, found it also empty. So was the kitchen…. Apparently, he'd left… And he hasn't returned. Guess he has no intention of coming home anytime soon.

I had come to the kitchen, after smelling the coffee and toast and hash browns searing on the griddle, and for a second, I had thought that it was Michael… But sadly, it wasn't. I finished my breakfast on my own, and wandered around the house, before finding my way back to the library.

I had lingered there, picking out more strategy books like *The Prince* by Niccolo Machiavelli — of course, he'd have Machiavelli in his collection — *Meditations* by Marcus Aurelius, *A Book of Five Rings: The Classic Guide to Strategy* written by someone called Miyamoto Musashi who had been a Samurai centuries ago. OMG, does this man only read books by dead men or what?

Well, he also has more eclectic books in his collection, like *Man's Search for Meaning* by Viktor E. Frankl, the entire collection of *The Hitchhiker's Guide to the Galaxy* by Douglas Adams, *Jonathan Livingston Seagull* by Richard Bach....Apparently, there is a thinking side to the alphahole, not that I had doubted it.

Michael has a streak of cruelty a mile wide, but he also has a lot of depth. Bet if he put aside that simmering resentment for all living things, we could have an interesting conversation on anything under the sun. I move to another shelf, spot some well-thumbed volumes of poetry by Byron, Pablo Neruda, and a few other familiar names. Poems, huh? Does he actually read these books? From the well-used condition of them, I'd say yes. Plus, he quoted Byron the first time we met.

Also... I see Harry Potter. WTF? He reads Harry Potter? Does that mean he's also a romantic and somewhat of a dreamer deep inside? Does that dark soul of his also harbor something as mundane as emotions? At least, that's what his book collection tells me. And books, as we all know, don't lie... Unlike people. They don't go about trying to kill their husband to get away from him, or hold a grudge against their wife, so they end up withholding orgasms.

My pussy instantly spasms in sympathy. *Stupid pussy! You've become such a greedy little thing. Can't stop begging for his fat cock to be buried inside of you, huh? Great, now I am talking to my cunt.* Heat flushes my skin and moisture laces my core. The emptiness inside of me writhes and moans. I squeeze my thighs together, then slide my fingers under the waistband of my jeans. I part my legs, play with my clit and a shiver of pleasure runs up my spine. I press down on the already engorged bud, and goosebumps pop on my skin. I slide my fingers down between my pussy lips, thrust one finger, then another inside my aching channel. I weave my fingers in and out of my melting channel, again and again. The vibrations shiver along my nerve-endings and my toes curl. OMG, a few more seconds of this and I am going to come...

My fingers tremble and I pull them back. I lower my hand, press my elbow into my side, and blow out a breath. My knees tremble and I lean against a book case. Raise my cum-soaked fingers. Shit, why the hell did I stop? I could have gotten myself off so easily. And I hadn't. Just because that stupid douchebag had told me to not to come. And of course, much as my body wants the relief, something inside me insists that I can't come. Not yet. Not until he gives me permission. Argh! I dig my fingers in my hair and tug. *But I wanna come! And right now.*

Which means, there's only one way out. If the alphahole won't come to me, I'll have to go to him, to paraphrase one of those popular sayings. I pivot, walk out of the library, and up to my bedroom. I mean, he hasn't said that I can't leave the house. He hasn't told me that I have to stay here. Which means that it is up for interpretation. Which means, fuck it, I am going in search of him. But first, I have to wear something that reflects the mood I am in. Which is… I am not to be taken for granted. I am not to be pushed aside and made to feel like I am a spare wheel… Or a docile wife who will float around her husband's house waiting for him to come to me.

Nope, no way, no siree, I am going to him and that is that. I head up the stairs, fling open the closet door, and examine my limited options. Unlike the island, alphahole hasn't filled the wardrobe with dresses. Which is good…considering I hadn't exactly liked his taste… But the gesture had been sweet. As much as the lack of his thinking about my needs here is…a little worrying.

Well, what do you expect, after you tried to kill him, not once but twice? Hmm. Okay, guess it's reassuring that he did let me live and he hasn't tried to off me since I stumbled back into his life, so there is that. Also, he had remembered to bring one of the dresses that he'd bought from the boutique in Palermo. I run my fingers down the fabric, then turn to the only other dress in the closet, the one I had been avoiding looking at. My wedding dress. It's freshly laundered, but not in good shape.

The bodice is torn, one of the sleeves is in tatters, and the long train that I had stitched on lovingly takes up a lot of space in the closet. The skirt grazes the floor of the wardrobe, the black of the fabric so dark that it absorbs all of the light in the area. A creation that truly represents what I am… What he is… What we are together. A perfectly black object, a completely clandestine crush, an enigmatic love that is, surely, fated to be doomed before we can start anything together. A gaze, a touch, a fleeting glance, a connection that binds us together for better or for worse. I rub the ring on the finger of my left hand.

Oh, Michael, are we fated to implode? Are we but ships that pass in the night…with a bridge thrown across our decks for a short span of time? Are we lovers? Are we enemies whose chemistry turns our every meeting to kryptonite? Are we…nothing but dust, sparks that fade into the dark, fireflies with a short life that burn out before they even start living? A teardrop rolls down my cheek and I brush it away.

Hell, what's wrong with me? From where did these thoughts tumble into my mind anyway? There can't be anything lasting between us. So what if, I've fallen for that rat's ass of a man. He is a bloody criminal… which only makes him all the more appealing. He is a sadist…who speaks to the masochist in me. He is…a Capo… I am a seamstress… And never the twain shall meet.

So, I have nothing to lose by seeking him out, and insisting that he put me out of my misery. As long as he will give me an orgasm… Or two… Or a whole bunch… Hell, I'll be happy. The answer to all your problems is sex, and don't let them tell you otherwise.

I grab the green dress from the hanger, and turn to find Cassandra in the doorway.

She glances at the dress, then at me, "Want help getting changed?"

Forty-five minutes later, I glance up at the facade of the four-story building…all of which is, apparently, Venom—the nightclub and offices owned by Michael's clan. I push open the door of the car in which Cassandra had driven me here. She had not only helped me get dressed, she'd also handed over an entire bag of cosmetics which she'd, apparently, bought for me when she'd been out of the house yesterday. I'd protested and she'd insisted that I keep it. That it would help me look my best for the Capo, and honestly, I couldn't resist taking it then.

Only, I want to look good not just for him, but for myself, know what I mean? Though, why has she been this generous with me? Maybe she feels sorry for me? Maybe it's because of that word which Michael scrawled on me?

I'd almost told her that it was nothing to feel sorry about. The very fact that Michael had felt angry enough by my actions to do that to me, that he'd etched a part of himself into me, that even though it said 'whore,' it was as close to an endearment as any I'd gotten from him.

Shit, why had I not realized that earlier? Maybe my subconscious mind had known, which is why I hadn't gone completely ballistic in response to what he'd done. I had been enraged but not over the top, tear your hair out, going on a killing rampage like the bride from *Kill Bill* furious. Nor like *Dominic Toretto* in *Fast and the Furious* upset. Ugh, clearly, Summer's movie trivia references are rubbing off on me, if I am taking refuge in Hollywood movies to express my frustration at why I had not realized this earlier. Which means, it is doubly important that I get to him, and confront him and say... Well, I'll think of something to say when I come face-to-face with him.

"So," I turn to the car and Cassandra rolls down the window of the passenger seat. "His office is on the top floor, eh?" I ask.

She nods, "You sure you want to do this, *Signora*?"

She just used the word as a form of address in the Italian language to indicate that I am a married woman. I bite the inside of my cheek. Shit, I am married to him... He is my husband... And I could be pregnant with his child... Something which I have avoided thinking about since I went back to Michael. Not sure why it popped up in my mind now... except... If I am pregnant, it would be a hell of an incredible way to ensure that I change the tone of our relationship into something a bit more...permanent? Another reason to walk up there and confront my husband. I swallow the ball of emotion that crowds my throat.

Shit, my husband. The one person I can actually call mine. I have to find a way to, somehow, get through that cloak of hurt he's donned since my ill-fated attempt to escape him. I need to get through the barriers he's building between us, somehow make him see, just how much I regret what I did to him.

"Yeah," I jerk my chin, "I am sure. Wish me luck?"

14

Michael

"What makes you think I want to do a deal with you?" I glance across the conference room table in my office. The man sprawled out at the foot of the table chuckles.

"Come now Capo, you and I both know that you need allies on your side in your quest to bid for the role of Don."

"I don't need you for that, Nikolai." I yawn. "I am the son, the heir; the title of Don is as good as mine."

"If that were true, you wouldn't be meeting with me." Nikolai's lips twist, "You not only need to show that you have built up your association with the strongest organized crime syndicates in your region, but you also need us in your corner should the Don, for some reason, decide to turn on you."

I stiffen, then force my muscles to relax. Fucker is good. As strategic as me. As ruthless as me. As power-hungry as me... Which is why he hadn't hesitated to accept meeting me on my own turf in my office. Not that it was my idea, but I have to give Seb credit. By asking Nikolai to come here, he'd shown that he was thinking ten steps ahead. Nikolai accepting it? It shows that he needs me as much as I need him.

"The same can be said of you." I tilt my head, "You're here meeting me on my turf, unarmed—"

"But not alone," He spreads his arms wide, drawing my attention to the two men who stand on either side of him. His younger brothers Roman and Victor stare back at me, their faces impassive.

"Brothers, eh?" I jerk my chin toward mine who stand behind me, "Can't live with 'em, can't live without 'em."

"That's family for you." Nikolai chuckles, "In our business, it's all about blood ties. You may not get along with your family, but you can trust them to have your back."

That's what I had thought too. Then Luca decided to turn everything on its head.

"The times are changing," I murmur, "enemies become friends become enemies."

He frowns, "I am not following."

"We've never been on the same side of the fence before—"

"Yet you reached out to us, and offered us a proposal we couldn't resist."

He's referring to our earlier agreement where Nikolai agreed to stop targeting our ships in return for a cut of the money we make on the shipping routes.

"The enemy of your enemy is a friend, too." I allow my lips to kick up.

Niko's forehead creases. "The Kane Company."

"Indeed." I lean back in my chair. "They've become more daring, of late."

"Are they responsible for—" He nods toward the bandage on my forehead.

"No, that was me."

I jerk my head around in the direction of my wife's voice. She stands by the now open door, Antonio, hovering behind her.

"Sorry, Boss," he raises his hands, "she wouldn't take no for an answer, and—"

"You did the right thing," I wave my hand and he steps back.

Beauty walks over to me. She's wearing one of the dresses she'd chosen from the boutique in Palermo, where I had taken her. Where I had pushed her up against the wall of the changing room and ripped the dress she'd been wearing and thrust my fingers inside her sopping wet cunt, and she had come. She had moaned loud enough for everyone in that boutique to hear her. The blood drains to my groin and my balls tighten. I move around in my chair, trying to ease the strain on my pants. That's when I notice that the gaze of every single man in the room is on her. *Che palle.* I rise to my feet, "This meeting is over."

Nikolai glances between my wife and me. "Indeed." His lips curve, "Aren't you going to introduce us to the beautiful *signorina?*"

"*Signora,*" I clarify as Beauty pauses next to me. "This," I wrap my arm around her and pull her stiff body against mine, "is my wife."

"Ah!" Nikolai finally gets up from his seat, "*Ocharovannyy, printsessa,*" He half bows.

Why is it that every man who comes across her seems to be enchanted by her? Can't the fuckers see that she belongs to me?

I yank her even closer and she digs her elbow into my side. My cock instantly jerks. Fuck. Hasn't she realized by now that any hint of violence from her only turns me on? Maybe it's why she's tried to kill me twice, and both times, the connection between us has only grown stronger. What the hell? Why hadn't I realized this before? That the more she tries to hurt me, the more I want her. The more she wants to push me away, the more I need her. The more she tries to prove to me that she can do without me...the more I want to imprint myself on every pore of her body.

"And you are — ?" Beauty holds up her hand.

"Leaving," I snap at the same time that Nikolai walks around the table to take her hand in his.

"Very pleased to meet you..." He tilts his head.

Beauty laughs. "Karma," she murmurs, "call me Karma."

"A fitting name for the woman who has brought the Capo to heel." He kisses her fingers and every muscle in my body goes on alert.

"Relax, Capo," Nikolai drawls, "I pose no threat to you or your family."

"Didn't take you to be a liar," I say through gritted teeth.

He releases her hand and I shove her behind my back.

"Hey," she protests, "what are you doing?" She tries to step around me and I wrap an arm behind and around her, keeping her in place. She digs her fingers into my arm, and a shudder shivers up my spine.

I glare at Nikolai, who meets my gaze. He doesn't back away, doesn't lower his gaze either. For a few seconds our staring match goes on, then he jerks his chin. "You protect what's yours." His lips twist, "I respect that."

"Then you'll also respect when I say that you need to leave now."

"A straight shooter, too." He chuckles, "We are cut from the same cloth, Capo. I do believe we have more in common than we realize."

"We'll see about that."

"Until next time then," he nods at me, then pivots and stalks out, followed by his brothers. The door shuts behind them.

I release Karma who stomps out and around to stand in front of me. "Jesus, all that posturing. It was highly entertaining—not." She fumes, "If you dare try to control me again in front of your acquaintances I will—"

"How are you Karma?" Xander cuts in. "Haven't seen you since your unexpected arrival at the chapel."

Karma scowls in his direction as he walks toward her. Her forehead smoothens out. Typical. No woman can resist the lure of the beauty of my youngest brother.

Karma smiles at him, "You must be..."

"Alessandro, but people call me Xander."

"At his insistence." Christian steps forward, "Personally, I think he does it because it annoys the Capo."

"Does it?" She shoots me a side glance. "And why is that?"

"He claims it's a bastardized version of Sandro, which is, of course, the Italian version of my nickname."

"For the record, I prefer Xander." Her smile widens, "Reminds me of Xander Cage in the xXx series."

"Love action-packed Hollywood movies, eh?" Xander laughs.

"Also, video games."

"SIMS 4?"

"Wha-a-t?" She tosses her head, "Give me some credit, yeah? Call of Duty, all the way here."

"Holy shit, you don't say, you—"

"Okay, that's it," I step between them. "Out, you guys."

"But, *fratellone*," Xander's smirk widens, "we were just talking."

"And now, you've finished talking." I nod my chin toward the door, "Don't call me, I'll call you."

"Aww," Xander chuckles, "and I was only trying to be friendly."

"Well, take your friendliness somewhere else." I fold my arms across my chest, fix him with my most stern gaze. "Now," I say in a low voice and that wipes the smile off of his face.

"You got it, Boss."

He walks past us without saying another word. The rest of the guys file out with him. Antonio closes the door, and I turn to find Beauty staring at me with an incredulous look other face.

"Don't call me, I'll call you?" She huffs, "You really do need to work on your dialogues."

"Is that right?"

"Yeah," She swipes her hair over her shoulder, "I mean, how trite can you get?"

"Trite, eh?"

"Seriously, every part of you is a cliché." She sniffs, "From your dark suits, to your glowering face, to..." She glances around the space, "To this office, on top of a nightclub."

"What's wrong with having an office at the top floor of a nightclub?"

"It's predictable."

"It's convenient."

"Why? So you can have women service you as you are working?"

"Hmm." I stroke my chin, "Now that you mention it, that is a fringe benefit."

"What the hell?" She pushes against my chest. "How dare you say that to me?"

"I'm not the one who brought it up, Beauty; you did. Speaking of," I peer into her face, "what are you doing here?"

"I wasn't aware that I was a prisoner."

"My point, exactly." I hold her gaze, "You could have escaped, Beauty; you could have walked out of the house—"

"Which I did."

"Or called your sister—"

"You didn't give me my cellphone, and if I had called from your home, no doubt, you would have found out about it right away."

"You could have called her from somewhere else, once you left the house.

She blinks, "True."

"But you didn't think of it?"

She shakes her head.

"Why is that?"

"For the same reason that you didn't imprison me in your home, this time," she murmurs.

"What reason is that?" I fold my arms across my chest.

"I know why you carved out the word 'whore' on my back."

"Oh?" I tilt my head.

"It's because you feel something for me."

"You're right about that."

"Oh, yeah?"

"Apathy." I look her up and down. "You're a nice hole to bury my cock in, but considering I've already sampled what you have to offer," I raise a shoulder, "I think it's time I set you free."

"You're lying!" She bursts out.

"Am I?" I round the desk, drop into my seat, then flick on my laptop. I busy myself looking at the figures from last month's sales...which has taken a hit, thanks to the Kane Company hijacking our gun shipments in and out of Eastern Europe. Fuck... Something I need to deal with right away. I glance up at her, "What are you still doing here?"

She opens, then shuts her mouth.

"You're free to leave."

"What will it take for you to realize that this connection between us cannot be broken so easily?"

"There's no connection...and even if there was one, it shattered when you took the oar to my head."

"Oh, my god!" She throws up her hands, "Your stupid ego is going to be the death of me."

"That day can't come soon enough."

"And yet you faked your death so I'd come back to you," she points out.

"I faked my death so I could draw out my brother who betrayed me; you were a fringe benefit."

Her features crumple, hurt writ large across her features. My heart twists and I glance away to stare at the computer screen. The figures fade in and out in front of my eyes.

Cazzo! What's wrong with me? Why does she still affect me so? When she had walked in here, it had felt as if the world had finally tilted right on its axis. Then I had seen the men in the room look at her and had experienced the kind of jealousy that had twisted my guts, that had made me want to whisk her away somewhere, away from all of them, hide her in a place where no one else could see her or talk to her or glance at her.

Then, I'd realized that I have to let her go. If I continue to hold onto her, she'll completely undo me. She'll make me weak, expose my frailties, derail me from the course I have set for myself. Something I can't afford.

As for her relationship with the Seven and how that would have strengthened my own bid to be the next Don... Well, I'll just have to do without it.

"So, this is it?" she whispers. "This is what it's come to? You asking me to leave because you can't deal with your own insecurities?"

"Interesting theory," I drum my fingers on the table, "but I'm afraid I am not in the mood to listen to it."

She stiffens. Anger pours off of her. Then she straightens her back, "You're going to regret this."

"I regret the day I saw you in that park. I should have turned around and left. Sadly, you seemed too easy an opportunity to pass up."

"That's all I am to you, then? After everything we've been through, it's all you view me as?"

"You know the answer to that already." I glance away, pretend to focus on my work.

She stays motionless for a second, then out of the corner of my eyes I sense a flash of movement. I turn to find her pulling off the ring from her finger. "Here." She slams it on the table. Turning, she walks out.

15

Karma

The ring, which had refused to come off my fingers all this time, had finally slipped off in there. Maybe it was a sign that he's right? Maybe I had been wrong to come back for his fake funeral?

He had written 'whore' on my skin, and I guess he really meant it. He doesn't really want me. In fact, he'd rather let me go than admit that he feels something more than hatred for me. Hell, the *stronzo* is half in love with me. Only, he doesn't want to admit it. And hell, if he hasn't converted me to using Italian words in my vocabulary in a matter of weeks. I have only known him for a fraction of my life, and already, it feels like he is a part of me in a way that nobody else has ever been before. Why am I still so attracted to him? Someone who is a psychopath...and a criminal...probably, a murderer.

I draw in a breath and my lungs burn. I stomp down the steps of the nightclub, past the bar on the ground floor that has two bartenders restocking the shelves behind the bar. I reach the door, push it open, and step into the early afternoon.

A cool breeze blows over me and I shiver. The weather has been so pleasant even for early December. Shit. It's already early December.

Soon it will be Christmas... Will I be home for Christmas? Where is home? Here, with the alphahole Mafia Capo? Or in London with Summer and her new husband, who, I confess, I don't know well at all?

Not like I have a choice. After all, he had thrown me out... Well, he'd kidnapped me, so it was his prerogative to let me go. Hold on... What prerogative? He had taken me and married me... The least he could have done was share his feelings with me. Not to mention, at least, gotten me off.

Now, here I am, walking up the road in the center of Palermo, with nothing but the clothes on my back, and nowhere to go... I need to get to a phone and call Summer. I pause. Maybe if I turn and go back to the nightclub, I can ask to borrow a phone or something? And risk running into my husband—well, my not-husband, to be precise... Nah, no way. It would only give him a chance to smirk. Maybe a chance to tell me to get out, all over again.

Nope. N-a-h. I am going to have to do this without him. Gonna have to find someone with a phone, or someplace which will allow me to make a call. Aren't Italians largely warm-hearted people? Or at least, that's what I had read somewhere. I walk up the road, which features other bars, eating joints... No other nightclubs on this street. Guess when the Mafia runs a nightclub, no-one wants to go head-to-head against them. They'd lose. As I had.

I'd thought I could go toe-to-toe with this man, and see what happened? Asshole really did do a number on me. Why the hell did he have to be so...hot? So sexy... So irresistible. Why did he have to show a glimmer of humanity under all that alphaholeness, eh?

If I were truly convinced that he's evil, I would be jumping for joy right now. The problem is, I now know he isn't as mean as he pretends to be. Nor as unfeeling as he'd like me to believe. Unfortunately, nothing I've said or done so far has convinced him to open up to me either. Jerk.

To think, we actually had a chance to make a go of it. We could have had a future together; a possibility of a life together. Gah! I really have done it now, falling in love with him so completely. I knew I was attracted to him, that I was falling for him, but to be in love with him? Shit, shit, shit. A pressure builds at the backs of my eyes. I am in love with him and he... He, clearly, hates me.

Nice one, Karma. The story of my life. Why do I always realize what I want a little too late?

I had gotten into Goldsmith to study fashion design, then in a fit of rebellion, dropped out... Only to figure out later that I could have done with that little bit of extra guidance... I mean, I was rushing to break the rules without first learning what the rules were. So, in the end, the only person who was hurt by the entire process was me. Just like now, when I am the only person mourning the end of a relationship that wasn't.

I continue walking up the street. The bars and restaurants have given way to shops that look more run down. There is a coffee shop with a group of men standing about it. Some are seated at the tables outside, drinking coffee, talking together. Many are dressed in pants and vests. Their forearms tattooed. One of them raises the espresso cup to his lips. The guy opposite him says something, and the man throws the coffee in his face. The guy screams. The second man jumps to his feet, smashes the cup into the first guy's temple. The cup shatters. Blood pours down his face. Shit, I really am in Mafia land, huh?

I pause, glancing up and down the street. I could turn back...but... nah, I am not conceding defeat. I need to keep going. I cross the street, to the other side, then stay close to the wall. I continue walking, keeping my gaze forward. My palms begin to sweat, and I wipe them on the silk skirt of my dress. Shit, why had I worn this outfit? It had seemed like a good idea then. But on the street and trying not to draw attention to myself...? Yeah, think again.

A wolf whistle rings out from the other side of the street. I wince, but don't look in their direction. Hell, the one thing I know is self-preservation. If I don't pay attention to them, hopefully, they'll lose interest. Another wolf whistle sounds, this one louder and accompanied by kissing noises. Ugh. I draw myself up to my full height, keep my pace even. If I run, they'll know I am scared... And while I am—shitless, to be honest—I am not going to give these assholes the satisfaction of knowing that.

A bead of sweat trickles down my spine. The hair on the nape of my neck rises. The sound of a vehicle accelerating reaches me. I stiffen, turn to find a van overtaking the car in front as it hurtles up the road. The hair on the back of my neck rises. My senses jangle. Somehow, I know the van is headed for me. *Run! Get out of here.* These blasted heels I borrowed from Cassandra are not meant for running. My ankles wobble, I cry out, then kick off my stilettos, and break into a sprint. The soles of my feet hit the hard concrete. Vibrations of pain race up my legs. I wince, but keep going even as the sound of the vehicle's engine draws closer. It draws up next to me and the door slides open. A man jumps out in my path. I careen to a stop, pivot to find another man behind me. *No, no, no.* I throw up a fist, then scream when arms wrap around my center. I am lifted straight off of my feet, and even as I try to kick out, I am flung inside the van. I jump up, but something hits me on the head from behind. Then everything goes dark.

16

Michael

Shit, shit, shit. I shouldn't have let her go. I snatch up the ring that she had flung down on the table. I close my palm around it and the edge of the diamond seems to bite into the flesh of my palm. Shit, what was I thinking, letting her leave like that? I slide the ring inside my pocket, then pull out my knife and flip it, catch it by the handle. I stare at the polished blade. The edge of which I had sunk into her skin when I had carved the mark of my possession of her.

Was she right? Did I do that because I wanted to own her? To make her mine. To have her as my wife to cherish, to protect, to love… No… Not that. I am not capable of that emotion. No, my feelings for her are already way more complex than that. If I had asked her to stay, if I had given in to the temptation she is… In that gorgeous dress which had clung to her like a second skin, outlining the thrust of her breasts, the curves of her hips, and pulled tight across her thigh… I would have never been able to let her go.

And would that have been so bad?

Pain slices my palm. I glance down to find the blade has nicked the flesh at the base of my thumb. *Che diavolo.* I stick the knife into the wooden surface of the desk, then bring my palm to my mouth and suck on the wound.

The door to my office bursts open and Seb stalks in. His features are set in hard lines, his forehead furrowed.

"What is it?"

"Karma." He scowls, "They took her."

My heart slams in my chest. My pulse rate ratchets up. "What do you mean, they took her?"

"That's what he says." Massimo drags in a guy by his collar. The man is bleeding from his mouth; blood stains his vest. A sleeve of tattoos covers one arm and runs up the side of his throat.

"Who is this?" I growl.

"Found him bragging to one of the dancers downstairs, that he saw a woman being kidnapped. She reported it to me, and I got suspicious. I collared him, asked him to describe what he saw, and from his description, I am positive that he witnessed Karma being taken."

I rise to my feet, slam my palm into the table with such force that a glass crashes to the floor. "Will one of you tell me who the fuck would dare come into my territory and take my wife from me?"

"You did let her go," Seb reminds me. "You sent her out there unprotected."

Anger squeezes my guts and pain slams into my chest with such force that my lungs burn. "Shut the fuck up," I growl.

"Am I wrong?" Seb tilts his head.

"Don't fucking talk to me like that."

"Someone needs to, considering you are letting your ego blind you to what's there right in front of you."

"And what's that?"

"That you love her."

Something hot stabs at my chest. I round the table, throw up my fist. He doesn't duck... He had enough time to evade my blow, but he doesn't. My strike hits home. I connect with the side of his face and he grunts. I raise my fist again, but Massimo shoves the man he's holding at Antonio.

He steps between us, holds up his hands, "Enough, Capo, you need to get a grip on yourself."

"I am going to kill him."

"For telling the truth?"

I freeze, "What the hell is wrong with all of you?"

"What is wrong with you?" He snaps. "Your woman has been taken... This time, likely, by our enemy, and you're standing here fighting with your own clan? With people who are on your side, in your corner. You need to rein in your temper, *fratellone*, and focus on what we must do next."

I lurch back, shake my head. Fuck, fuck, fuck. What's happening to me? I drag my fingers through my hair, then jerk my chin at him. "You can step aside," I murmur, "I won't attack him."

Massimo lowers his arms and I brush past both of them. I stalk over to the *figlio di puttana* who's struggling to get away from Antonio. I swipe out my arm, bury my fist in his face. Blood blooms from his nose, drips down his chin.

"What did you see?" I growl.

"I had nothing to do with." His throat moves as he swallows, "I swear, on the holy Virgin Mary, I was minding my own business when she comes along. I only noticed her because... Well, it's difficult not to, the way she was dressed, and her figure, I—"

I bring my fist up, sink it into his stomach this time. He gurgles, bends over, and would have fallen if Antonio hadn't jerked him back upright.

I slam my fist into his shoulder, then raise it again, only to be grabbed and yanked back.

"*Fratellone*, stop." Massimo grips my shoulder, "We need him to tell us what he saw."

"I'll kill him." I say in a low voice. "I'll tear him from limb to limb, then smash all his bones and throw him in a barrel of acid while he's still alive."

"If you did that, we'd never be able to find her."

Find her. Find her. The anger drains away and silence fills my head. I step back, look the *bastardo* in the eye.

"Who took her?"

"I don't know, I swear," he warbles. "I was watching her... Hell, we were all watching her—"

I fold my fingers into fists. I will not kill him. Not yet. Not until he's told me everything he witnessed."

"And then?" Massimo prompts, "What happened after that?"

"A van drove up the road, pulled to a stop in front of her, and they took her."

My vision tunnels and a coldness grips me. "What kind of a van?" I ask in a low voice. "Did you notice the numbers on the license plate?"

"The license plate was c-covered in dirt," he stutters. "It was a white Fiat Ducato," he adds.

"Like that is helpful," Massimo growls. "There must be a million of them on the road."

"Any other distinguishing features?" Seb walks up to stand on my other side, "You'd better come up with something that is going to help us, if you want to live."

The *testa di cazzo* blinks, then glances between us.

"Or maybe, he wants to die right now?" Massimo raises his fist and the man yells.

"Wait, wait, let me think."

"Think fast," Seb prompts him. "Else your insides will be gracing the floor very soon." He pops his knuckles and the man pales.

"A...a...flower."

"What?"

"I saw a design of what looked like a flower on the windscreen."

"Are you sure?" I scowl at him.

"Yes, no, I don't know," he pants. Sweat drips down his temples. "It... It...looked like it, but I can't be sure."

"What kind of a flower?" I glare at him and he blinks rapidly.

"I am not sure."

He glances between us, "Please, just let me go. I promise never to look at her again."

Fuck, if I don't want to pull his eyes out for daring to look at her in a lascivious way. And if I did, I'd never have witnesses come forward in the future with information. I roll my shoulders, narrow my gaze on him. "Get out while you're still alive," I snap.

The man turns and scampers out.

I fold my arms across my chest, "I am going to find whoever did this, and when I do... I am going to destroy their entire bloodline. Every. Last. One of them."

Neither Seb nor Massimo contradict me.

"There are only two gangs who would dare do this," Massimo murmurs. "It can't be the Bratva because we've struck a deal with them. Which leaves—"

"The Kane Company." I roll my neck from side to side "Would they dare come right into my territory and do this?"

"They attacked you on your turf." He's referring to an incident a few months ago when four unarmed men had attacked me. I had managed to overpower them, and even brought two of them in for questioning. One of them had swallowed poison and died, the other, I had knifed. We hadn't gotten much from either of them, but it stood to reason that it was the Kane Company who were behind both incidents.

"They are the only ones with enough gumption to attempt something like this." Seb scratches his chin. One of his eyes is half closed, a ring of black already showing up around it, thanks to my hit. "They probably wanted to get your attention," he warns.

"Well, they have it."

"They, clearly, wanted to make you angry enough to commit a mistake." Massimo tilts his head.

I glare back at him. "Fuck that," I growl. "They took what is mine and now they have to face my wrath."

I brush past both of them, head for my desk. Working the knife from the surface of my table, I slide it back in its sheath. Then I pull out my drawer, snatch up my gun, check to make sure it's loaded before I slide it at the back in my waistband holster. I grab another gun, repeat the actions to ensure that it's loaded, then slide it into my underarm holster. I snatch up a third gun, bend and raising my pant leg and slip it into the holster around my ankle.

I straighten to find both of them watching me.

"What?" I snap.

"You don't think you are going in alone, do you?" Seb drawls.

"It's my fight."

"It's our territory," he counters.

"She's our family." Massimo frowns, "And if you think you...our Capo is going there on your own—"

"You are wrong," Christian says from the open door.

"Thought I told the lot of you all to head off and get on with your work."

"This is work," Xander prowls into the room. "Much as I hate bloodshed, I am afraid this is one time I can't help but back you up."

"They dare to raise a hand on our flesh and blood," Christian growls. "They'll answer for this with their lives."

"I can't allow everyone to come with me on this."

"But—" Christian begins to protest, and I raise my hand.

"If this is some kind of trick, and I'm not saying it is, but if it is, then with the lot of us heading out together to confront them, we are playing right into their hands."

Xander nods, "So what would you have us do instead?"

"Stay back," I glance between the twins. "Monitor for any unusual activity within our network. Anyone who could have leaked news of what happened here. They were keeping a close eye on us. There's no doubt about that. It's how they knew the moment she walked out on her own." I widen my stance. Whoever is leaking information needs to be brought to heel, before any more damage is done." And her... What about her? If my actions led to her being hurt... I'll never be able to forgive myself. I won't stop until she has been avenged. And how will I live after that? How will I continue without her? I roll my shoulders. Only one way out. I need to get to her before anything happens.

I stalk past the men and to the door, then pause to glance over my shoulder at Seb and Massimo, "You two coming?"

17

Karma

Darkness presses in on me. Pain thuds at my temples, between my eyes. I turn on my side and the throbbing in my head ratchets up. Red sparks flare behind my closed eyelids. I groan and the sound seems to echo in the space. I crack my eyelids open, wince when the brightness overwhelms me. I turn on my back, lay still. Take a deep breath, another. Shit, why won't the pain recede? I swallow and my throat hurts. I take a mental inventory of my body, but nothing else seems hurt.

I open my eyes again, slowly, and this time they seem to adjust to the brightness which is sunlight pouring in from a window to my right. I glance around, take in the empty room I am in. Well, except for the bed that I am on. I attempt to sit up, then almost cry out when the headache worsens. I bring my hand to my head, then wince when I feel the bump at the back. No wonder I have a headache... I hit my head. OMG, the van. I had been trying to get away from those men in the cafe, when the van...had drawn up next to me. One of the men had grabbed me and thrown me inside, and then... Someone had hit me on the head, I think. Bloody hell, I've been kidnapped... Again? What the hell?

Is it just my bad luck, or do I walk around with a target painted on my forehead to attract all of the creeps around me to come after me? Not that Michael is a creep… No, he's worse… He's an asshole. A jackalope. A douche canoe of the nth degree. Gah! And here I am, back to being a captive. My freedom had lasted roughly half an hour, if that? And am I going to, once more, lay here waiting for someone to tell me what to do next? Whoever these guys are, they're surely as dangerous as, if not more than, Michael.

Of course, it's also thanks to him that I am in this situation. If he hadn't turned me out, I would never have been kidnapped. A-n-d hold on… If he hadn't kidnapped me in the first place, then I wouldn't have been kidnapped again, either. Yeah, everything that's happened to me is because of him. He's the one to blame. When I see him again, I am going to yell at him, slap him, then…fling myself on him, climb him like a tree and kiss him. The sound of the door being opened reaches me. My heart jackknifes in my chest. My pulse rate ratchets up. I jerk my head toward the doorway, stifle another cry when the headache seems to intensify.

A man walks in. He's tall—as tall as Michael, maybe—and broad, but in a way that hints at him spending too much time in a gym… That, and steroids. He is definitely on something, to have his biceps balloon in that fashion. His shirt strains at the seams and outlines his chest, as well as the making of a flabby belly…which is a weird combination. He stops at the foot of the bed, looks me up and down. My skin crawls. The hair on the nape of my neck rises. Shit, this man, he is up to no good. His gaze comes to rest on my chest—asshole—before moving in a leisurely path down to the apex of my legs.

"You're awake?"

"No, I am sleeping. And clearly, I like to talk in my sleep too."

He blinks, jerks his chin up. "Har, har." His lips kick up, "You have a sense of humor."

"That makes one of us." I scowl at him. "How dare you kidnap me?"

He opens and shuts his mouth. Evidently, I have rendered him speechless, which is a start. I lever my body up, swing my legs over the side of the bed and stand up. My stomach lurches, bile boils up my throat and I swallow it down. My head spins. I draw in a breath, and the world rights itself again. I take a step forward, then another. I walk to the door, grab the handle and twist it. I try to open it and the door resists. Shit. I jiggle the handle, try to pull it back again, "Come on, come on."

I hear his footsteps approach, feel him close enough for his body heat to envelop me. My stomach ties itself in knots. I slide away, just as his heavy hand lands on the door, which shudders. Shit. If he'd grabbed me, he'd probably have broken a bone or two. I turn to face him. He takes a step forward and I stumble back against the door. *Don't show him how scared you are. If you do, it will only make it worse.* And there is no one looking for me.

Alphahole has no idea that I've been kidnapped again, and if he did, would he come for me? My heart stutters. He would. I have no doubt about it. He may be upset with me, enough to have cast me out, but there's no doubt that his ego would not permit him to allow anyone else to take what is his. But does he still consider me his? What if he really is done with me? Shit, what if I am doomed to spend the rest of my days here, in this stupid room, with this horrible, overgrown gorilla of a man, whoever he is? Trying to come on to me... Who definitely wants to do worse than just come on to me. Gross!

He rolls his shoulders, no doubt, to impress upon me just how much bigger than me he is. *Bloody baboon.*

He cracks his knuckles and I pretend to yawn. That wipes the smile off of his face. *Stupid shitstain.* He lunges forward and I bring my knee up and smash it into his center. He roars in pain. I slide aside, as he bends over and grabs his nuts. I race for the door, hammer on it, "Let me out of here. Let me out. Let me out right now." My head throbs each time my fist connects with the door, but I don't let up. I sense him straighten and begin to lumber toward me. I pivot, bring my fist down on the door with such force that the entire frame shakes. Pain ripples up my arm, and I cry out. "Open the goddam door. Please open the door, please—"

He grabs my hair and pulls me back with such force that I scream. He shakes me, and I see sparks behind my eyes. Tears squeeze out from the corners of my eyes and my legs seem to give way from beneath me. He releases me and I sink to the floor. He steps toward me, when the door is wrenched upon.

"The boss wants to see you," someone says from outside the room. The man hesitates when the voice speaks again, "You know how he doesn't like to be kept waiting."

The man grumbles under his breath, then turns and walks out of the door. I lay where I have fallen on the floor. My headache seems to have grown exponentially, now filling the entirety of my head. I groan, then stagger to my feet. I manage to stumble to the bed and sink down onto it. The scent of stale cigarettes and other assorted smells I don't care to identify assails me. I cough, turn my head away, throw my arm over my eyes and curl into myself.

When I open my eyes again, it's dark outside. My headache, at least, seems to have receded. Thank God. I sit up, then groan when every part of my body aches. My tongue seems to be stuck to the roof of my mouth. I swallow and my throat hurts. The soles of my feet throb, probably from that hasty run to get away from my kidnappers earlier. I glance around the empty room again. I hate this... Sitting here, waiting to be rescued. Not that there is anyone coming to get me. I hunch my shoulders as a tear makes its way down my cheek. I sniffle, then wipe the back of my palm against my nose. Goddammit, how the hell am I going to get out of this situation?

I rise up to my feet, then hobble over to the window. I glance outside, and blink. We must be on a hill or something, for the lights of the city stretch out in the distance.

I glance down and realize I am on the second floor.

I reach for the handle on the window frame, try to pull it down but it won't budge. Dammit! I grab it with both of my hands, tense my biceps, then yank it down. Still, no movement. Argh! I draw in a breath, then brace my feet on the floor. I throw the entire weight of my body behind it, and it moves, maybe, just a centimeter. I collapse against the windowsill, panting. A headache knocks behind my eyes, but I ignore it. I grab the handle and twist it. My muscles protest; my arms hurt. My biceps feel like they are being put through a wringer. The handle slides down a little more. Oh, my god! I sink down onto the floor, lean my head into the wall.

I close my eyes, draw in a few deep breaths. Close my eyes and focus inside myself. If my hippie mother were here, she'd tell me to center myself. Zoom in on the intention. Ground myself, draw on the energy of the earth and—I hear the sound of footsteps approaching. I snap open my eyes, then spring up, turn to the window, then grab the handle and yank on it. It moves down a few more millimeters. "Goddam it!" I cry out as I hear the door open behind me.

I throw everything I have into grabbing the handle and hang off of it. Metal against metal screeches and it slips free. I turn around to find the guy from earlier entering the room. My heart slams into my ribcage.

My pulse rate spikes. Adrenaline laces my blood. I turn back to the window, fling it open. Then pull myself onto the window sill.

He reaches for me and I clamber out onto the ledge. He leans out of the window, and I evade him. My feet slip on the ledge and I cry out, then right myself. I slide forward, out of his reach, and plaster myself against the wall. I turn to find the bastard trying to pull himself up. His shoulders fill the window, his frame, clearly, too big for the space. As I watch, he maneuvers himself onto the window sill, then shoves one leg over the frame. Fuck!

Sweat trickles down my spine and my dress sticks to my back. I glance down at the ground which, despite the fact that I am on the second floor, seems way farther down than I'd like, then back to where the gorilla climbs out onto to the ledge. He bares his teeth, and my stomach twists. No way, am I going to be a sitting duck, waiting for him to get his hands on me again. Wait—I am standing; does that make me a standing duck? Ugh, not the time for wordplay, Karma! Just this once, can karma be on my side?

He edges toward me and my heart gallops in my chest. Adrenaline laces my blood. My vision tunnels, I stare down at the ground, then toward the horizon.

He gets closer, close enough for him to swipe out his arm. The tips of his fingers brush my hair. I duck, hold up my middle finger at him, then jump.

18

Karma

I squeeze my eyes shut and prepare for impact. I crash into something hard. Solid. The shock smashes through my system. I groan. This is not going to be pretty. Am I going to look like one of those people who jump from a height and ends up splattered over the sidewalk? Not that I have seen any in real life, thank God... But I have seen enough movies to know it's a gruesome sight.

The ground under me moves... Huh? I snap my eyes open, stare down into blazing blue eyes. Gone is the coldness, the remote look he had worn when I had last seen him. This man is angry...livid with the kind of rage that vibrates off of him and slams into my chest.

"You jumped." he growls, "you fucking jumped."

"It was only from the second story, besides I...I didn't have a choice."

Debris rains down on us and Michael steps aside, his movement so graceful I can only blink as he stares up. I don't take my gaze off of his beautiful face as he growls, "Who the fuck is up there?"

"One of the men who kidnapped me."

His features harden. All emotion drains from his face. His gaze narrows as he walks back a few paces.

"Wh…what are you doing?"

He merely heaves me over his shoulder like I am a sack of potatoes.

"What the fuck?" I yell as I stare at his perfectly hard backside. My hair streams down about my ears and down to cover his gorgeous rear. I sense him move, then hear a shot, and the ground seems to shudder. "Fuck." I close my eyes as a trembling grips me, "Fuck, fuck, fuck."

Footsteps approach us, then Michael snaps, "Make sure you kill every last *figlio di puttana* inside the house."

"Will do," a voice replies.

Seb? Is it one of his other brothers. Michael's body moves, then he lowers me down and back into his arms. I turn my face into his chest, breathe in his dark, edgy essence, fill my lungs with his scent, and burrow into him. His grip tightens around me.

His voice rumbles above me and the vibrations resonate up his chest, sink into my blood. His voice fades in and out as I begin to drift.

"Set fire…send a message…taking her home."

He turns and walks away, as the sound of gunshots reaches me, then wanes as he moves further away. His grip tightens around me, then he brushes his lips over my hair. "I need to lower you to the ground so I can open the car door," he murmurs.

"No," I grip the front of his shirt, "no, no, no."

"Shh!" He presses a kiss to my forehead, "You're safe with me."

Tears fill my eyes and run down my cheeks. How the hell am I ever going to feel safe after what happened? After I was kidnapped, twice, in quick succession, in such a short time? And to think, my once kidnapper is the only person in whose arms I now feel safe. I am such a bloody mess.

"Don't cry," his voice catches, "please don't cry, Beauty."

Of course, that only makes me sob harder.

He walks around the car, then bends and manages to open the door on the driver's side. He slides inside, shuts the door behind him as I cling to him. Gah, shrinking violet, I am not. But right now, if I let go of him… What if someone else tries to take me away? What if he decides, again, that he doesn't want me?

Fuck, I am conforming to every damn stereotype of a damsel in distress that I hate. My throat closes and another wave of trembling grips me. My teeth chatter and my bones feel too brittle for my body.

I draw up my legs, try to conserve what warmth I have left in my body.

He wraps his arms around me, plasters me to his chest, then lowers his head to kiss the skin between my eyebrows, my eyelids, the tip of my nose, my mouth. I moan, part my lips, and he sweeps in. He dances his tongue across mine, closes his mouth over mine in a deep, draining kiss that seems to suck every last thought from my head. His chest heaves, his breath grows shallow, a hardness digs into my side, and when he finally breaks the kiss, I can't think anymore. Maybe that was the point. When he lowers me onto the seat next to his, I don't protest.

He yanks on the safety belt, snaps it into place. Snatches up a bottle of water from the holder between the seats and hands it over to me. I gulp down the water, then close the bottle and hand it over to him. He tosses it back in the holder then reaches over to grab my hand. He places it on his thigh. The strength in that thick, hard column sinks into my blood. A warmth steals up my arm, fills my chest. My head throbs and I lean back into the seat, as he sets the vehicle in motion.

How did I put myself in this position? Since when do I need a man to take care of me? I have navigated life on my own terms since a very young age, yet a few weeks with this guy, and I am dependent on him for my security. When he's the one who kidnapped me in the first place. Since when has my kidnapper become my protector?

"How—" My voice cracks and I clear my throat. "How did you know where to find me?"

"Someone saw you being taken. He was bragging about it at Venom. When Seb heard it, he realized that he was talking about you."

"How did you track me down?"

He turns down a road, and the muscles of his forearms flex as he steers the car. "The man who saw you noticed a symbol on the windshield. One that, as we found out, is associated with the Kane Company. From there, it was a matter of raiding each of their strongholds. If we had gotten to you even a few seconds later—" His jaw tics, "I'll never forgive myself for letting you leave unprotected. If it were up to me, I'd tie you to me and never let you leave my side. If I could, I'd take back everything I said."

"But you can't."

He grimaces, then turns onto another road. "I am going to try my very best to make it up to you."

"I... I'm not sure that's a good idea."

"What's that supposed to mean?" he growls

"We are not good for each other, Michael." I firm my lips, " For heaven's sake, I tried to kill you. Twice... And you forced me to marry you, then turned me out when you felt like you didn't want me around anymore."

"That's not true," he says through gritted teeth, "I turned you out, because..."

"Because?"

"Because I knew if I kept you around, I'd end up falling for you."

"Huh?"

"Surprised?" He peers at me from the corner of his eye, "Didn't think I could admit that to you, huh?"

I swallow, "It still doesn't change the fact that every time we are together, we bring out the worst in each other."

"That's how the best relationships are." He stares through the windshield. "We are not a normal, staid couple meant to have a normal, staid marriage, where the husband holds down a desk job and makes an appointment to have sex with his wife—"

"You're right."

"I am?"

I nod, "We're the kind of couple who needs to steer clear of each other if we want to survive."

"Survival is overrated." His lips curl. "We bring out the darkness in each other. We speak to each other on a primal level. Even now, as we maintain the distance that society asks of us, our bodies hunger for each other, our flesh wants to reach out to the other, and our souls? Our souls recognize the twisted, fuckedupness that each of us has tried to hide from the world, but which we haven't been able to hold back from each other."

"My point, precisely." I pull my hand back from his thigh, but he captures it and imprisons it between his big palm and the solidness of his thigh. My core flutters.

Shit, even as I am trying to put distance between us, I can't stop being aware of him. Can't stop myself from being turned on by his strength. Can't stop myself from wanting to turn to him and crawl into his lap and feel his arms around me as he hides me from the world. Tears prick at the backs of my eyes. Goddammit, since when have I become so needy?

Is it his dominance, his need for control that brings out the feminine side in me? Is that why I veer toward him for safety? Is that why, despite everything in me knowing how wrong it is to want to be with him, I want to trust him?

"We need to have nothing to do with each other."

His fingers tighten on the wheel.

"You did the right thing in turning me out earlier." I set my jaw. "It was my bad luck that I ended up being kidnapped again. But I'm safe now, so there's no reason for you to hold onto me."

He doesn't answer, simply keeps his gaze forward.

"If you return my phone back to me, I can call Summer and have her send someone to help me leave here."

"No."

"What do you mean no?"

"If you think I am letting you go that easily, you are mistaken."

"I thought you said that you were falling for me."

"All the more reason to not let you go."

And there…he is. The big, bad, alphahole Capo. Guess it was too much to hope that he was actually revealing his more sensitive side. Not that I doubt he has it. Not that I want him to share it with me. Somehow, it's easier if he continues to stay in his arrogant, over-the-top, alpha persona. It's much easier to deal with him that way. It's so much easier to hate him when he doesn't reveal the man behind the ruthless Capo. Yeah, I'd much rather he be unreasonable, and inconsiderate, and conceited.

I whip my head toward him. "I thought you said you were going to try to make it up to me."

"Doesn't mean I am going to let you go free."

"Then your idea of making it up to me and my idea of your making it up to me are, clearly, different."

"We'll see."

19

Karma

As it turns out, his idea of making it up to me is to transport me back to his island. He'd first driven me to a house in Palermo where a doctor — one he trusts, apparently — had checked me out. He'd checked out the wound at the back of my head, treated it, then given me a shot to help ease the pain. Guess Michael didn't want to risk taking me to a hospital, though the doctor had been competent and very professional.

Then he had driven straight to the pier and whisked me up in his arms, despite my protesting that I'm not some stupid, helpless female. To which he'd retorted that he had rescued me, so perhaps I am more help-less than I thought. Which had promptly upset me more, but he'd ignored my reaction. He'd marched to his yacht... Yeah, there was a freakin' yacht that he'd had anchored at the pier. He'd carried me aboard, parked me in a chair in the captain's cabin, then had shrugged off his jacket and wrapped it about me. I had shoved one arm, then the other, into the sleeves, pulled it close — even as I had hated myself for snuggling into the comfort it offered, even as I had berated myself for being stupid enough to turn my nose into the collar and sniff, drawing his dark, edgy, masculine scent into my lungs. As he'd started the boat and steered it across the water, I had watched his broad back, his powerful shoulders, the corded strength in his arms as he had steered the boat, and my heart had stuttered. Hell. I had just told him that I wanted nothing to do with him, yet watching him maneuver the boat with that innate confidence that defines my Capo had turned my insides to jelly. I had slipped off the chair, walked up to him, and he had pulled me close to his side.

I had slid my arms about his lean waist and clung to him as he piloted the craft to the island. By the time we had reached it, I could barely keep my eyes open, thanks to whatever it was that the doc had given me, I guess. He had swung me up into his arms again, and I had fallen asleep as he'd carried me inside, only to wake up in the middle of the night screaming.

In my dream, I was back in that room, with that same gorilla of a man on top of me, threatening to...not only kill me, but first, to do much worse. He slapped me about, tore my clothes and... That's when I woke up and found I was clinging to Michael.

His arms around me, he held me close enough for my breasts to be crushed against his massive chest. "Shh!" he soothed me, then rocked me and made these rumbling noises that seemed to emerge from deep within his chest. It soothed me enough to fall asleep, until I woke up this morning, alone...in his bed...in his room. Huh?

I stare about the space, wondering what it means? The last time I was on the island, I was his prisoner. Well, I still am, considering he said that he's not letting me leave, despite my stated desire to do so.

I roll out of bed, trudge to the bathroom, and make the mistake of looking at myself in the mirror. I look terrible, downright frightening. The dark circles under my eyes are almost as dark as my favorite goth make up, which I don't have with me to cover the ravages of my recent ordeal.

I shower, carefully wash my body, then shampoo all of the filth from my hair, wincing only a little when my fingers encounter the bump on my head. When I emerge, I find a set of newly-laundered and folded clothes, along with fresh underwear.

Was it him? More likely, Cassandra, assuming she returned to island as well. I pull on the jeans and T-shirt (both black), along with the socks and the sweatshirt (both grey), and walk down to the kitchen to find Cassandra at the stove cooking.

She turns to me with a smile on her face, "How do you feel?"

"Not too bad," I concede as I take a seat at the breakfast counter. "When did you get here?"

"Earlier this morning." She pours out a glass of orange juice, then places it in front of me.

I glance at it, then fold my hands in my lap.

"The Capo wants you to drink that."

"No doubt." I scowl at the glass of juice, "Where is he, anyway?"

"He had some business to see to."

"Is he still on the island?"

She nods.

"So why isn't he here?" Jesus, why do I sound so whiny, so needy? Everything I had sworn to myself I never would be. Summer had taken good care of me, and had ensured that she had moved me out of the state's foster care system as soon as she was old enough to be able to do so… Still, the time we had spent apart had taught me that, ultimately, the only person I can depend on is myself. "Forget I said that," I clear my throat.

"No need to explain." She slides a plate of pancakes in front of me, then places a jar of honey next to it, along with butter. As well as a cup of espresso. "I'm just glad you are safe."

"So, you heard what happened?"

"The Capo was beside himself. He didn't rest for one second, not until he had found you. He contacted me early this morning and told me to get here so I could help make you more comfortable."

"Oh," I glance down at the pancakes, "maybe that's what he wants you to believe." I raise a shoulder. "Or maybe, it's just that he can't bear the thought of anyone else getting ahold of what he considers his."

"And is that so bad?" She murmurs, "I'd give anything to have a man look at me the way he looks at you."

"What do you mean?" I frown, "I am not exactly his favorite person."

"That's not true, you—"

"Cassandra." His hard voice rings out from the doorway.

Both of us turn to face him. I expect Cassandra to get nervous, or at least be startled at having been interrupted half-way through a conversation, which I am sure would have shed some more enlightening details on the Capo. Instead, there is no change in expression on her features. Huh?

She merely nods at me, "I'll see you later, Karma." She walks over to the doorway and he steps aside to let her pass.

He prowls over to pull up a chair opposite me. "You aren't eating."

"Neither are you," I retort.

"I ate already."

I lean back in my chair, "Why did you bring me here?"

"How's your head?" He rakes his gaze across my features, "No headache or anything?"

"I'm good," I say grudgingly, "and you are avoiding the question."

He quirks his mouth, "I'll make you a trade."

"Huh?"

"One answer to one question that you can ask me for every mouthful of food."

"It's a terrible deal." I purse my lips.

"How do you know without trying it?"

"Sometimes you don't need to try to know you are being set up." I scowl at him, then glance down at the pancakes. My stomach grumbles. My mouth waters. Damn it, they look so good. I pick up my knife and fork, cut a piece and raise it to my lips. I chew on it, then tip up my chin, "So, will you answer my question now? Why did you bring me here?"

"That's two questions," he retorts. "Also, it's safest for you here."

"You mean because you can keep me prisoner?"

He stares at me, looks down at the plate, then back at me.

Yeah, yeah, whatever. I cut into the pancake again, pop it inside my mouth, then glance at him."

"I brought you here to ensure that no one can get to you."

I shoot him an icy look, "So you *are* keeping me prisoner?"

"Does it look like you are a prisoner here?" He raises his hands, "You are free to come and go as you wish."

"A gilded cage is still a cage."

He tilts his head, "Not if you're safer within the walls than outside."

"Is that what you think?" I scoff, "That I am safer inside here?" I shovel more of the pancake inside my mouth.

"Considering the last time you managed to find a way out, probably not." His lips quirk, "It's why I have taken certain precautions."

"Precautions?" I narrow my gaze, "What precautions?"

"There's still time to discuss that." He nods at my plate, "Finish your food."

I scowl at the remnants of the food on my plate, "I am full."

"Only one more bite," he coaxes me. "Come on, you can do it."

I blow out a breath, "Oh, okay." I scoop up the last mouthful, chew on it, swallow. "Happy?" I place my knife and spoon in the plate.

"Finish your juice."

"But—"

"Karma," his voice lowers to a hush, "do as you are told."

"Fine, fine, I'll do it." I squeeze my thighs together. "No need to go all alpha on me."

"You like it when I do."

"That's what you think." I toss my head as I grab the glass of juice and sip from it.

He merely arches an eyebrow, indicating he knows that I am lying. Hell, I know I am lying. But so what? It's either that or confess that I want him to own me, to possess me, to wrap his arms around me, before he grabs my throat, pushes me up into the wall, then shoves his thigh between mine and sinks his— I cough and sputter as the juice goes down the wrong way. Damn it. I place my glass back on the table.

Once the coughing subsides, I frown at him, "So, what are the stupid precautions you wanted to talk about?"

"I'll tell you when the time is right." He rises to his feet. "Meanwhile, I have something I want to show you."

20

Michael

I had woken up in the early hours of the day to find her thrashing about and screaming, trapped in the throes of a nightmare. I had brought her to the island because it's the only place where I can control everyone's comings and goings…After making sure that the boathouse no longer holds any boats that she could use to get away from me again…that is. Then I'd taken her to my bedroom…

There is no question in my mind that she belongs here. Not that I am going to touch her. She needs time and space to mend from what happened, not just physically but also emotionally. And clearly, I had been right in bringing her here, for she'd jack-knifed up in bed panting, no doubt, from the images of the debacle she'd been through… Which had been my fault. Because I'd let her leave… I'd told her to leave… Something I am not going to do again… And…

I am going to makes sure that if, for some reason, she does… Or if, somehow, someone else dares to take her away from me, I'll know where to find her.

All of those thoughts had run through my head as I had reached over to her side of the bed and drawn her close to me. I had made sure to sleep on top of the covers, putting as much distance as possible between us. Because, truly, I don't want to be tempted to touch her. But comforting her? That's completely different. She needs me and I am not going to let her down. Not when she, clearly, aches for comfort.

I had wrapped my arms around her, pulled her close, and tucked her head under my chin as I had tried to soothe her. She'd cried in my arms, until finally she'd quietened and fallen asleep. I had held her through the night, and sworn that I'll never allow her to be in this situation again, where she's helpless and a victim.

It's my fault she was kidnapped. By taking her, I had drawn the attention of all of my enemies to her. By keeping her and deciding to marry her, I had proclaimed to the world that I have a weakness—her. I had given those who hate me an opportunity to get to me... Through her. It's why it's doubly important to keep her safe. And there is only one way to ensure this. I'm not egoistical enough to think I can keep her 100% protected all the time.

Sooner or later, if someone wants to get to her, they will. And while I will do my utmost to ensure that won't happen... If... In the event that, God forbid, someone else does get to her again, I have to ensure that I will be able to track her down.

I was lucky this time that Seb had heard about the guy who had seen her being taken and put two and two together. Next time, I may not be this fortunate. She may not be this fortunate. Which means I have to tip the odds in our favor...

There is only one way to ensure that I never lose sight of her, no matter what happens. And while it's not something I want to do... It's something I have to do... Something for which she is going to hate me... Something she'd never agree to... Something I don't have a choice but to impose on her. Something which will make her loath me... That is inevitable.

So, before that happens, I have to sweeten her up to me... Hey, I'm only human, after all. And while I can live with her hate—as long as she is safe, that is—I can, at least, try to get into her good books beforehand, right?

At least, that is my reasoning as I push open the door to what had been her room previously. She walks inside, then halts. Her gaze widens as she takes in the space. Where her bed had once been is a sleek sewing machine. I had bought her a sewing machine to sew her wedding dress, but I decided to replace it with a state-of-the-art, most expensive model on the market. Next to it, the yards of fabric that she had purchased from the fabric shop, along with the various sewing tools that she'd bought that day, are neatly folded and organized. And, yeah, I had added to it by asking that *stronzo* Giorgio to bring in anything that she had left behind, just to be safe.

"Wh...what is this?" She blinks rapidly, as she turns to survey the space. "You changed the room completely?"

"It would seem that way, yes." I watch closely as she takes in everything in the space.

She walks over to the worktable next to the sewing machine, opens a sewing kit. She stabs her thumb into a thimble then holds it up, "I see you've been shopping."

"Do you like it?"

She drops the thimble back in the kit, then folds her arms around her waist. "When," she says without turning to face me, "when did you manage to do all of this?"

"Don't worry about that." I take in her flushed features, her bright eyes, "I take it that you *do* like it then?"

"I... I am not sure what to say." She shuffles her feet.

"Everything you might possibly need to create is here."

"I can see that," she murmurs, still not meeting my gaze. She walks over to the mannequin in the corner, and runs her finger along the curve of the figure. "I don't think this is enough."

"It isn't?" I frown as I take in the mirror on the opposite side, the adjustable shelves with cubbyholes, the rectangular table in the center of the room with enough surface area for her to work on.

"Nah," she turns to me, "I think you left out something very important."

"Eh?" I run my fingers through my hair, "What did I miss? I swear, I bought out that entire blasted shop."

"Clearly, you didn't research what goes into making a design studio."

Heat flushes my neck. Truth is, I had merely told Giorgio that I wanted everything that she'd possibly need to create in her studio. I hadn't exactly researched it myself though. *Merda!* Typical, that she had to catch me out on that, huh?

"So, what's missing?" I scowl, "Tell me and I'll make sure to get it for you."

"You sure about that?"

"Of course, I am."

Her lip curves, "No backing out after I tell you what it is."

I plant my palms on my hips, "Try me."

"Last chance," her smile widens.

I draw in a breath, "Do you want me to get it for you or not?"

" A cat."

"What?" I blink.

"A cat." She saunters over to me. "C-A-T, cat. You know, the furry thing that says 'meow'?"

"I know what a cat is."

"Good." She flicks some imaginary dust off my collar, "Now you can get one for me too. Make sure it's cute."

I gape as she sashays over to the fabrics and begins to examine them.

"Let me get this right, you want a cat to complete your studio?"

"Do I need to repeat myself?"

What the —! That little thing; she dares to talk that way to me? I take a step forward, then pause. Of everyone I have met, she is the only one who doesn't take shit from me. It takes some guts to stand up to me too... Especially after everything that we've done to each other. But then, Beauty, isn't just anybody. She's special. She's always known which of my buttons to press to get a reaction from me.

I thought I'd surprise her, but yet again, she's managed to throw me for a loop. A chuckle rumbles up my chest, turns into a full-blown laugh. I throw my head back and guffaw until tears run from my eyes. I wipe them away, then straighten to find her watching me.

"You okay?" she asks, her tone hesitant. "Not coming down with something, are you?"

"No," I shake my head, aware I am still wearing a smile on my face, but fuck, there is no one else here. Only this pint-sized woman who always knows how to put me in my place. "Why do you ask?"

"Never seen you laugh like that before. Hell, I've never seen you smile properly, let alone...give in to a full belly laugh like that."

"I've never been asked to buy a cat before."

"Never?" Her forehead creases.

"Never."

"Oh," she raises a shoulder, "guess there's a first time for everything."

She turns back to playing with the fabrics, before reaching for the sheets of paper next to them. She picks up a drawing pad, and a pencil, then turns to glance at me over her shoulder.

"What are you still doing here?" She scowls, "Leave, so I can work."

21

Michael

And I had obeyed her. Fuck me, but she had asked me to leave—not very politely either—and I had turned on my heel, skulked out of there, and left her in her studio. Me, the Capo with enough kills under my belt to warrant most people in Sicily warning their children at night that if they don't go to sleep, I'll kidnap them… Yeah, that's the kind of myth that accompanies my reputation… And I had simply acquiesced and left her to work. Maybe it's because she had seemed so happy to find herself surrounded by things that bring her pleasure. Maybe I had seen the sheer joy in her eyes in finding a space where she can work to her heart's content?

She had been taken aback, but also, there had been relief in her eyes. Has she missed her art that much? I raise the glass of whiskey to my lips and take a sip as I stare out of the double doors of the living room, which are flung open to face the sea. The evening sun slants its rays, lighting up the waves. The colors of the impending sunset bleed across the skies. Reds, pinks, golden hues… As pretty as her eyes. As gorgeous as her lips. No… She's more beautiful than nature's treasures. *Che cavolo*... Now I am waxing poetic about her while watching a sunset? Next, I'll be writing odes in her honor.

I left her room a few hours ago, and haven't seen her since. Cassandra had informed me that she had taken lunch up to Beauty's room and that she had eaten it all, as evidenced by the empty tray that had been deposited outside the door. Which is progress. At least, she is eating and happily ensconced in her studio. Which is more than I can say for myself. I glare at the fast-sinking sun on the horizon. Damn it, why is it that my thoughts are still on her?

A knock on the door interrupts my thoughts, and I confess, it is with relief that I turn to find Christian walking in. I nod to my brother, then turn to the woman at his heels.

"Doc," I jerk my chin, "he's briefed you on what I need?"

She draws herself up to her full height, "I have been told what you'd like me to do, but I must record my complete disagreement with what you have proposed."

"I wasn't asking for your opinion."

"I am giving it to you anyway," she firms her lips. "As a health care provider, as a professional, and as a woman, I must protest in the harshest of terms."

"Noted." I tilt my head, "If there's nothing else then—"

"I have something to say as well." Christian folds his arms across his chest. "You know I would never interfere with your personal relationships. I respect you too much for that, *fratellone*..."

"But?"

"But," he shuffles his feet, "I have to say that this is taking things too far."

"You think so?"

He nods, "I definitely do. Why not just speak to her first? Why not tell her what you have in mind?"

"And if she refuses—and you know she will—what then?"

"Then," he rubs the back of his neck, "then maybe you find another way to reach your goal without having to hurt her along the way."

"If this is what is needed to keep her safe, then I am not sorry."

"What if you are afterward? What if she hates you so much that your relationship with her breaks down completely?"

"It's not like the relationship between us is all that healthy right now."

"But at least, there is some semblance of one, isn't there?"

"Is there?" I rake my gaze over his features, "I'll take the risk, if it means I can keep her safe."

"I take it that's the most important thing for you, her safety?" the doctor murmurs and I turn to her.

"What did you say your name was again?"

"Aurora." She tightens her fingers around the sleek briefcase-like bag that she holds, "Doctor Aurora Garibaldi. My father is unwell, so I am here in his stead."

"I assume you are reliable?"

"My father wouldn't have sent me if I weren't."

I arch an eyebrow, "You do realize who you are talking to?"

"To the Capo of the Cosa Nostra," she says in a tone that is respectful, while her gaze is anything but.

"Everything you say and do here is confidential," I murmur. "If I hear of anyone getting wind of what you did, you are dead. You realize that."

"It won't come to that," Christian angles his body, half-blocking her from my view. *Interesting.* "I vouch for her, *fratellone*," he adds.

The woman jerks her head in his direction. She firms her lips but doesn't say anything. *Very* interesting.

"Do you now?" I stroke my chin. "Can I trust you to keep an eye on her?"

"I don't need anyone to keep an eye on me," she snaps at the same time that his features brighten.

"With pleasure." The bastard all but rubs his hands together.

"Meet me in my office in ten minutes." I walk past them and to the exit.

As I leave the room, I hear her say, "I don't need you to vouch for me." Her tone is so chilly that it could freeze a gelato in seconds.

I can't stop the smirk that curls my lips. This, whatever it is between them, is going to be fun to watch. I head up the stairs and to Beauty's room.

I walk into her room and find her bent over the table. Her back is to me and that gorgeous peach-shaped behind of hers wriggles as she focuses on whatever it is that she is working on. Around her, there are crumpled pieces of paper on the floor. More paper is strewn all across the table. As I watch, she straightens, then balls a piece of paper and tosses it over her shoulder. I reach forward, snatch it up and out of the air. I straighten it out, take in the half-sketched design which looks like the outline of a woman with the dress sketched on her.

"It's called a croquis."

"Whatquis?"

"A croquis," she replies without turning around. "A quick sketch of a human body that serves as a template for a fashion designer piece of clothing."

"I knew that."

"No, you didn't."

"You're right," I agree and she turns to scowl at me over her shoulder.

"What are you doing here?"

"Glad to see you are enjoying yourself." I toss the wadded-up piece of paper in the general direction of the piles of paper she's abandoned on the floor. "We do have a wastepaper basket in the room."

"I'll clean up the room once and for all at the end."

"What are you drawing?" I step behind her, try to peer over her shoulder. She moves to block my view.

"None of your business."

"Everything about you is my business."

"Don't you ever give your alphaholeness a rest?" She huffs.

"Do you want me to give it a rest?"

She raises a shoulder, "I am not sure I'd recognize you if you ever started conversing like a normal person."

"Normal is boring, Beauty. No-one understands that more than you."

"Oh?" She turns to shoot me a glance over her shoulder, "How do you know that?"

"Haven't we established many times over that I know you better than anyone else?"

Her forehead furrows. "It's true, actually," she concedes. "Only, I don't understand how someone like you can be intuitive enough to understand what I like."

"I know what you don't like, too."

She arches an eyebrow, "And what would that be, Mr. Capo of all he surveys?"

"I know that you don't like to be manhandled, for one." I wrap my fingers around her nape, and she shivers. "I know that you don't want to be urged to bend over your drafting table." I apply enough pressure that she lowers her upper body to the surface. "That you don't want me to palm your butt." I do just that as I place my palm against the curve of her denim covered backside, "And that you don't like being spanked." I bring my palm down against her ass and she draws in a sharp breath. "And that you don't like being spanked again," I slap her other asscheek, "and again." I smack both her asscheeks, alternating between them, and she groans. Her entire body shudders.

She slaps her palm onto the paper strewn the table, "Bloody hell." She groans, "Oh, my bloody God."

"And you don't like your pussy being fingered either, do you now, *tesoro mio*?"

I step behind her, fit my tented crotch against the valley between her butt-cheeks. She huffs, then parts her legs further — so I can push my throbbing shaft into her butt. I reach around, to lower her zipper, then slide my fingers inside the seam of her panties.

I brush against her pussy lips and she whines. "Oh, Mika, please... please —"

I slip one finger inside her sopping wet channel and she moans, then clamps down on my digit with her inner walls. The blood rushes to my groin. I thrust a second finger, then a third inside her, as I lean over to press my chest into her back, then bite down on the skin between her neck and the curve of her shoulder.

She yells, "Ouch, you neanderthal, what the hell was that for?"

I lick the abraded flesh and a whine spills from her lips. Moisture drips from between her legs and my cock instantly lengthens. Fuck, I had come here because I need to complete the one thing that will keep her safe, but one look at her, one glance at her delicious behind, one whiff of her sugary scent, and hell, if I can keep away from her. I hesitate with my fingers still inside of her when she frowns at me as she gives me side-eye.

"Either put it in or get away from me, you ass."

A chuckle rumbles up my chest. "Challenge accepted, *piccolina*." I pull my fingers out of her and she scowls, "What the hell, you horrible man, why do you have to tease me so, why —"

I yank her jeans down to her mid-thigh. I reach for the thimbles in her sewing kit, slide one onto my middle finger —thank the *Vergine Maria* that they fit—then another onto my forefinger, and she blinks, "What the hell are you doing?"

"What the hell does it look like I am doing?"

"I don't know. That's why I am asking you...oh!" She gasps as I shove the gusset of her panties aside then play with her pussy lips. "Oh, my," she gasps, "wha...what are you up to?"

"Shh." I finger the opening of her pussy, then slide my thimble-wrapped middle finger inside her channel.

"Gah!" She opens and shuts her mouth, "You didn't just, you didn't—"

"Oh, I most certainly did, my little wife." I add my thimble-wrapped forefinger, then my ring finger, and stretch her channel. She trembles, then clamps down on my fingers and I feel the pull all the way to the tip of my cock. "*Gesù Cristo*, you can take everything I can give you, can't you? You'll take it and you'll ask for more. Your greedy pussy will never have enough. It wants to be fucked and torn into. It wants every filthy thing I can do to it. It wants my cock and my fingers in at the same time so I can stretch it and fill you up until you have no idea where I begin and where you end, isn't that right?" I pant... "Beauty?"

She moans loudly and the sound snaps something inside of me. I release my hand on her neck, spit on my fingers, then slide one inside the opening of her backhole.

"Fuck you," she growls, even as she parts her legs even more, giving me better access. I add a second finger to her back channel, then begin to move my fingers in and out of her. At the same time, I fuck her pussy with the thimble-covered fingers of my other hand.

"Oh, hell. Oh, my bloody hell!" she yells as her entire body shudders. Her shoulders snap back, she thrusts back with her hips, trying to take more of my fingers inside her, then propels her hips forward, chasing her climax. "Mika, Mika," she chants, "I am going to—"

"Come for me, Beauty; come all over my fingers."

22

Karma

His command cuts through the thoughts in my head. Something primal inside of me rushes to obey him, and the vibrations which had been threatening at the base of my spine gallop out and up my back, to spark behind my eyes. I throw my head back, open my mouth and a soundless cry emerges. The climax crashes over me, and seems to go on and on. When I open my eyes, I am in his arms and being carried to the bathroom.

He seats me on the sink, pulls off the thimbles from his fingers before he reaches over to wash his hands.

"Guess it's a good thing that you ordered leather thimbles big enough to fit your fat fingers, eh?"

"You weren't complaining when I had said fat fingers inside you," he chuckles.

Heat sears my cheeks again. Can't believe I let him fuck me with thimbles. OMG, I let him fuck me with his thimble-wrapped fingers. Ugh, and I also enjoyed it. Double ugh. I glance away from him, reach down for my jeans, which are down around my ankles, but he grips my wrist. "Let me," he murmurs, and I straighten.

I watch as he wets a towel, then presses it between my legs.

Heat sears my cheeks, "You don't have to."

"I want to."

"None of this will change how I feel about you."

"I don't expect it to."

"If you think setting up a studio for me will get you into my good books...then you are... " I hesitate and he peers up at me from under those thick eyelashes.

"I am..."

"You are absolutely right," I mumble under my breath.

He smirks, then urges me down from the sink. He turns me to face the mirror then drags the washcloth between my arsecheeks.

"Oh, geez," I squeeze my eyes shut, "you really don't have to do that."

"Let me take care of you," he murmurs as he pats me down once more, then throws the towel aside. He reaches for the cabinet over the sink, opens it and grabs an ointment.

"What's that?" I ask, then gasp when he applies it to my smarting backside. Coolness soothes the skin instantly. I glance over my shoulder to find him administering more of the soothing ointment to my other butt –cheek.

"It's aloe vera," he replies as he continues to massage it slowly into my arse. The rhythmic movement sends pulses of awareness up my spine.

My core stutters, my belly flip-flops, and I squeeze my thighs together, chew on the inside of my cheek to stop myself from moaning aloud. *Down, slut, down. How much more will you humiliate yourself today, hmm?* I choke down all possible sounds of pleasure that threaten to spill from my lips. Watch as he finishes his task, then caps the ointment and places it aside. He pulls up my panties, then bends and yanks my jeans. He turns me around and I glance away as he zips up my jeans. He fits a knuckle under my chin, and angles my face toward him. "Of all the things I have done to you, you find this embarrassing?"

"Of all the things you've done to me, this is the most intimate," I shoot back. "You really didn't have to."

"I really did have to." He leans in closely enough for our eyelashes to tangle. His breath merges with mine; his lips almost brush mine. Those blue eyes of his seem to come alive with an emotion I don't dare put a name to.

Shit, of all the things that have taken place between us so far, this… This is, by far, the most threatening. My heart rate spikes and my pulse thuds at my temples. Heat from his body slams into my chest, and I gasp. The force of his personality is a heaviness that pushes down on my shoulders and holds me in place. It's a kind of safety blanket, like one of those weighted-down duvets that hold you in place, that keep you secure, that envelop you with a sense of safety which lulls you into a state of contentment. The hair on my forearms rises.

"What are you going to do?" I whisper, "Why are you being so nice to me?"

His features freeze for just a millisecond, then he brings his big palm up to cup the nape of my neck. "So fucking intelligent, my Beauty. You make a worthy opponent, you know that?" His fingers are long enough to meet around the front of my throat.

I bring my hands up to grab his thick forearm. "Please," I murmur, "don't."

"Do you trust me?" He lowers his forehead to mine, "Do you, Beauty?" He peers into my eyes, holds my gaze with those hypnotic depths of his. "Do you?" He asks again, "Do you trust me?"

"Yes." I whisper, and in that moment, I know I do. Damn it, why do I have to give him this part of myself too?

His fingers around my neck tighten, specks of black flicker at the edges of my eyesight, I draw in a breath and my lungs burn, then everything goes dark.

I hear voices as if from far away. "What did you do to her?" A man's voice—not Michael, one of his brothers maybe—asks.

"It's for her own good. I told you already," Michael rumbles back. "Don't question me again, *fratellino*."

"I must warn you again that what you are doing is unethical, and goes against everything my profession stands for." A woman's voice, this time. Her tone is filled with concern. For me? What's happening? What is he doing to me?

I try to stir, and must succeed, for the next moment, Michael's breath brushes my cheek. His scent fills my senses as he presses a kiss to my forehead. "Shh, baby," he murmurs, "you're safe with me."

I shouldn't believe him. Why the hell do I *want* to believe him? Why do I still trust him? I swallow, try to ask him…but can't seem to string the words into a sentence. I turn my face toward him, and his warmth envelops me. His arms come around me and he hauls me close to his chest. I try to open my eyes, but my eyelids are weighed down.

"Go on, Doc," his voice rumbles, "don't delay further."

"I must formally record the fact that I am doing this under duress."

"You are boring me, Doc." Michael's voice is impatient, "If it weren't for the fact that my brother, here, seems to have taken a shine to you, I'd have killed you by now."

I sense the woman stiffen in shock. Huh? You'd think she'd be used to the ways of the Mafia if she works for them? Or maybe she doesn't? Is that why she sounds so...above-board...so normal? Enough to protest against whatever it is that Michael wants done to me? Holy shit, what does he want her to do to me? Whatever it is, it can't be good. But I do trust him, don't I? I had told him so... So why is it that all my instincts insist that I don't want whatever it is that is going to happen? I try to push against him, but his arms tighten.

"Doc," he growls, "do it now."

Wh-a-t the — I open my mouth to protest, but his mouth covers mine, and the kiss... OMG, his kiss is soft, tender, sweet... WTF? Michael Byron Domenico Sovrano can kiss with so much emotion? So much tenderness...so much...devotion? He swipes his tongue across the seam of my lips and I open my mouth. He slides his tongue over mine, deepens the kiss, opens himself up so his presence seems to invade my mouth, my throat, my chest... Every cell in my body is filled with Michael. Michael. Michael. I sink into the kiss, surrender to his strength, his complete dominance, that absolute force that is my husband. I push into him, aching to be near him, wanting to be closer to him, needing to feel his skin on mine. He brushes the hair away from my ear, holds it to the side, then grips my jaw, holding me in place.

Something—no, someone—pulls back my ear... The same ear from which he had brushed away my hair. Something pricks me behind my ear. I stiffen, try to turn, but his grip on my jaw tightens. He licks into my mouth and my belly trembles. My pussy clenches, my thighs spasm, and I moan deep in my throat, thrust up and into him. He drags his arm over my butt, grasps the curve of my hip and holds me immobile as he thrusts his tongue in and out of my mouth, in and out. His complete mastery over me something I cannot deny as my head lolls back and I surrender to him, as he deepens the kiss even further. Even as I sense another prick behind my ear...this one a pin-prick that I might have missed if it were not for the fact that a part of me is still resisting him, the part that has allowed me to survive thus far. The part that insists I give in to his ministrations now—or at least, pretend to. That part insists that I close my eyes and drift with the warmth, the comfort that he provides. I allow his presence to engulf me, let the darkness pull me under.

When I awake, I am in his bed and it's dark outside. I sit up, and when a shape looms over me, I scream.

23

Michael

"It's only me." I hold up my hands.

She draws in a breath, "Michael?" Her hushed voice shudders across my skin, and a shiver runs down my spine. My nerve endings pop. The blood drains to my groin as I lean forward in my seat.

"How are you feeling?"

"A little dazed," she yawns, then looks around the room, "Where am I? What happened?" She runs her fingers through her hair. "One moment you were kissing me, the next moment, I think I blacked out..."

"You were out for a little while," I concede.

"Why are you sitting in darkness?" I sense rather than see her scowl. She reaches over, flicks on the light next to the bed, then winces. She blinks her eyes as her eyesight adjusts, then glances over at me. "You going to tell me what happened?" She folds her arms about her waist.

I rise up to my feet and walk over to her. Sink down next to her on the bed. Reach for her, but she pulls away.

"Oh, no," she shakes her head, "no, no, no." She throws up her hands. "Keep your distance, buster..."

"Or what?" I smirk.

"Or… " she glances about the room, then grabs the book next to the bed, "or I'll throw this at you."

"You sure you want to do that?"

"Why wouldn't I?"

"Have you seen what the book is about?"

She frowns at me, then lowers the book, "It's a fashion sketchbook." She turns it over, then flips the pages. "With readymade templates I can use to sketch my fashion designs…"

"And…"

"And plan my outfits; and for my illustrations; also, a diary to take notes when inspiration strikes." She lowers the book, "If you think you can distract me that easily—"

"That's not all," I nod toward the side table.

She glances down and her gaze widens. She places down the sketchbook, then picks up the other slim volume, *"25 Cats Named Sam and One Blue Pussy."* Her voice hitches. "Am I the *Blue Pussy?* Is that why you bought this for me?"

"You're my pussy, regardless of the color, *Bellezza.*"

"Ha, you're funny." She laughs nervously as she swipes her palm across the book.

"I mean it."

She peers into my face. "You really do mean it, don't you?" she says in a low voice.

"You know, I do." I jerk my chin toward the book, "Open it."

"Is it what I think it is?" she murmurs.

I chuckle, "Only one way to find out."

She flips open the cover and draws in a breath. "It's the original illustrated manuscript by Andy Warhol." She glances up at me. "It *is* the original illustrated manuscript, isn't it?"

I arch an eyebrow, and she blows out a breath. "Shit, it really *is* the original manuscript." She glances down at the book again, "I didn't think this was available to buy."

"It wasn't."

"Then, how—?" She glances up at me, "I have a feeling you may have had to spill a little blood to get a hold of this."

I stare at her and her gaze widens. "In fact, I am *sure* that you had to spill more than a little blood to get ahold of this, but you know what…?"

I tilt my head.

"In this instance, murder may have been justified."

I blink. "Say that again?"

"I said, you may have had to commit —"

"I heard you." I reach for her, and this time, she doesn't shy away. A hot sensation stabs at my chest. I push a strand of hair behind her ear. "I had a dream, which was not all a dream..." I whisper.

She swallows, "The bright sun was extinguished, and the stars..."

"Did wander darkling in the eternal space..." I lean in close enough for us to share breath.

Her pupils dilate, "Rayless, and pathless, and the icy earth..."

"Swung blind and blackening in the moonless air," we say in unison.

"Byron," she murmurs.

"Lord-fucking-Darkness himself."

"What is with you and Byron?" She peers into my face, "Why do I get the feeling that there's more to why you recite him than what meets the eye?"

I pull away, then stand up, "Because there is."

I turn to walk away, and she grabs my wrist, "That's it? That's all you are going to give me?"

I glare down at her fingers and her grip tightens. "You can scare your men with that Michael Byron stare, but it doesn't do anything to me."

"Is that right?"

She stares at me with a strange look on her features.

"What?" I scowl, "What is it?"

"Michael Byron," she murmurs.

"Yeah, that's my name."

"Were you named after Byron, as well?"

I drag my fingers through my hair, "It's also my father's name."

"The two of you share more than your first name, huh?"

"Cursed to have not one, but all four of my names in common," I reply bitterly.

"You don't like him, huh?"

"Did you like your father?"

She shakes her head.

"There you go."

"Still, you are following in his footsteps, so I assume it's not all bad when it comes to the relationship between the two of you?"

"Some things I do only because it's tactically the right thing."

"You love plotting your moves, huh? You love to move people

around like they are pawns on a chessboard, and only you have control over their futures."

"I am the only one who has control over the destinies of my clan."

"And that includes me?"

"You're my wife, so you're part of the clan; ergo..." I raise a shoulder.

"That's why you did whatever it is you did earlier?"

"What did I do earlier?"

"Don't bullshit me, Michael." She places the book back on the side table with care, then throws off the cover and rises to her feet. "What did you do, earlier? Tell me."

"I don't think you want to know."

"You mean, *you* don't think I want to know," She scoffs.

"Getting sassy, Mrs. Michael Byron Domenico Sovrano?"

"I didn't say that I have accepted being your wife yet."

"Not giving you a choice, Beauty."

"There's always a choice." She tosses her head, "Also, if you really did think of me as your wife, you'd tell me what happened earlier." She scowls at me, and there's something in her eyes, some kind of knowl-edge...a suspicion, maybe, of what happened earlier.

Merda, I ball my fingers into fists at my sides. Why the hell am I second guessing myself here? Why can't I just tell her what I did? Since when have I become so...worried about someone else's response? She's my wife. She'll damn well take whatever I do to her... And if I had wanted someone meek and servile, I'd have married someone from my clan a long time ago. Maybe I had been holding out for someone like her, and I hadn't even been aware of it. I shake my head to clear it. And since when have I begun thinking in such emotional terms about her? Love is for fools and poets, neither of which I am.

"You going to tell me about it, yet?" She scowls.

"Do you want me to tell you about it?"

She throws up her hands, "What else have we been talking about all this time?"

"Okay, then."

"What does that mean?"

"It means, okay. I'll tell you about it."

"So, what are you waiting for?"

There's a knock on the door and I smirk at her, "This." I pivot, walk over to the door, and open it just enough to accept the covered basket that Seb hands over to me.

"You owe me, *fratellastro.*" He scowls.

I nod, "I won't forget this." I shut the door on him, then turn back and prowl over to her. I plant the basket at her feet.

"What's that?"

"Open it."

She hesitates and I chuckle, "Not like you to be uncertain."

"Hmm, let me see... A surprise given to me by the Capo himself," she jabs a finger in her cheek, "why does that not reassure me?"

I laugh, "I promise, this one won't bite you... Well, not unless you provoke it."

"Huh?" She scowls, "Now *that* has piqued my curiosity."

Bingo! I can't stop the smile from curving my lips as she bends, then grabs the cloth and whisks it off.

Stunned, she stares into the basket. "What...what is that?" she splutters.

"What do you think?"

"I... I..." she reaches for the tiny creature that stretches and yawns. "It's a...cat?"

"A kitten," I correct her.

"Oh!" She rubs the forehead of the little thing that mewls pitifully. "Oh, you beautiful, beautiful creature." She scoops up the kitten and holds it against her chest. The animal nestles against her breasts. What the fuck? When I had bought her a pet, I hadn't anticipated competition for her attentions. I scowl at the beast, which nuzzles into her palm.

"What's your name, you sweet little thing?"

"He doesn't have a name, yet" Shit should have bought a female kitten. Now, I have another male in the house who is closer to her than I am.

"Andy," she murmurs.

"What?"

"His name is Andy."

"Because I bought you a book by Andy Warhol?"

"D-u-h!" She smiles without look at me. "Are you hungry, Andy? Do you want something to eat?"

"There's cat food in the kitchen, if you want to feed him."

She stares at me, and I scowl back, "What?"

"You bought cat food?"

"I got you a kitten. Of course, I also bought cat food." I shrug. "Well, kitten food, to be exact."

Her gaze widens.

"What?" A flush heats my neck. "I am not completely heartless, you know?"

"Hmm." She bites down on her lower lip, and hell, my groin instantly hardens.

"How did you know that I wanted a Savannah?" she murmurs.

"Lucky guess?"

"And how did you find out that Andy Warhol is one of my fave artists ever?"

I raise a shoulder, "His style of expression seemed closest to how I see you."

"How do you see me?"

"You don't get to ask me the questions." I scowl and her smile widens.

"Humor me on this, Capo."

Fuck, when she calls me that, I'll do anything for her. Good thing she doesn't realize that.

"So," she urges, "how do you see me?"

"I see you as being original, unique, someone who stands apart just by being herself."

"Wow," she breathes, "that's a huge compliment."

"Saying it as it is, Beauty."

The kitten mewls again and she frowns, "I think he's getting hungry."

"Why don't I call Cassandra and ask her to feed it."

"What?" she cries. "No way. " She pulls the creature closer to her chest, "No one feeds my baby except me."

Ten minutes later, I am seated at the table in the kitchen, nursing a glass of whiskey as she watches the kitten eat from his bowl. Yeah, I bought not just cat food, but also all of the shit that the beast would need — bowls to eat from, more bowls to drink from, a basket in the corner of the kitchen with the softest blankets that can be used for his bed. She kneels down next to the kitten, pets him as he eats. She makes little cooing noises and I stare. Her entire attention is focused on the creature. I take another drink of my whiskey, place the glass down on the table with a *thwack* that echoes around the room. She doesn't even look up.

Gesu Cristo, maybe this hadn't been a good idea. On the other hand, she hasn't breathed a word about what had happened earlier, so there's that.

"Don't think your buying me a kitten has bought you into my good graces," she murmurs at me over her shoulder.

"Me?" I raise my hands, "I'd never think that."

"Ha," she scoffs, "why don't I believe that? Speaking of," her forehead furrows, "I only told you that I wanted a cat last evening, and you've managed to get me one in what...twelve hours?"

Nine, but who's counting?

"How did you do that?"

I smirk and she rolls her eyes, "Why do I even bother to ask these questions?"

She continues to pet the creature and it's like I have been dismissed. *Che cazzo?* Have I been usurped by a few weeks old kitten, and in my own home? I drag my fingers through my hair. And why the hell am I even threatened by that beast? Is it her proximity that's making me weak? Is it the fact that by falling for her...

Hold on. Back up. Who said anything about falling for her? I want her to stay my wife. Doesn't mean I have feelings for her...do I? And if I do? What then? What am I going to do about that, eh? I lower my chin, narrow my gaze on her, "I chipped you."

24

Karma

"What do you mean, you chipped me?" I rub Andy's head. He's stopped feeding and proceeds to curl himself in my arms. Aww, sooo cute. A melting sensation coils in my chest. Just a few hours after I told him that I wanted a cat, he got me one. Not to mention, that Andy Warhol book, which was, like, totally unexpected. Okay, so he has more money and power than anyone else I've met in my life, but still... It means something that he noticed my tastes enough to actually buy me things which reflect who I am. No one else has done that before. Maybe Summer... I suppose, but she is my sister. She is supposed to know these things. This man, however, is practically a complete stranger, and in a few weeks, he has really gotten to know me well on so many levels, he— *hangonabloodysecond*. I whip my head around to face him. "You *chipped* me, chipped me?"

He nods.

"You..." I bite the inside of my cheek, "you put a GPS tracker in me?"

He nods again.

"Holy shit." I glance around the kitchen, find a basket that, no doubt, the faithful Cassandra must have organized for the kitten. I walk over and place him in the bedding which is of the softest cotton, by the way. Nothing but the best for the pet of... His pet, huh?

I straighten, then turn to face him. "That's what all that activity earlier was about, huh? I thought maybe I'd dreamed it, but I didn't."

He simply holds my gaze.

I slide a finger behind my ear, feel the slight bump. "Holy hell," I burst out. "It's true; you actually put a tracker in me."

"Told you I did."

Anger surges through my veins. My heart slams against my rib cage. "Why would you do that?" I cry. "And you didn't even ask my permission to do so, you asshole!"

"I don't need your permission. Have you forgotten?" He looks me up and down. "You are my property — mine."

"I am my own person. I don't belong to anyone else, least of all, you."

"Then why did you come back?"

"That was only to make sure that you were actually dead...you...you bastard."

He laughs, "That's a lie and you can do better than that insult, Beauty."

"Don't call me that," I snarl. " I should have known there's an ulterior motive behind everything you do. The studio, the books, the kitten... It was all so...what? So you could distract me? Or maybe, you thought that you could buy me off with expensive gifts?"

"Maybe, it's because I want you to be happy?"

"How can I be happy when you chipped me like.... I am an animal?"

"Did it ever occur to you that I did it because I don't want to lose you again?" The skin around his eyes tightens. For a second, I am sure he's afraid... Of what? He's the bloody Capo of the Cosa Nostra. What could he possibly be afraid of, eh?

"You could have told me that's what you intended to do," I snap.

"You wouldn't have agreed."

"You don't know that."

"Would you have?"

I look at him, then away.

"That's what I thought." He pushes back his chair, then rises to his feet. He prowls over to me, pauses when he's right in front of me. "Look at me, Beauty."

I scoff.

He notches his knuckles under my chin and raises my head, so I have no choice but to meet his gaze. "Maybe I put a tracker in you because you are what's most precious to me."

"Maybe I don't care why you did it," I try to pull away from him, but he tightens his grip.

"Maybe you need to care more. Maybe you need to come clean about the fact that whatever is between us is not going away any time soon."

I stare into those blue eyes of his. He holds my gaze, and in them I see...the same helplessness that I feel.

"You know, I returned because I couldn't believe that I had killed you. I prayed that you were still alive, that there had been a mistake. I had hoped that if you were... Perhaps, we could find a way to be together. But all you were interested in was revenge. Then, when I was taken from you, I guess you had a change of heart or something. And just when I think that perhaps I can find a way of being with you, after all... You do this." I wave a hand in the air, "You chip me, without batting an eyelid, like I'm your pet. This is not normal behavior, Michael."

He opens his mouth, but I shake my head. "No, don't give me your bullshit about me not being normal. I know I am not. It's why, all my life, I've hoped to find someone who could give me the kind of normalcy that I have missed all my life."

"You don't mean it," he growls.

"Oh, but I do." I swallow. "All this time we were together, not once, did you ask me what I wanted."

"I didn't need to," he jerks his chin toward where Andy is sleeping in his basket, "I know exactly what you need."

"Maybe that is the case," I murmur and he glares at me. "Fine, fine," I pull away from him, and this time, he releases me. "I don't deny that everything you did...from refurbishing the studio, to the books to the kitten, was spot on. It's what I'd have chosen for myself... Still, it's just politeness to ask me what I want."

"You don't want me to be polite."

"See?" I turn on him, "This...this is what I am talking about. You assuming you know my mind."

"I do."

"You don't."

"Yes, I do."

"Argh," I dig my fingers in my hair and tug, "this is going nowhere."

"It can go exactly where you want it to."

"Where I want it to go is…" I tip up my chin, "far away from you."

"Don't lie to me." He scowls.

"I am not." My heart hammers in my chest. My pulse rate spikes. I square my shoulders, hold his gaze. "If you think I can forgive what you did to me, then you have another think coming. I may have been able to look past the kidnapping, even, but this…this. What you did… It's… I can't even pretend to understand it. It's the worst kind of violation, ever."

His jaw tics. A dense cloud of anger spools off of him and smashes into my chest. I gasp, take a step back.

"If you think I am letting you leave, you have another think coming," he growls.

"Fine," I snap.

"Fine."

25

Karma

That stupid conversation was yesterday. I haven't seen the alphahole since. I had wanted to leave the bedroom I've been sharing with him and move into one of the guest rooms, but he wouldn't hear of it. He had commanded me to stay and had walked out. He hadn't come to bed, so I guess he's sleeping somewhere else. Whatever. I'm not going to feel sorry for depriving him of his own bed. Not after what he did to me.

I woke up early this morning and he was gone. Good riddance! I took a quick shower, then headed down to the kitchen to check in on Andy...who had already been fed by Cassandra. I tried not to be jealous about that.

I grabbed his basket, as well as two bowls, one for his food and one for water, and a can of cat food, and brought them up to my studio with me. I settled him a corner, before continuing to work on my latest creation.

I'm not quite sure what it will be yet. I am still in the doodling stage. And yeah, I refuse to use the sketchbook he got me. I also haven't touched the Andy Warhol book because... Well, I want to spite him. Maybe I'm spiting myself. But whatever.

I draw a design, then crumple up the paper and throw it aside. Draw the design again... Ugh! It sucks. I scrunch up the paper, toss it aside. To be honest, I don't know exactly what it is that I am drawing here.

It's often like that for me. I need to doodle first, wait for the design to emerge from my subconscious mind. Often, I have to draw for days on end before the motifs begin to reveal themselves. It's like, by drawing, I plumb the images in my subconscious mind. I stare at my scribblings... The wide forehead, the hooked nose, the square jaw. Gah, it's an outline of his stupid face.

Shit. Clearly, I have his features imprinted on my brain. OMG! This is soo not happening. I design clothes. I don't draw people or profiles... but somehow, I have ended up etching his likeness instead of focusing on my new creation. I crush the paper between my palms, toss it over my shoulder.

"Ouch," a female voice protests, "I've never had a patient deck me with a paper ball, and that too, on our first meeting."

I turn to find a woman I have never seen before standing in the doorway.

"Who are you?" I scowl, "And haven't you heard of knocking before entering?"

"I'm Doctor Aurora Garibaldi," she murmurs, "and I'm sorry, we're normally not that formal in this part of the world."

"Well too-bloody-bad." I sniff, "In my part of the world, it's polite to knock and ask permission before you enter a person's room, and—" I stiffen, "did you say that you are a doctor?"

"I am." She tilts her head, "May I come in?"

My heart begins to beat faster and I don't know why. No, I do know why, but I don't want to acknowledge it. Yet.

"If I say you can't," I say in a low voice, "what then?"

She blows out a sigh, "I think you'll want to hear what I have to say, Karma. May I call you, Karma?"

"You know my name."

"Yes," she nods, "that's what I want to talk to you about."

"Oh, hell."

I stare at her, and an uncomfortable silence descends between us, broken by a soft mewling from Andy's basket.

I turn toward him at the same time as the doctor. I watch as Andy peeks over the side of the basket. He mewls again, then crawls out and my heart stutters. I walk over, lift him up in my arms.

"Oh, wow, you have a kitten?"

I don't reply. Instead, I walk over to the arm chair near the window and sit down with the kitten in my arms.

"So sweet," she murmurs, still hovering by the doorway.

"I'm not sweet," I snap.

"The kitten, she's—"

"He," I interrupt her. "It's a he; his name is Andy, and I suppose you had better come in."

She nods, steps inside the room and shuts the door behind her. She walks over to take the chair on the opposite side of the table, then places the sleek satchel she's brought with her on the floor. One thing about Italy—everyone seems to be dressed and carrying designer wear, like it's the norm. Which, I guess it is here, considering that so many well-known designers are of Italian origin. Both of us watch as the kitten purrs in my arms, then snuggles in.

"How old is he?"

"Nine weeks," I reply.

"He's beautiful," she says, her tone sincere.

I can't stop the smile that curves my lips, "He's a Savannah."

"Have you had him long?"

"No," I rub my finger over Andy's tiny forehead and he yawns, "Michael gave him to me yesterday."

She blinks rapidly, "The Capo gave you a kitten?"

"Umm, yeah." I scowl at her, and she stares at me with a strange look on her face.

"What?"

"Nothing."

"Out with it." I point a finger in her direction, "It's not nothing when you have that weird look on your face."

She tilts her head, "It's just... The Capo, getting you a kitten...is—"

"What?"

"It's out of character."

"Hmm," I bite the inside of my cheek. "Well, I am his wife, after all." Not that you'll catch me saying that to him, but he's not here in the room, so it's fine to say it aloud in front of a stranger, isn't it? Speaking of... "Why are you here, Doc?"

"Call me Aurora." She half smiles. "I came to check on you, Karma."

It's my turn to blink, then I square my shoulders. "You're the one who did it." I touch the slight bump behind my ear which, while I had managed to push it to the back of my mind, in all honesty, I haven't forgotten about. "I heard your voice last night. I thought maybe I had dreamed it, but guess I didn't."

"I was there," She folds her hands in her lap. "It's why I had to come and check on you today."

"You were there and you didn't stop him from tagging me?" I say in a low voice. "What kind of a doctor are you that you were actually part of this process? Isn't this going against the Hippocratic oath or something?"

She glances away, then back at me, "You have to understand that this is the Capo you are talking about. I am but a lowly doctor. I have to do as he says, else —"

"Else?"

"He'll kill not just me, but every member of my family. He'll wipe out all trace of us if we defy him."

I take in her wide gaze, the white skin around her lips. "Wow, you really do believe that, don't you? You are afraid of him."

"He's the Capo," she says simply. "His word is law."

"And I am his wife. Supposedly." I scowl, "And this is what he does to me." I rise to my feet with the sleeping Andy in my arms, then walk over to the basket. I place him in it, soothe him when he wakes up so he falls asleep again. If only it were that easy for me to forget everything he's done to me. I turn to face her. "You know this is wrong... So wrong," I ball my fists at my side. "He tagged me like I am some... some...animal with no rights."

"He," she clears her throat, "he only wants to keep you safe."

I stare at her, "I can't believe you are taking his side."

"I am not really." She swallows. "If I were, I wouldn't have risked his anger and insisted he allow me to come check on you this morning."

"Fat lot of good that will do." I begin to pace. "You were there and you didn't stop him."

"I tried, believe me. His brother and I begged him not to do it, but he was most insistent. I got the impression that he —"

"What?" I scowl, "Say it."

"That he's afraid for your safety. That he'd do anything to protect you. That he doesn't want you out of his sight. That he wants to make sure that if, for whatever reason, you are separated from him, he'll know where to find you."

"Ha," I scoff. "All this is just a power play. It probably turns him on to know that he can do anything with me. That he could even...even... put a bloody tracker on me so he'll know exactly where I am every minute of every day."

"And you like that?"

"What?"

"That he's so...focused on you. That all of his attention is targeted on you."

I flush. Honestly, there's a part of me that revels in it...but damn, if I am going to admit that aloud. "Frankly, I don't care for it. Especially not, if it means that he virtually has me on a leash here... Besides, it's wrong. Can't you see that? You don't go around tagging another human being just because of your own insecurities."

"You're right," her shoulders slump. "It's not the 'done' thing. But then, when have the Capo and his brothers ever conformed to the 'done' thing?"

"You sound like you know them well."

"No one knows them well." She half smiles. "They are a force all their own. I went to the same school as them, though they are all much older than me. All the boys wanted to be them and all the girls...couldn't take their eyes off of them." She adds, "Even our teachers were afraid of them in school. They could do pretty much whatever they wanted and no-one would dare stop them."

"Sounds like nothing has changed." I scowl, "Once a bully..."

"They weren't all bad though."

"No?"

"They helped my father when he needed money the most."

"Oh? How did they help?"

"The Capo paid off his mortgage, paid for me and my sister's education."

"Only so he could buy your father's loyalty."

"That may be the case," she raises a shoulder, "but just the threat of his power would have been enough to have my father fall in line. He needn't have done everything else that he did. I know he comes across as gruff and uncaring—"

"You have no idea."

"—But that's just the persona he's had to create to survive in the Mafia world."

Maybe I did guess that. Maybe a part of me has hoped that's true. Maybe, in the moments that we had been intimate, I had glimpsed the tenderness that he is capable of... But then he had gone and chipped me, and without even asking me. He may claim that it's to keep me safe, but surely, I should have a say in it too?

"I am afraid I don't buy it." I square my shoulders. "Why are you here anyway? If you came to make sure that I am alive, then you can rest assured that I am."

"It's not only that." She bites her lower lip, "I guess, I just wanted to make sure that you are okay."

I scoff.

"Maybe I just want to help?" she offers.

"You can help me by getting rid of this microchip."

She shakes her head, "I am sorry but I can't do that."

I push my hair back from my face, "Then get me out of here."

"What?" she says in horror. "I... I can't. If I go against the Capo, he will have me killed."

I can't stop the smile from curving my lips, "You owe me, Doc."

She shakes her head, "No, please don't ask me to do that." She rises to her feet and picks up her bag, "I guess it was a mistake coming here. I should have realized there was nothing to be gained from it."

"Sit down," I say in a hard voice. Shit, some of Michael's assertiveness is rubbing off on me. Hell, I even sounded like him there for a second.

She blinks, but sinks back slowly into the seat. "You are not letting me leave without some kind of a deal, are you?"

I smile wider, "You guessed right, Doc. You can make up a little bit for what you were part of."

"How?" She swallows. "He has you chipped. Even if you did manage to escape, he'd be able to track you."

But if I manage to get to a phone and call Summer first, she'll be able to help. "Let me worry about that," I murmur. "Your role is only to get me out of here."

She locks her fingers together, "The moment you go missing, Michael will suspect me. Also, I was checked thoroughly on the way in, and they are bound to repeat the procedure on the way out again."

"Hmm," I tap my finger against my chin, "you're a doctor, right?"

She frowns, "You know I am."

"So, if I were unwell enough that you couldn't treat me here, you'd have to take me out of here to a hospital, right?"

She peers into my face, "You really are a devious woman, aren't you?"

"You have no idea."

"Does he know that you can run circles around him?"

"*He* has no idea." I chuckle and a reluctant smile curves her lips.

"So, I was thinking…"

"Stop," she throws up her hand, "whatever it is you're thinking, don't tell me. I trust you to plan the events. Then, I'll be called in and when I am, I'll simply be the concerned doctor who insists on doing the right thing by you."

She rises to her feet, "Now, may I check you out, to make sure the wound behind your ear is healing properly?"

"That was like barely a prick."

"Regardless, Capo's orders."

I take my seat again and she checks me out. When she's satisfied, she packs her bag, and straightens, "Right then, I'll leave you here." She glances around the studio, "The Capo had this set up for you, didn't he?"

"Are you surprised?"

"Not anymore. When it comes to his wife, I am realizing, the Capo will do just about anything for you."

She heads toward the door. Somehow, I get the feeling that my only friend in the entire world is leaving. Not that I know Aurora that well, but with some people you just know that you can trust them, right? Maybe it's because she's a doctor… A doctor who is in his employ, who was the one who implanted the tracker. But still… She's also a woman. Surely, she understands why it's important for me to leave here?

"Aurora!"

I call out and she stops. She turns to me, with a quizzical look on her face.

"Thank you."

She tilts her head. "Don't thank me, yet," she murmurs, "you don't know if this plan of yours is going to succeed."

26

Michael

"Goddamnit, missed again," I straighten, then slam my cue against the edge of the billiards table. It promptly snaps in two. "*Che cazzo!*" I glower at the half-broken cue in my hand, then raise my hand to hurl it.

Seb steps aside. "Watch it, Mika," he murmurs. "Your temper is getting the better of you."

"There should be a rule that you cannot defeat the Capo at a game," I lower my arm and glare at Massimo—the *pezzo di merda* who smirks at me from across the table.

"Giving up so easily, *Padrone*?"

"*Vaffanculo!*" I growl as I fling the broken half of the cue on the floor. It's her fault that I am in this state. Every night I sleep next to her... No, not sleep. I lay awake next to her, breathing in her sweet scent, aware of her luscious curves next to me on the bed. And the little noises she makes sometimes in her sleep, or the way she sometimes turns over and snuggles into me. The first time that happened, I tried to move away — yeah, me, the man who never denies himself pussy, tried to put distance between himself and his wife... So, yeah, tell me again, how that happened? — and she simply followed me, insisting on cuddling into my side, as I lay there with a fast-thickening erection, that I had to jerk off to in the bathroom, trying not to make too much noise before leaving before dawn. And even after leaving and trying to get some work done in my study, the scent of her followed me. Images of her assailed me, as if determined to burn right into my brain.

Che cazzo! I am really losing it. I glare around at the faces of my brothers. "What?" I growl at Christian who's staring at me over his knitting needles. What the— I do a double take. "Is that what I think it is?"

"You mean this?" He holds up the knitting needles, and nope, na-a-h I wasn't imagining things. *Stronzo* actually does have a pair of—you heard that right—knitting needles, held between his fingers.

"What are you doing?" I snap.

"What do you think I'm doing?"

"I am not sure." I rub my eyes, "Tell me you are not knitting."

He glances down at the needles. "I am…not…knitting." The clack-ity-clack of the needles fills the space.

"Shit, he's actually knitting," Massimo turns to gawk at him.

"Why the hell are you knitting?" Seb mutters from his position against the wall—he's put a fair distance between us, I notice, *bastardo.*

"Maybe he's trying to get in touch with his feminine side?" Xander offers.

"That's the kind of shit we expect you to pull," Adrian retorts, "But Christian? Naw." He scratches his chin, "It must have something to do with a chick."

"A chick?" Seb scoffs, "If that were the case, surely, he'd need to be using a completely different kind of needle?"

Adrian shoots him a sideways glance, "Was that a joke? Because I don't get the joke."

"You wouldn't get the joke because you have no sense of humor."

Adrian laughs, "So speaks the most serious of all the men in Sicily."

"I'm not serious; you are serious."

"I'm afraid, in this regard, I have to side with Adrian," I state. "You are going to make a very effective Capo, but you could do with a little bit of loosening up."

"Yeah, you take everything too seriously," Christian drawls from his position in the armchair. Fucker is sprawled out, and with the reading glasses he has on… He resembles a more serious version of the brother I know.

"Not all of us can be happy-go-lucky and waste time trying to explore our feminine side or some such shit," Seb growls. "Some of us have had to fight for everything that comes our way."

"Here we go again," Christian mutters, "like we haven't already heard about how your being the half-brother means you always get the raw deal. When you know it's not true. Not only did our mother embrace you as her own son, but she also worked herself to an early grave taking care of the both of you, in addition to her own five sons."

"And look where that got her," Seb pushes away from the wall. "Her own son, your own brother turns on his own flesh and blood and helps his Capo's wife escape... Now, that's something to make her turn in her grave, for sure."

"Don't talk about her that way." Christian rises to his feet, still holding those goddamn knitting needles. He takes a step forward and the ball of yarn falls to the floor next to him.

"I ain't telling a lie here and you know that," Seb scoffs. "Ask *fratellone*, here, and he'll only confirm it."

"Don't bring me into this, you guys," I mutter. "Luca has his punishment coming to him, when I finally catch up with him. So, whatever this unresolved business is between the two of you, it's up to you guys to sort it out."

Christian glowers at Seb, "You've always had a chip on your shoulder about being the illegitimate bastard. Time you moved on from that, don't you think?"

"Who are you calling a bastard?" Seb prowls toward Christian, who takes a step forward as the yarn winds around his ankle. He takes another step, stumbles, then rights himself. *"Che cazzo!"* He glares at the ball of yarn, "Why is it that the shit that seems so easy is the most difficult to master?"

"Is that a rhetorical question?" I ask.

"Are you sure you're talking about the knitting, or is this about women?" Massimo arches an eyebrow.

"You mean 'are you talking about one particular woman,' right?" Xander inserts.

"Shut the fuck up." Christian glares at Xander.

"You're twisting yourself up in knots." Seb smirks.

"No, I am not." Christian scowls at Seb, "And what the fuck are you smirking at?"

"Me?" Seb's grin widens, "I am not smirking."

Christian throws up his fist, "You laughing at me, *stronzo?*"

"You talkin' to me, *stronzo*?" Seb retorts.

"*Vaffanculo, testa di cazzo.*" Christian lunges forward. This time, he does actually trip on the yarn. He crashes down, just as Seb gets out of his way.

"Shit, you're a mess," Seb shakes his head. "Alas, poor Christian, he did mean well."

Christian pushes up to his feet. He grabs his now crooked reading glasses and flings them on the table. "First, you quote *Taxi Driver*, then Shakespeare. Make up your mind, asshole." He swipes out his fist; Seb ducks. Christian hurls his fist again. This time, Seb steps aside. Christian stumbles past him. Seb's on him in a flash. He steps up behind Christian, wraps his arm around his neck, and yanks. Christian growls. He grips Seb's arm, bends forward, heaves, and Seb goes flying over his shoulder. He lands on his back with a crash that seems to reverberate through the room. Christian rushes forward, only his foot slips on the damn ball of yarn again. He falls over and hits the ground next to Seb. The two lay there, chests having, breaths coming in pants.

I swallow my laughter, walk over to stand between them. "You guys done, yet?" I hold out both of my arms.

Christian grabs my left hand, and I pull him up. I stare down at Seb, who glowers at Christian. "This is not over yet," he growls as he grabs my hand. I haul him to his feet, as well.

"You two need to sort out your shit before we meet the Kane Company. I can't have bad blood between the two of you weakening our position."

"I am not the one with issues; he's the one with issues," Christian glowers back.

"No bad blood here." Seb shrugs. "Only a man pretending to be bad, when he'd rather be playing doctor with a certain...doctor."

"Doctor, huh?" Just as I thought. I jerk my chin toward Christian, who glares at Seb.

"I have no idea what you're talking about."

"Don't think I haven't noticed how you keep finding excuses to see the doctor. She's something, eh? That figure, that fair skin, those tits…" Seb cups his palms below his chest, and Christian's features harden.

His nostrils flare, and a growl rumbles up his chest. "Stop talking about her, you *pezzo di merd*a." He starts to dive toward Seb, only I slap my palm in Christian's chest.

"Back off, you complete idiot. He's trying to get under your skin."

"Oh, he's succeeding, all right." Christian lunges forward, and this time, Massimo grabs him from behind.

"Shit, you're pussywhipped. You haven't even slept with her and you're already protecting her honor?"

Christian struggles against Massimo's hold. He manages to break free, but Adrian grips his other shoulder. "Chill the fuck down, *stronzo*," he snaps. "Asshole's simply trying to make a point."

"I'll make a point all right, with him." Christian rolls his shoulders. His biceps bulge, he rolls his neck, and his shoulders seem to grow even more massive. He's not the tallest nor the broadest of all of us. That honor belongs to Massimo. But Christian also never gets angry enough to lose his cool and fight, so guess this is a first, all around. He rushes forward, with both Massimo and Adrian still holding onto him, before Massimo throws his arm around Christian's chest, and manages to halt him.

Seb laughs, "That all you got in you, you pathetic piece of—"

I turn and sink my fist in his face.

"What the fuck?" he roars as he stumbles back.

"Back the fuck off, Seb. Stop trying to bait him." I turn on Christian, "And that goes for you too, Christian. Get a grip on your dick, or your emotions, or both."

"You mean like you have?" Christian mumbles.

I freeze.

So does every other person in the room.

"*Minchia*," Christian swears. "I'm sorry, I shouldn't have said that."

I glare at him, and he holds my gaze, "No, seriously, *fratellone*. I didn't mean it."

"Sure, you did," I glance around at the rest of them. "Is that what this is about? Is that why there's unrest among you lot? You think I've lost control of my personal life; that's why you bastards are picking fights with each other, as well?"

The guys look at each other, the expressions on their faces ranging from embarrassment to unease to discomfort.

"*Che cazzo!*" I growl, "This is about me, eh? You guys don't trust me to figure out my own shit?"

"It's not that, Mika," Xander murmurs.

"Then how do you explain that your twin, who is normally as even-tempered as you, lost his cool today?"

"It's to do with a woman," Massimo offers.

"Bull-fucking-shit," I snap. "You going to feed me that line, as well?" I scowl at Massimo, "You, who is the most straight-talking of all of us?"

Massimo's face reddens. He glances away then back at me, "You're right." He adds, "It is about you… Partly." He raises a shoulder, "Okay, it is definitely… Probably…only about you." He releases Christian; so does Adrian. Christian straightens his collar, as Massimo steps back. "Look, Mika, you've just been a different man, is all. You've, uh, changed, since you met her."

"Changed?" I scowl, "How have I changed?"

"For one, you're wearing jeans," Massimo points out.

I glance down at my clothes, then swear aloud. Fuck, if I am not wearing jeans. "What's wrong with wearing jeans?" I glare at him, "You wear jeans. Hell, we all wear jeans."

"But not you, Mika." Adrian shuffles his feet, "You hate being dressed in anything except formal pants, and that too, only made by our family tailor."

"These are stitched by our family tailor." I glance around at their faces again. "*Porca miseria*. These aren't stitched by our family tailor?"

Xander shakes his head, "Sadly not, *fratellone*. They're off the shelf, *Levi's*."

I wince. How the hell had I gotten hold of them? How the hell do I even own a pair? "I had no idea…" my voice tapers off. "It's only jeans." I scowl at Xander, "It's not like it's the end of the world."

"To quote you, *fratellone*," he smirks, "wearing jeans is the end of the world."

I glower at him and he raises his hands, "At least, that's what you said not too long ago."

"*Merda*," I run my fingers through my hair, "I'll fix it." I scowl down at the offending garment I have on. "Still, it's hardly a sign that I don't have things under control."

That's when there's a knock on the door. I frown. The staff knows not to disturb me when I am in here with my brothers. It's a billiards room, but the rest of my team knows that this is where I discuss business. So, they wouldn't disturb me, unless… I stiffen. My heart begins to race. I pivot, head for the door and pull it open. "Is she all right?"

Cassandra peeks behind me and her lips firm. I glance over my shoulder to find Adrian hovering behind me. I turn back to her, "Well," I snap, "is she okay?"

Cassandra pulls her gaze back to my face. "She fainted."

27

Karma

I hear the door open and I squeeze my eyelids shut. My heart begins to race and my pulse pounds at my temples. In all honesty, I don't have to pretend that I am unwell. The sheer nervousness of what I am trying to pull off here has me feeling faint. Oh, also the fact that I haven't eaten in nearly a day. It's been twenty-four hours since Aurora left. I'd told Cassandra to leave my meals outside my door and she had obliged. I had then flushed the food down the toilet... Ugh, I know, one shouldn't waste food. But it was either that or involve Cassandra in my scheme. And while I had been tempted, I hadn't wanted to put that heavy of an onus on her. It would have meant putting my trust in her, and while I sort of do trust her, especially since she helped me the last time around... But this...this is different.

I am throwing everything I have behind this. This time, I am going for broke in trying to escape, and if Michael ever found out that Cassandra had helped me, he wouldn't hesitate to kill her, and honestly, I can't live with her death on my conscience. This is what I get for becoming close to her. Damn it.

Guess that's why Michael prefers to keep his emotions bottled up inside and not get too involved with anyone…Except for his brothers, of course. The way those men look out for each other, it totally reminds me of Summer and me and our relationship.

Shit, Summer. I really do miss my sister. Hopefully, though, I'll be out of here and with her very soon. If everything goes well, that is. Footsteps approach and the heavy tread, the even gait, proclaims it's his. I sense him sink down to his knees next to me… Yeah, I had pretended to faint in front of Cassandra, and hit the floor…which had hurt, but it had been worth it.

Fingers touch my cheek and my pulse rate spikes again. I flutter open my eyelids, gaze into his burning blue eyes. "Mika," I whisper, "you came?" Ugh, drama much? But Michael doesn't seem to suspect a thing. His features pale. A groove appears between his eyebrows as he scoops me up in his arms. His heartbeat thunders against my cheek, in synchrony with mine, as he walks over to place me on the bed.

He sits down next to me, leans over, and place his palm on my forehead. "What happened?" he murmurs. His voice is so soft, so gentle, so unlike how he's ever spoken to me before that a tear squeezes out from the corner of my eye. Shit, shit, shit. Why the hell am I feeling so weak in front of him? And all because he showed me a little tenderness.

"Shh!" He leans over and kisses my forehead, "Are you okay? When I saw you collapsed on the floor I…" His shoulders seem to shudder. Umm… What? Is he faking it? But why would he? On the other hand, why does he seems so upset that I am unwell?

He pulls back and I clutch at his arm. "Michael," I cough, "I…I don't feel so well."

He frowns, then places a palm against my forehead, "You do seem warm. Is that why you fainted?" He glances around the space, "Is it too stuffy in here? Should I change the location of my bedroom?"

Eh? He'd change his bedroom to another room in the house, rather than just move *me* to another room? Hold on, he's offering to change rooms because he thinks I'm uncomfortable in this room? In his room? "You'd do that for me?" I whisper.

"Of course." He cups my cheek, "I'd do anything for you, *amore mio*, don't you know that by now?"

"Only, you won't release me."

His jaw hardens, "You know I can't do that, *tesoro mio.*"

I swallow. Bloody hell when he uses those gorgeous Italian words on me, words which I now know the meaning of, then he completely slays me. I bring my hand to my chest and press it against my heart thumping against my rib cage.

"What's wrong?" He scowls, "Are you okay?"

"I..." I clear my throat, "I... I am fine." I only partly lie. Truth is, my stomach has tied itself up in knots, and a coldness has wrapped itself about my shoulders. I glance away from him, as I bite the inside of my cheek. "I... I am sure it's nothing."

His frown deepens.

"I am sure I will be okay," I cough. "I just need to... Maybe close my eyes for a little bit." I do just that, allow my shoulders to shudder.

I hear him inhale a sharp breath. "You are definitely not fine," he growls. He places his palm on my forehead, and honestly, it feels cool against my skin.

Shit, I am not really running a fever, am I? A shiver grips my body. I turn over on my side, curl into myself. "I... I'll be okay," I whisper.

"Bull-fucking-shit," he growls, then grips my shoulder. "You're not okay at all. What's happening? Talk to me, baby."

I freeze. Baby? He called me baby? Shit, why does he choose now to call me baby? Now, when I am trying to pull another fast one over him. Deceive him. Try to escape him. NOW is when he decides to show that humane part of him hidden behind that mafiahole facade?

I cough, try to swallow it, and end up choking. That sends him into a veritable tizzy.

"*Che cazzo!*" he swears, his voice almost hoarse with panic. I sense him pull out his phone, dial a number. The phone rings once, then a male voice says, "*Pronto?*"

"Sebastian," he snaps, "ready the chopper! I need to take my wife to the hospital."

My muscles freeze. Chopper? He has a bloody helicopter on the island? Of course, he has a bloody helicopter on the island. But why hadn't he mentioned it to me so far? Not that I can fly a helicopter or anything. Not that he's had any reason to tell me. So, if he hadn't mentioned it to me, does that mean he was hiding it from me? What else has he conveniently failed to tell me? My stomach twists. Bile bubbles up my throat. I sit up so suddenly that my head bumps his chin. Pain whispers down my spine. The phone slips from his grasp and hits the bed. I slide down the bed, then around him and swing my legs to the floor.

"Where are you going?"

I point in the direction of the bathroom as I take off toward it. I dive across the floor to the commode, then bend over it as the contents of my stomach gush out. Gross. I puke what little food I have left inside, considering I haven't eaten for the last twenty-four hours. A cool hand grips my forehead. He gathers the hair back from my face as I continue to dry heave. My head spins and darkness laces the edges of my vision. I blink it away, reach for the toilet-paper, but he's already there. He rips off a few sheets, hands them over to me, and I clean my mouth. He reaches over, flushes away the evidence of my being sick. I wince as I slump down onto the tiled floor, but of course, he catches me.

He swings me up and into his arms, and I turn my head away from him. How embarrassing. He saw me being sick. Can things get any worse from here? He carries me over to the sink, then lowers me to the floor. "Rinse your mouth," he orders, and I lean over and do as he commands. This once, I have no strength to disobey him, and not only because I need to get rid of the funny taste in my mouth.

Also, what's wrong with me? In pretending to be sick, I seem to be honestly coming down with something. That's all I need right now, some stupid virus to get a hold of me. I shut off the faucet, and he hands me a towel. As soon as I pat my mouth dry, he, once more, scoops me up in his arms. He carries me out into the bedroom, then out of the door.

"I can walk," I mumble. My voice trembles, and shit, I wasn't even pretending that time.

"I don't know what's wrong with me," I say truthfully. "One minute I was fine, the next..." I swallow down the rest of the words. Can't really tell him that I started out pretending to be sick, only to find out that I am really sick, can I?

"Don't worry, Beauty." He tucks my head under his chin, "You'll be fine, I promise. Once you are at the hospital—"

"No," I turn to him, only half-faking the alarm. I really do hate hospitals. So, it's not a complete lie when I say, "Why don't you simply fly the doctor here, instead?"

"I'll call ahead when we are on the way and have her meet us there."

"But Michael, please, I don't wanna go to the hospital," I whine.

"When it comes to your health, I will not take any risks," he says as he stalks down the stairs. When he reaches the bottom of the steps, Seb joins him.

"How is she?" he murmurs.

"Not good," Michael replies without glancing down at me once.

"Christian's readying the chopper for us." Xander joins us as Michael continues without pausing. He reaches the main door and Cassandra pushes it open. We walk down and Massimo turns to us. "Christan's already called for the doctor to meet us at the hospital."

"Of course, he did." Seb smirks, and Michael glares at him. "Sorry, Boss," he mimes zipping his lips, "won't mention it again."

"You better not," Michael growls. "Things are complicated enough without you and Christian coming to blows over something that, clearly, hits a nerve with him."

I glance between them. *What the hell are they talking about?*

"It hits something," Seb agrees, then quietens when Michael shoots him a glance.

"I won't warn you again, Sebastian," he says in a soft voice. It's his 'killer' voice, the one that says that he means business, that he won't hesitate to take action if anyone dares go against him or his orders. The one he'd probably use with me if he found out just how I am double-crossing him…again.

I shudder and he pulls me closer to his chest. "You okay, *Bellezza*?" His voice is soft again…but in a different way. It's more tender, more caring. More…everything. Everything I've wanted from him, he's now willing to give to me. If I asked him now, I have no doubt, he'd hand over his very business to me. Not that I'd want that. In fact, the opposite. Given a choice, I'd put enough distance between me and his Mafia state of affairs… Only, I can't separate the made-man that he is from the man who is my husband.

I curl my fingers into a fist. He hasn't returned my ring yet. I had returned it to him, but he hadn't trusted me enough to put his ring back on my finger. That's my fault though. I had felt the need to rub it in when I had left him the last time. If only I hadn't, I'd have the ring still with me, when I walk out on him again. A part of him would, at least, stay with me. Not that I need that to remind me of him. His scent, his heat, his sheer dominance…and his unexpected tenderness… All of it has spoiled me for anyone else.

Once I leave him… I'll probably spend the rest of the days trying to fill the void that his lack of presence in my life will create. My heart begins to race and the band around my chest tightens. I cough again, and this time, he hurries his pace until he's almost running. The guys follow us. As we reach the helicopter, Antonio reaches for him, but he declines, holds onto me as he navigates the steps. Once inside the chopper, he sinks into a seat with me in his lap. Seb reaches over to buckle both of us in. Xander and Massimo slip into the seats behind us as Christian readies for take-off.

"You sure you don't want me there, Boss?" Antonio hesitates and his features wear a worried look. "I'd feel much more comfortable knowing I'm there with you."

Michael chuckles, "I have my brothers with me; I will be more than fine."

Antonio frowns.

"Stay with Adrian, hold down the fort here."

Antonio looks like he's about to refuse when Michael jerks his chin, "You're delaying us from taking off."

Antonio nods, then steps off the helicopter. Seb shuts the door behind him and straps in, and the chopper instantly lifts into the air.

28

Michael

I pace the corridor outside the hospital examination room. What the hell is taking them so long? We'd made it to the hospital in Palermo in under fifteen minutes, thanks to Christian's expert flying skills. A team had been ready and waiting for us when we'd landed on the makeshift helipad next to the hospital. One that Christian had organized at the same time as he'd called ahead to alert the medical staff. They'd rushed her over in a stretcher, and all through, she hadn't let go of my hand. She'd also seemed to grow paler by the second. Even more than when we'd been in the air. Throughout the trip she'd clung to me, her shoulders shaking every time the helicopter had banked. I had yelled to Christian to take it easy with the chopper and he had managed to smooth out the helicopter and still get us here in record time.

I owe him for that. Hell, I owe all of them for dropping whatever is important in their lives and coming over with me. Not that I didn't expect it, considering I am the Capo. But still... They are also human. They have their own lives, their own...women?

Holdonasecond. Not one of my brothers... Not even Seb or Adrian have ever introduced me to any of their women... Or ever been serious

with anyone, so far, as far as I know. Xander has his childhood crush…
but he is far from admitting his feelings for her. Then there's Adrian. He
seems to have noticed Cassandra; and Christian seems to be taken in by
the doctor…but that's just speculation on my part. None of them have
ever confessed to ever being in love…

Cazzo! What am I doing thinking about my brother's love lives?
Sure, I want to see them settled and have families… And not just
because it is important to ensure continuity of power, but also because I
want them to be happy. So why is it that not once in all these years, have
any of my brothers ever mentioned anything about finding someone
special?

A touch on my shoulder and I turn to find Sebastian at my elbow.
He hands me a paper cup filled with a dark brew. I take a sip and the
liquid warms me. I toss the rest of it back, feel it rejuvenate me somewhat. I crumple the cup in my fist, walk over to the waste paper basket
and deposit it. I turn to find the four of them watching me. Xander is
sprawled out in a seat that looks too small for him. Christian is seated
opposite him, his elbows digging into his thighs. Massimo leans his hip
against the wall, watching. Seb stands where I had left him, his gaze
ticking my progress as I walk over to them.

"Why the hell haven't any of you married before now, huh?"

"Eh?" Massimo blinks, "What kind of a question is that?"

"A straight one." I scowl, "It's not normal that none of you have even
brought a woman home to meet the rest of us."

"And risk scaring her away?" Xander snorts, "Not likely."

"But that isn't why you haven't brought anyone special over to introduce her to us, is it?" I scowl between them, "It's because none of you
have anyone important in your lives."

Massimo raises a shoulder. "I haven't met anyone. Not that I was
looking. Besides," he narrows his gaze on me, "since when did you
decide it's important to find out about our personal lives?"

"Guess because he's married now, for better or for worse; he's
hooked and he wants the rest of us to be balled and chained too," Seb
murmurs.

I frown at him, "That's not why I asked."

"It's the first time you've bothered to ask about our personal lives,"
Christian points out. "Like I said earlier, you have changed."

"Huh," I rake my fingers through my hair, "just because I thought to
ask after my brothers doesn't mean I have changed."

The four exchange looks.

"You also haven't asked us once if we've made any progress on finding Luca," Seb points out.

I glare at him. "Speaking of," I look him up and down, "your time is almost up on that, so have you any inkling on his whereabouts yet?"

"He's in—"

The sound of the door opening has me jerking toward it. The doctor steps out. She walks over to us and Christian instantly rises to his feet. His gaze eats her up as she comes to a stop in front of me. Yeah, there's definitely something there... I glance from him to the doctor who shoves her hand into the pocket of her scrubs.

"How is she? Is she okay?"

"She's fine, but we need to keep her overnight under observation."

"But she's not in any danger, is she?"

"She's exhausted, a little dehydrated; Also, her blood pressure and pulse rate are elevated. While she's not in any immediate danger—" She hesitates and my pulse rate instantly spikes.

"What is it?" I snap.

She stares at the rest of the men, then back at me.

"These are my brothers; you can speak in front of them."

"This may be something you want to hear in private?"

"Tell me, woman," I burst out, "or I swear—"

There's a touch on my shoulder. I turn to find Christian right behind me. He jerks his chin toward the doctor, then shakes his head. *Che cazzo!* Of course, he has to come to her rescue. Did I say that I wish my brothers would find their own women and settle down? Guess I wasn't aware of exactly how that would change the dynamics between us when that happens. I glare at him and he holds my gaze. Shit, he's serious about her? When the hell had that happened, eh? I shrug off his hand, turn to her.

"Look, Doc, I appreciate your being sensitive about the situation, but right now, I only want to find out what's wrong with my wife, so if you can just spit it out—"

"She's pregnant."

Next to me, Christian inhales. A pulse of shock runs through the assembled men. "What did you say?" I growl.

"She's pregnant," the doctor repeats herself.

"She's...." I swallow, "She's..."

"Pregnant." The doctor nods, "Your wife is pregnant, Capo."

"My wife is pregnant?" I open and shut my mouth, "She's having my child?"

A small smile curves her lips, "It would seem that way, yes."

My knees seem to give way from under me.

Christian grips my shoulder. "Steady, Capo," he murmurs.

I blink to clear my vision, then focus my gaze once more on the doctor.

"She's fine, other than that?"

The doctor nods, "Like I mentioned, it would be best if we kept her under observation overnight."

I nod, "Of course, whatever you think is best for her."

"Also," she glances to the side, "there was—ah— Something else that I think you should know."

"What is it?"

"I...ah..." She shuffles her feet, "It's just that—" She straightens her shoulders, "She needs to take better care of herself. She needs to eat well, sleep well, make sure she's getting her vitamins."

"I'll make sure of that." I run my fingers through my hair. "Anything else?"

She seems like she's about to say something, then shakes her head.

"Can I see her now?"

"Of course."

She turns and I follow her inside. I walk into the room, almost bumping into the doctor who's come to a halt inside the threshold. She's staring at the bed. The empty bed. I glance around the space. The entire room is empty. I stalk toward the door on the far side, peek inside. There's no one in the bathroom either.

"What the hell?

A draft blows in through the open window. I lunge toward it, glance down at the ground which is maybe five or six feet away. Not too close, but not too far either. Could she have jumped? The hair on the back of my neck rises. She did jump. She managed to get away. My pregnant wife managed to escape. Is she strong enough to have made the jump? How far can she go in the condition she is in? I had found her collapsed on the floor of the room, and now she manages to jump out of the window and leave? My guts twist and my stomach ties itself in knots. I bunch my fists at my side, "What the hell is happening here? Where is she?"

"She... I..." the doc's voice trembles. I glance at her, find her features have lost all color. She has her fingers gripped together in front of her; the skin over her knuckles is white.

Minchia! Why is she so nervous? I close the distance between us, and glare at her, "Something you want to tell me, Doc?"

"I... " she shakes her head, "it's my fault; I agreed to help her. I had no idea she was pregnant. As soon as I found out, I —" I raise my hand and she flinches. *Damnit!* I lower my arm, brush past her, then out the door. My brothers crowd around me.

Seb takes in my features and his own harden, "What's wrong, Boss? What happened in there?"

"She did," I point a thumb over my shoulder, "she helped my wife escape."

"Karma's gone?" Christian glances between me and the doctor who's standing behind me.

I pull out my knife from the small of my back, "I am going to kill her for it." I am about to turn, when Christian closes the distance between us.

"Leave her to me."

"What do you mean?"

"Don't waste your time on her. I've got this."

I peer into his eyes, then jerk my chin, "I am going after my wife."

29

Karma

When I'd been brought to the hospital, Aurora had examined me thoroughly, not just going through the motions, as I'd thought she would.

I had protested and she'd said it had been to make things look authentic. Authentic? When no one was around to see her? Hmm. When she'd completed her examination, she'd told me that she needed to run a few more tests. I'd asked her if something was wrong and she'd said, not really, it was just a precaution. But the look on her face.

Seriously, it reminded me of the time when the doctor had told me that I have a hole in my heart—that it wasn't dangerous yet, but that it needed to be fixed. Clearly, this was something similar. Either her examination had revealed my condition… Or it was something else. And either way, I was not staying to find out more.

I'd asked her if she had changed her mind about helping me and she had said, of course, not. That she'd do everything in her power to help me. And somehow, it had been the way that she'd said it, how she had avoided looking at my eyes when she said it, that had caused me to mistrust her. Something was up with her. Maybe she was getting cold feet, or an attack of conscience. Or perhaps, she had realized she could not go up against the Capo. Either way, I wasn't waiting around to find out. She had told me that she needed to access a few more things to run some more tests on me, and that's when I had decided, no way, was I going to stick around to find out what those tests involved. Likely, she was going to tell the Capo that I was planning on escaping. I had been sure of that. So, when she'd left the room, I had promptly pulled my clothes and shoes back on and rushed to the window.

The ground hadn't seemed too far, until I had jumped, that is. I had landed with a thump that had sent pain slicing through my body. I had picked myself up, then broken into a run. I hadn't dared to look back for fear that he'd have already discovered my absence. I'd raced out of the hospital complex, up the road, until I had reached a junction. I had glanced around, wondering which way to go, then decided to keep straight. I was on a road that was busy enough that I felt safe. If I was in a crowd, he wouldn't do anything, would he? He couldn't just drag me off kicking and screaming if he managed to track me down, could he?

I had taken off up the pavement, trying to not hurry too much, trying not to attract too much attention to myself. All the while my heartrate had skyrocketed; my pulse had kicked up…

Shit! Once more, I am pushing myself too much. My breath comes in puffs. I can feel my heart slamming against my rib cage. Sweat pools under my armpits, and overall, I don't fell so well. I slow down to a normal walk, but that doesn't help. My head spins and the edges of my vision flicker with dark spots. Shit, what the hell is wrong with me? Why am I feeling so woozy? I've never fainted in my life… Not counting the fake fainting spell earlier, which is how he had found me.

I hope this isn't my heart acting up. It can't be my heart acting up. It had better not be my heart acting up. I press my knuckles into my thundering heartbeats that vibrate through my chest. Shit, shit, shit, this is not good! I glance about the space at the people engaged in their day-to-day lives. The woman scolding her child, who seems to be on the verge of tears. The men crowded around a table outside a coffeeshop. A couple of boys on their electronic scooters driving by on the pavement. The man and woman holding hands as they peer into the shopfront. The image fades back and forth as I take a step forward, and another. My knees wobble. I throw out a hand as the ground comes up to meet me, stops, as arms grasp me. The scent of testosterone envelops me. Musky, like leather, with a hint of woodsmoke. The heat of his body envelops me as he swings me up in his arms.

"Foiled, again," I murmur. "I tried to run, I tried to leave you, but—"

"I found you." His blue eyes bore into mine. "I'll always find you, no matter how far you go. I'll always track you down, no matter how far you flee. You can try to escape me, but I'll never let you."

"Michael."

"Beauty?" He rakes his gaze across my face, "You should have planned better. I gave you more credit than this half-brained escape attempt."

"It wasn't half-brained. I had—" I chew the inside of my cheek. No way, am I going to give up Aurora, no matter that she had abandoned me at the last minute. Guess she's entitled. I would be worried for my skin, too, if my family was answerable to the Capo.

"You had help," he states.

"No, I didn't."

"I know it was the doctor," he says as he turns and begins retracing our steps. The smattering of people on the pavement glance at us, then away. No one tries to stop him. Not that I am struggling or anything. Still, apparently, it's normal for a man to carry a woman through the streets here…

Not that he is just any man. He is the Capo. *Their* Capo. Guess none of them would have stopped to help me even if I had been struggling to get away from him…which I am not, anyway. I snuggle into his chest, push my cheek against where his heart thuds steadily. It's beat slower than the organ that pounds away against my ribcage.

"I have something to tell you," I say at the same time as him.

He glances down at me, "You first."

"You first," I murmur as I reach up to touch his cheek. *So bloody gorgeous. Why couldn't you have been, at least, ugly looking?*

He chuckles and I realize that I have spoken the words aloud. Heat sears my cheeks.

"What did you want to tell me?" I ask, more because I want to divert his attention from my earlier faux pas. That's all I need, voicing my thoughts aloud… I mean, if he could read what my thoughts are when I am normally around him…then he'd know that I'm fighting a losing battle when it comes to him.

OMG, why are all of my thoughts so muddled? Why does my brain feel as if it's turned to mush? Why do my arms and legs feel so heavy? I squint up at him through the sunlight that pours over him, bathing him in a golden glow that brings out the hollows under his cheeks, the shadows under his eyes, the grooves on either side of his mouth. That stern mouth, those lips that had brought me so much pleasure, every time he's kissed me, every time he's sucked on my nipples, bit me on my pussy. I clench my thighs together, drag my fingers to his mouth, as his lips move.

"You're pregnant, Beauty."

I still, "Wh... what?"

"You're with child," his arms tighten around me, "my child."

"It's not possible."

"It's very possible."

"I... I mean. I can't be pregnant."

"You are."

"Who told you?" I firm my lips. "The doctor?"

He nods.

So that's why she had stepped out of the room to talk to him? To alert him first? Why hadn't she told me? This is what I get for trusting someone who is one of them... Clearly, they owe their loyalties only to each other, and I am not one of the Mafia. No wonder, she had pretended to be my confidant, only to betray me. It wasn't even the fact that she had mentioned it to him first. Why hadn't she shared it with me when she had found out? Because then she knew, I would never have allowed myself to be caught by him. No bloody way. I begin to struggle, but his grasp tightens about me.

I wince, "You're hurting me."

He eases his hold just a fraction, but keeps me plastered to his chest.

"Is that why you came after me? Because I am carrying your heir?"

"I came after you because you are mine."

And this child...would also be his. Shit, this is what I had been afraid of. That if I became pregnant, I'd never be able to leave him. That he'd become even more possessive, and stake his claim on me even more firmly.

Oh, hell. "Let me go," I say in a harsh whisper, and he shakes his head.

"You know I can't, especially not now that—"

"That I am carrying your precious child."

"Your child too."

No kidding. My stomach ties itself up in knots. The band around my chest tightens. "I... I don't want this child," I lie.

"Too bad, you don't have a choice."

I stare up at what I can see of his face. "Fuck you," I snap and he chuckles.

"I'd love to, but we may have to exercise caution until you are stronger."

"Nothing is wrong with me."

"Other than your being pregnant with my child, that is."

His child. His wife. What about me? What about what I want? I dig my fingers into the front of his shirt, "I can't do this."

"Yes, you can."

"I don't want to do this."

"Yes, you do."

"Are you hearing anything I am saying?"

"You're afraid," he murmurs. "It's normal."

"I am not afraid, you prick."

"Is that any way to speak to the father of your child?"

Oh, my god! I am pregnant with his child. Our child. Oh god, oh god. My stomach seems to coil in on itself. "I think I am going to be sick again."

He glances down at me as we reach the entrance to the hospital. He shoulders his way inside, then makes a beeline past the reception down the corridor. He shoves open the door, races to a bathroom stall and deposits me on my feet. I sink to my knees, and for the second time in twelve hours, I puke my guts out in front of him.

30

Michael

She sinks down onto the floor of the bathroom next to the commode. I place the wet cloth on her forehead, "How are you feeling?"

I had brought my wife home from the hospital two days ago, and since that vomiting bout at the hospital bathroom she hasn't stopped puking.

"How do you think?" She scowls back at me, before launching up again on her knees and hanging over the bowl. When she finishes retching, she collapses against the wall. "I am dying," she groans, "I am never going to make it through the next few months."

I flush away the evidence of her being sick, then gently pat her mouth, "The doctor said the morning sickness should fade by the end of the first trimester."

"Considering I am only a few weeks along, that doesn't comfort me very much." She scowls, "Besides, I don't trust him or his diagnosis."

When Aurora's role in my wife's escape had emerged, I'd wanted to make her pay for it. I'd come very close to pulling my gun on her, except Christian had stepped in. He'd insisted I spare her life, which I had. He'd wanted me to let her return to her previous life, which I had decided was unacceptable. The result is that she's currently locked up in a room in one of my safe houses while I figure out what to do with her. I can't simply let her go; that would weaken my reputation and my ability to stake my claim as Don when the time comes. On the other hand, I can't kill her, since I promised Christian I won't. However, there is no way I am letting her treat my wife. I've lost my faith in Aurora and I can't imagine any circumstance under which I would allow her anywhere near Beauty. The result is that I had a specialist flown in from Rome—had ordered him to relocate to be near us so he can come when needed.

"He's a perfectly capable doctor."

"I prefer Aurora."

"Considering she let you down when you needed her help to escape, I am surprised you want to be treated by her."

Beauty hesitates, "I admit, I was pissed off at her, at first, but I guess I do understand why she did it. I just don't understand why she didn't tell me I was pregnant, as well."

"Maybe she was trying to protect you and the child?" I raise a shoulder. "Frankly, I don't give a rat's ass about her intentions. She alerted me in the nick of time. Else not only would we not be here having this conversation, but I doubt she'd have made it out of that hospital alive."

She pales further and I curse myself. I really need to curb my vocabulary when I am around her in this state. Since finding out she's pregnant, Karma has done an about face. It's as if all of her hidden emotions and sensitivities have come to the fore. She's become needy, absentminded, and also, possessive. None of which I mind. She's also been very sick. Enough to make me think she might need to be admitted to the hospital a couple of times. Except, no way, am I letting her out of my sight.

Instead, I had arranged for the hospital to come to her. I had a complete suite in my home converted to a hospital room...which will also serve as the birthing room, when the time comes. Yeah, also a team of doctors and nurses are on-call around the clock, in case of any emergency. No, I am not being over-the-top about this... I am just being safe. No way, am I taking any chances when it comes to my wife's health or of that of my unborn child. I reach forward and push the hair away from her forehead. "How are you feeling now?"

"Hungry." She scowls. "I wish my body would make up its mind.

One minute, I am puking my guts out; the next moment, I am starving like I haven't eaten in days."

"Well, you are eating for two."

"More like I am eating for a crowd," She pouts as she pushes up to standing. Her color is better and she definitely seems stronger than even a few seconds ago. Her ability to recover from these bouts of puking never ceases to amaze me. All in all, since discovering she's pregnant, she's been too preoccupied with trying to keep up with the changes to her body to think of trying to escape... Or at least, I hope so.

I reach for her and scoop her up in my arms. She frowns, "I can walk, you know."

"Indulge me," I murmur as I walk out of the bathroom, past the bed in our bedroom, and down the stairs to the kitchen. When I found out she was pregnant, I moved her to my house on the outskirts of Palermo. Not the one I normally use, but the one I bought many years ago, with the hope of, one day, using it as a base for my family. The location of this place is known to only my brothers, and the closest members in my clan.

It's away from the city, which means she's also out of reach of our rivals. Not to mention that with the security I have placed about it, we'd spot anyone coming from a mile off.

Once in the kitchen, I place her at a chair at the dining table, then busy myself making breakfast. I sense her gaze on me as I move around, popping the bread in the toaster and whipping up the eggs for an omelet. I plate out the toast and the omelets for both of us, place them on the table, then pour her a glass of orange juice.

When I slip into the seat in front of her, she stares at me.

"What?" I arch an eyebrow, "Everything okay?"

She nods, "Everything is fine. Maybe too fine."

"What do you mean?" I jerk my chin at her plate and she begins to butter her toast before cutting a piece of her omelet and bringing it to her mouth. She finishes almost all of the food on her plate before she leans back and surveys me with a gaze.

"I don't understand why you are being this nice to me."

"I am always nice to you, Beauty."

"You weren't very nice to me when we first met."

"I didn't know you as well as I do now."

"You think you know me well?" She arches an eyebrow, mirroring my earlier gesture.

I smirk as I cut into my omelet and continue eating.

"Well?" She prods, "Do you think you know me well?"

"I think…" I pause as I survey her features, "I know you well enough, to allow you access to your phone again."

She huffs, "That doesn't mean anything. You allowed me access to my phone earlier, as well."

"Until you insisted on showing me that you couldn't be trusted," I glower.

"So, you trust me now?"

"Nope."

She gapes, "So you don't trust me now?"

"Not an inch, my darling Beauty." I place my knife and fork on the plate, before I push my chair back, "However, I do trust you enough to give you…" I slide my palm inside my pocket, pull out her ring.

"Oh," her chest heaves.

I go down on one knee in front of her—only because it's the only way to reach for her fingers as I slide the ring onto her left ring finger.

She draws in a breath. "I really don't understand you," she murmurs as she raises the fingers of her left hand.

"What do you not understand?" I push back a strand of her hair behind her ear.

"You say you don't trust me, yet you give me back my ring… I mean, your ring." She glances up at me, "Why would you do that?"

"Because you are my wife?" I cup her cheek, "And the mother-to-be of my child."

"This child means a lot to you, doesn't it?"

I tilt my head, "As do you."

"Do I?"

"Do you doubt my word?"

"You just said that you don't trust me…so…"

"I don't have to trust you to—" *love you*. Shit, did I almost say that aloud? I rise to my feet, and she grabs my hand.

"To—?" She tips up her chin, "What were you going to say?"

"To acknowledge you as my wife," I reply and her features fall.

"Oh, right."

I pull my hand away from her grasp, then nod to her plate, "You didn't finish your breakfast."

"I…I'm not hungry anymore."

"Have you told your sister yet that you are pregnant?"

She whips her head around to stare at me, "You'd be okay with that?"

"Of course."

"As well as if I told her that I am married?"

"Wouldn't expect you to say one without the other."

She screws her features, "See, this is what I mean?"

"What?"

"You being nice to me... It's weird."

"I don't see why that should surprise you so much."

"It's just..." She waves her hand in the air, "All this conversation, your cooking meals for me, taking care of me when I am sick... It's just..."

"Normal?"

She frowns, "In a way, and that weirds me out even more."

"So, you find it weird that we are actually getting along, and that you are not trying to escape me anymore?"

Her shoulders slump and I curse myself. Why the hell did I have to bring that up? Just as I was thinking that she was settling in here and she also seemed content, I had to go and spoil it all, eh? *Che diavolo!*

"I am not trying to escape you because, for some reason, I seem to be forgetting exactly why I wanted to get away from you in the first place."

My heart begins to race. "You are, eh?" I say softly.

"It's all your fault," She lowers her chin as she proceeds to polish off the remaining food on her plate. Then she takes a couple of sips of the orange juice from her glass before turning to me. "You're making me too comfortable here."

Good.

"You're spoiling me by how you take care of me."

That's the idea, tesoro mio.

"You're..." her chin wobbles, "you're confusing me, you know that? You're tying me up in knots, you're messing with my head, you...you..." her voice catches, tears slide down her cheeks, and my heart stutters.

It fucking stutters. I squat down in front of her, frame her cheeks with my hands, "Don't cry, Beauty."

She sniffles, even as she turns her head away from me, "You think I want to cry, you ass? It's these stupid hormones. They are all over the place, and half the time, I can't even understand why things set me off when they do, without any warning. I am making a fool of myself in front of you, and I still can't stop bawling, damn it." She balls her fingers into fists as I pull her into my arms. She stays rigid as I rub her back. She refuses to unbend as I haul her into my chest.

I hold her there until her muscles slowly unwind, one by one. When her breathing has evened out, I finally pull away from her. "Better?" I ask as she blinks away her tears.

"Sort of," she mumbles, as she reaches for the tissues on the table in front of her and blows her nose. I rise to my feet again, and keep a hand on her shoulder as she pushes back her chair and gets up as well.

"So, you going to call your sister?"

She shakes her head.

"Why not?"

"I am not ready to talk to her about...," she gestures to the space between us.

"Why not?"

"Hell, I am still digesting the fact that I am not only married but already pregnant, so please..." she tosses her hair. "Just give me a little time, okay?"

"Hmm." I stare into her features and she scowls back at me.

"I hate the sound of that hmm!"

"Hmm..." I scratch my chin. "Is it just time you need, or is it something else?"

"Like what?" She brushes past me, then heads out of the kitchen and down the corridor to the study, which is where she spends a lot of her time these days. When I had furnished the space with all of my favorite books, I'd had no idea then that my wife, the mother-to-be of my child, would love the space so much. If I'd known, I'd have made sure to have books which were more to her liking on the shelves... Not that she has complained about my taste in literature so far.

I follow her down the hall and watch as she sinks down onto the settee in front of the fire, then pulls her legs up under her.

"What else would I need?"

"You tell me," I murmur as I lean a hip against the back of the chair near her.

"No, why don't *you* tell me?" She scoffs, "Since you seem to think that you can read my mind or something." She sniffs.

"Maybe you are ashamed to be married to the Mafia? Maybe you don't want to tell your family that you are carrying the child of a criminal?" I lower my chin, "May...be...you are hoping that if you wait long enough, things will go back to the way they used to be?"

She flushes, then glances away from me, "Honestly, I want to deny all of that, but—" She raises a shoulder. "I won't deny that all of those thoughts have gone through my mind," she murmurs, "but I also know things aren't just going to go back to being what they were."

"Do you?" I cross the floor to stand in front of her, "Do you understand that you are my wife and I am not letting you go? Ever? That this child is the one thing that can ensure that my bid for Don is sealed?

She starts, "So that's the only reason you want this child? Because he or she guarantees your position as the head of the Cosa Nostra?"

I stare into her now flushed features, "What other reason could there be?"

31

Michael

I can't believe I actually said that. *What other reason can there be?* What other reason can there *not* be? Why is it that when it comes to the crunch, I'm unable to tell her how I feel? Why is it that when she looks at me with her big green eyes, I feel myself sinking into them, feel the barriers around my heart melting away, realize that somewhere along the way I've developed feelings for her, that I want her in my life, and not only because she is the mother of my child? I need her because she makes me feel… And maybe that's the problem.

Once you start developing an emotional connection to someone else, once you make yourself vulnerable in that way, you're opening yourself up to being hurt. Once my rivals discover that she and the child are the chinks in my armor, they'll never stop, until they've hurt both of them. They'll use them to get to me… Just as they had already tried once before.

Only now, the stakes are higher. She is pregnant. *Dio santo!* She is going to give birth to my child. A hot sensation stabs at my chest. I stare out of the window of my home office, where I had returned after hurting her with that last comment. I had wanted to hurt her. I had wanted her to feel a little of the agony I am going through, to understand how powerless I had felt in that instant when I had realized that I would do anything for her...for the both of them. I would give up my claim to being the Don if it meant that I could keep them safe...

And that...is non-negotiable. I owe it to myself to see this through. After coming this far, after taking on my own father, and facing my worst nightmares, I deserve to be the head of the *Cosa Nostra*. This is what I was born for. This is what my mother sacrificed herself for. To ensure that I, one day, displace my father and changed the face of the *Cosa Nostra*; modernize them so there will no longer be victims like my mother. And I thought I had been on track... Until she had come along and exposed just how frail my beliefs are.

I had thought I was not like my father, that all I needed was to seize power and I could wipe out all traces of how he had run our clans... But she'd shown me just how similar to him I am... When it comes to her... to my child. When it comes to what really mattered to me, I am as possessive as my father, if not more so. I am as controlling, as dominating, as hellbent on taking control and getting things done my way, no matter that it hurts the people I love most... *Che cazzo!* There is that word again.

Love; fucking love! I am in love with her; if only I could tell her that. Maybe then she'd understand why I act so over-the-top possessive with her? Why I want to stalk her, to ensure that she is safe. Why I want to follow her every move. Why I cannot bear to have her out of sight. Why I want to direct what she wears, who she meets, what she eats, where she lives... Why I put that stupid tracker in her... Because I want to take care of her. To protect her. To make sure that all of her needs are met. That she is provided for and happy and...

That will never work. F-u-c-k. I grip the edge of the window sill. That will only suffocate her. She is a wild thing, a woman who needs freedom to flourish. An artiste who needs to explore the world and take risks in order to create. Her imagination needs new experiences so she can reinvent herself. And me? I need her to be by my side, where I can keep her out of harm's way.

I curl my fist and punch it down into the window sill. Pain shoots up my arm. Good. This is tangible, this is real, this...pain I can deal with. But if anything happened to her or to my child... I would—

"Mika, you, okay?"

Xander's voice interrupts my thoughts. If it had been anyone else,

I'd have told them to fuck off, but Xander... Well, when he speaks, you listen. Doesn't mean that I have to come across as welcoming though, right?

His footsteps sound as he approaches me. There's a touch on my shoulder and I know he's paused beside me.

"Contemplating the view, eh?"

"I'm contemplating, something, all right," I mutter.

For a few seconds, he stands there without speaking. That's the thing with Xander. Unlike my other brothers, who prefer to voice their concerns through speech, he prefers to use silence to convey his worry instead.

"It's normal, you know," he finally says, "to feel insecure."

"Me, insecure?" I chuckle, "Now I know I've heard everything."

"Even big bad Capo's have an Achilles heel."

"I didn't think I had one until..." I pause, not sure how, exactly, to voice the words in my head without giving myself away completely. And some things...a man has to keep close to his chest. Not even for my favorite brother, am I willing to lay my feelings out there completely.

"Until her?" Xander says softly.

I blow out a breath, "This...sucks."

"You mean, you're finally realizing that you are not as invincible as you thought you were?"

"Is that what this is?"

"It's...something you are lucky to face, *fratellone*."

"Eh?" I shoot him a sideways glance, "I don't feel lucky."

"That's only because you haven't acknowledged the true extent of your feelings for her."

"That fucking 'f' word."

"Yep," he laughs, "the one and only one that has brought the strongest of men to their knees, so you don't stand a chance."

I turn to face him, "What are you trying to say?"

"That," he glances at me, "you are fighting too hard. Putting too much pressure on yourself and her. You're allowing the past to dictate your future, brother, and that's only going to lead to misery."

"You have no idea how it feels to find out that your wife is pregnant, that you are going to bring a child into this world. How am I going to protect him or her from the evils out there? How am I going to protect all of them from what I am?"

"Ah," he nods, "I see now."

"See what?" I scowl, "I hate it when you are so cryptic."

"You're scared, *fratellone*."

"Me, scared?" I scoff, "What do I have to be scared of?"

"Yourself?"

I laugh, "Now you're taking the piss, as the Brits say."

"You're worried that you won't measure up to the needs of being a husband and a parent. You are unsure if you will be able to meet the demands made of you. You think you are not good enough to be either. You are afraid that—"

"Stop," I growl, "just shut the fuck up, Xander."

He tilts his head, "Hurts to hear the truth, eh?"

I push away from the window and begin to pace. "Why is it that this feels so..difficult...so monumental? Like something that cuts through all the bullshit I have been spewing all this time, something that slices me to the core, and cuts me off at the knees? Something that makes me feel so exposed that I am sure I am going to be sick?"

"Welcome to the human race," he murmurs. "It's not all fun and games when you begin to experience the emotions, but with great vulnerability, comes the gift of extreme joy."

I wince, "Doesn't sound like my cup of espresso."

"It's good, what you are going through."

I laugh as I rub at my chest, "If you say so."

"I know so." He walks over to me and grips my shoulder, "This is all good, brother. This, what you are going through, will make you stronger, more powerful, more resilient to face what is to come. Your ability to be a little more sensitive will only make you a more insightful leader."

"When did you become this wise?"

He smirks, "I was born wise, big brother."

I ruffle his hair, "Don't let my praise go to your head."

"Not likely," he snorts, "considering you are only telling me what I already know."

"Right," I murmur, "so what now?"

"Now you go back and apologize to her."

"Apologize?" I lower my hand, "What do I need to apologize for?"

"For whatever it is you did?"

"Why is it something I did?" I frown.

"It's always the man in a relationship who is wrong. Time you accept that."

"So, you admit that you are the one who's in the wrong when it comes to not acknowledging your feelings for Theresa?"

His features tense, then he forces his expression into a semblance of a smile, "You got that right."

"What are you going to do about it?"

"Nothing."

"What?" I gape, "You give me all this sage advice, and when it comes to confessing your feeling for your childhood friend, you get cold feet."

"It's not cold feet."

"What is it then?"

"It's just…" he rubs his fingers across the back of his neck, "it's complicated."

"And you sound like a cliché."

He stares at me and I raise my hands in the air, "Okay, all right, I admit I sounded like one too, earlier."

"See how much easier it is when you simply own up to your faults?"

I laugh, "Don't kid yourself, *fratellino*." I ruffle his hair, "Just because you happen to be right about some things doesn't mean you're right about *everything*."

He chuckles, "I wouldn't dare claim that." He punches me lightly in the shoulder, "Now, go back there and talk to your wife."

32

Karma

I rub Andy's forehead and he purrs, then snuggles closer into my chest. When Cassandra had arrived with him, I had been so damn happy that I had almost shed a tear. Gosh, I'd missed the little guy, and also her, if I am being honest. I've never had any close friends, mainly because Summer has always fulfilled that role. But since she is not here with me right now, and since Cassandra is really the only other woman around now, I find myself turning to her more and more.

I glance up as the door to my bedroom opens. After that last conversation of ours, I'd told Michael that I preferred to stay separately from him. He hadn't seemed happy about it, but he hadn't pushed it either. Maybe he thought it was best not to push me further in the condition I am in. Of course, he'd insisted that Cassandra check in on me every hour to make sure I was okay and, while it's annoying, I'll take that any day over having to sleep next to him at night. Which, unfortunately, also means that I miss him at night. Gah, there really is no winning for me, right? Now, his shoulders fill the doorway and I stiffen. Think of the devil…and there he is.

He hovers at the threshold of the room, glances about the space before his gaze finally alights on mine. "May I come in?" he asks and I blink. *What the —? Did he just ask my permission?*

"Umm… Excuse me?" I blink rapidly, "I don't think I heard that right."

He flushes, then draws himself up to his full height, "I asked if I can come in?"

"If I say no, would that stop you?"

"No?" He smirks, then sobers, "If you'd rather that I not come in then just say the word. I'll leave."

I take in his gorgeous features, the hint of something like…indecision in his eyes, the way he holds himself stiffly, like he's about to face an exam or do something that he's not completely comfortable with… Shit, the very fact that he did not barge in like he owns the place, but opted to wait for my consent before he walked in is…surprising enough that I want to find out what's on his mind. I blow out a breath, then jerk my chin, "You can come in, on one condition."

"Oh?"

I nod, "I'll tell you what it is, as long as you agree to it."

"Come now," he tilts his head "that's no deal at all."

"I'm not negotiating at all."

"Hmm," he looks me up and down, "fine, then tell me what it is."

"A Christmas party."

"Eh?" He seems taken aback, "A Christmas party?"

"It is the second week of December already," I point out. "Isn't it traditional in Italy for Christmas decorations to go up by December 8?"

"You've been researching Italian customs?" He smirks.

Cassandra had mentioned it to me, but I am not going to tell him that. "All I'm saying is that it's time we start planning for Christmas."

We? Shit, I said *'we.'*

He doesn't seem to notice though. "You want to start planning a Christmas party?" He rubs his jaw.

I nod. To be honest, I am not huge on Christmas gatherings, as such. But maybe I am lonelier than I thought… Or m-a-y-b-e, finding myself pregnant makes me want to surround myself with more people, I guess? Andy wriggles in my arms and I place him on the floor. He instantly pads over to Mika who picks up the kitten. He cuddles Andy who coils up against his chest. *Traitor.* And I thought he owed his allegiance to me. Apparently, not even kittens are exempt from the Capo's charm.

"I also want to invite Aurora to the Christmas party."

"No," his lips firm, "I can't allow that."

"Why not?"

"She conspired with you."

"She told you I was pregnant so you came after me."

"She—"

"Deserves another chance," I cut in. "Come on, she's a doctor, and she's helped you out when you needed her services, hasn't she?"

He hesitates.

"Also," I bat my eyelashes at him, "I really am starved for feminine company."

He tilts his head, "If feminine company is all you want, I could invite my Nonna..."

I gape at him, "You're kidding me, right?"

He frowns, "Why would I do that?"

"Your Nonna hates me. The last time she saw me, she slapped me."

"Only because you stuck a knife in me."

"Can't promise not to do that again," I mutter under my breath.

"What's that?"

I swear, it looks like he's repressing a smirk.

"Nothing." I clear my throat. "So, about the party—you'll let me invite Aurora to it?"

He grimaces. He bends and places Andy on the floor. The kitten walks toward the basket that has been made up for him in the corner of the room. He climbs in, turns around and begins to wash himself.

"Aww come on, Mika." I turn my gaze back on the glowering man, "It's Christmas! Isn't this when you forget the sins of your enemies and all that stuff?"

"I'll invite her, on one condition."

I scowl, "Thought this was my gig?"

He raises a shoulder, and I draw in a breath, "Fine, tell me your condition."

"You promise not to sulk in your room, and to eat well, and to get plenty of fresh air."

"If you think your fake concern for me is going to help you wheedle your way into my good books then..." I tilt my head, "you're going to have to try harder."

"So, you will eat well, get plenty of fresh air, take your vitamins and—"

"—yes, yes," I mutter, "I will."

"Promise?"

I throw up my hands, "I told you I will."

He prowls across the room to stand in front of me. Gosh, he is so big, his shoulders so massive, that he blocks out the sight of everything else. It's as if he's absorbed all of the oxygen in the room. I try to breathe and drag in his dark, edgy scent. The heat of his body curls around me, envelops me. The force of his dominance holds me immobile as he bends his knees and peers into my eyes. "There's one more thing I want."

"Wh...what?" I clear my throat, "What is it?"

Ask me to move back into your bedroom, ask me to throw myself down on my back on your bed, part my thighs and invite you to bury yourself inside me again. My core clenches. I tip up my chin, part my lips as he leans in close enough for his chest to brush mine. My nipples harden; my belly flip-flops. Those cold blue eyes of his flare with an inner fire as he drops his gaze to my mouth.

"Promise me you'll create your own Christmas dress?"

"What?"

He raises his gaze to mine, "I want you to start creating again, starting with the dress you'll wear to the Christmas party."

"That's what you wanted to ask me?"

He straightens, then kisses me on the cheek. His scent deepens, then fades as he takes a step back from me. "What else did you think?" he says, his voice so bloody innocent. Argh! I set my jaw and a low chuckle rumbles up his chest. "Wait... Surely, not..." he clicks his tongue and slowly shakes his head, "you didn't think I was going to fuck you, did you?"

Hearing him say that four letter word? OMG, it's so hot, so erotic. Not like he hasn't said that before. But considering I almost came just from hearing him do so... Hell... Is this a side-effect of pregnancy hormones? When I am not sick, I want to either eat or have sex. Is that how it's going to be from now on?

"Of course not," I sniff. "I thought no such thing."

"Good." He notches his knuckle under my chin, "Because I am not taking any chances with this pregnancy."

He turns to leave, and I call out, "Wait, what do you mean by that?"

"By what?"

"By not taking any chances with this pregnancy?"

He pauses at the door, "Just that." He turns to face me, "As long as you are pregnant, I don't plan on fucking you."

"Eh?" I open and shut my mouth, "Why the hell would you do that?"

"You need to rest and take care of yourself. Besides, I don't want to do anything to endanger the baby."

"You wouldn't be endangering the baby if you shagged me."

"Still, there's a chance that it would be uncomfortable for you."

"I am willing to take that risk," I cry.

He clicks his tongue, "It's noble of you to offer to do that, but I will not allow the mother of my child to be inconvenienced in any way."

I take in his determined stance, the set of his jaw, and blow out a breath, "Bloody hell, you're serious about this, aren't you?"

"Deadly."

I take in the set of his features, then scowl, "Wait, are you thinking of fucking someone else, maybe?"

"Do you think that I am going to fuck someone else?"

His blue gaze bores into me. I shuffle my feet, then glance away, "You tell me."

"Look at me, Beauty."

I hesitate.

"Now," he orders.

I find myself turning to face him. Dammit, what power does he hold over me that I can't disobey him.

He rakes his gaze across my face, then steps closer to me. He bends his knees, then peers into my eyes, "I am not going to fuck anyone else Karma, *caspice*?"

"Hmm," I twist my lips, "what about Larissa or that...that stewardess on the plane? You're not going to see them on the side, are you?"

His features harden, "I am not. Going to fuck. Anyone else. I take my vows to you very seriously. You understand?"

I nod.

"Say it aloud," he commands.

"I understand." I blow out a breath, "So, this means, you and I will continue to stay in separate rooms, until the baby is born?"

"Isn't that what you wanted?"

No.

No.

"Yes," I nod.

His features brighten, "Good." He curves his beautiful lips in a smile. "See? We are already getting along so well."

He straightens, turns to leave, then pauses once more. "One more thing, Beauty."

"Now what?"

"We may have arrived at a temporary truce, of sorts—doesn't mean I am not watching you."

33

Karma

If he's watching me, it's not because he has cameras in this room. I glance around the space again, taking in the light fixtures, the air vents, the shelves in the room—hell, even the corners of the ceilings, where a camera would have most likely be hidden—but can't see anything. Which is not to say that there can't be cameras in the mirror that is pushed up against one wall, or even embedded in a piece of furniture or something, but somehow, I doubt it. In the few days since Michael had made that statement, I had slept well, hadn't had the sensation of being watched in any way—not in my room, definitely not when I go walking in the large garden that surrounds the house, or even on the beach, for that matter.

A few hours after Michael had left, Cassandra had hauled in yards of different fabrics. Then Antonio had shown up carrying a sewing machine—a new one, by the looks of it—followed by a drafting table, and all of the other instruments I need for sewing.

The result is that half of my bedroom has been transformed into a studio, and honestly, I am not complaining about it. I had also asked Cassandra to fetch me additional supplies that I'll need for the creation I have in mind, and she had done it very happily. Andy is now a permanent fixture in my room and he keeps me company as I sew.

I've taken to having my meals with Cassandra in the kitchen, and while I have not seen Michael on any of those occasions, she has assured me that he is very much around, and working hard, both in his study as well as at meetings that he has had to attend out of the house. Something to do with a flare up of tensions with a rival clan. Which is none of my business, really.

I have less than two weeks to come up with a creation which will blow his socks off, and I intend to make the most of that time. I have also drawn up a guest list for the event, which is beginning to look like an evening party, which is good. It means there's no need to sit around a table and endure uncomfortable silences. No, for my Christmas party, which is going to be goth themed—surprise!—there are going to be lights and music...and a DJ. Yep, definitely need a DJ to get the crowd going.

I run into Michael briefly in the hallway and ask him who he wants to invite, and he says I can decide. When I tell him I want to get in a DJ, he flat out refuses, though. No strangers are to be allowed. Only close family i.e. his brothers, and yeah, unfortunately, that also includes extending an invitation to his father and his Nonna, I guess. So much for getting to decide who to invite.

I head back toward my room, grumbling under my breath. I don't want to. But clearly, the man is close to his grandmother... As for his father... Well, he is family...so it makes sense to have him. And his brothers...of course. Not that I have a problem with any of them. Speaking of, I wonder what's going on with Luca? Anyway, we'll invite Antonio, Cassandra, and Aurora, as well. Which still leaves the question of the DJ. Damn it! I reach my room and start slamming things around on my work table. "What's a party without a DJ?" I muse aloud.

"Someone mention a DJ?"

I jerk my head in the direction of the voice and find Xander, standing in the open doorway.

"Didn't realize I had mumbled that aloud." I redden.

"I heard you were organizing a Christmas bash and figured you could do with a hand." He ambles in. "Mind if I take a seat?" He nods toward the chair by the window, then before I can agree, he wanders over and sits down on it. Apparently, all of the Sovrano brothers are confident enough that no one will refuse them. Of course, whether that confidence is a result of respect or fear is another story. Oh, well.

He kicks out his long legs, clad in tailor-made slacks, no doubt, cut by the same family tailor who creates Michael's clothes. He taps his long fingers on his thigh, "So, you need a DJ for the party, huh?" Xander asks.

I nod.

"And I guess my brother did not want anyone from outside our immediate circle of family and friends at the party?"

"You know your brother well," I mutter as I place my scissors down by the cloth that I had been cutting earlier. I lean a hip against my work-table, "Do you have any ideas? I mean a party without a DJ is like a rose without thorns."

"Or the sixties without the Beatles," he smirks.

"Or *Apocalypse Now* without music by the Doors," I chuckle.

"Or like *Harry Potter* without Draco Malfoy," he offers.

"OMG!" I gasp, "Seriously though, sometimes I am sure I am more of a Dracohead than a Potterhead."

"You always fall for the bad boy, huh?"

I firm my lips, "You have no idea."

He raises his hands, "I didn't mean anything by that statement."

"I know you didn't," I murmur, then hunch my shoulders. "How are you in here anyway? I thought the Big Bad Capo had forbidden even his brothers from coming in here."

"Not me, though."

"Not you?"

"The rules don't apply to me." He grins and whoa, his charm hits me full whack, like the fireworks over the Thames on New Year's Eve. Jesus, these Sovrano brothers sure pack a punch. Each of them is deadly in his own right. Though Michael is, by far, the most dominant, the most mesmerizing of all of them.

"Is it because Michael doesn't consider you a threat?"

He blinks then chuckles, "You think fast, don't you?"

I raise a shoulder, "You're here, so yeah, it's not rocket science."

"Let's just say, Michael is aware that I'd never do anything to hurt him."

"You care for him deeply," I murmur.

"I'd give up my life for him."

"Oh," a ball of emotion sticks in my throat. "It's what I'd do for my sister Summer."

"She's older than you?"

I nod, "We only had each other growing up, so we learned to take care of each other."

"You miss her?"

I nod again.

"Have you called to let her know that you are here?"

I hesitate, then walk over to sit down in the chair opposite him. "I've been texting her regular updates, enough so she does not worry about me."

"But she's not aware that you are married."

"Or that I am pregnant."

I follow his gaze to my stomach and find I've placed my palm against my belly, as I seem to do so often nowadays.

"Why is that?" His voice is gentle and when I look up, the look in his eyes is even gentler.

A thickness clogs my throat and I swallow it away. "I just wasn't sure where to start, really." I wring my fingers together, "I am not sure she'll really understand what happened. More likely, she's liable to fly down here and demand that I return with her—"

"And you don't want to?"

"No," I say so softly that I can barely hear myself, but he catches it.

He leans forward and grips my shoulder. "You are not alone. We're your family now, and we are all here for you."

I sniffle.

"And Michael, regardless of his growly, grumpy nature... He does care for you, in his own way."

"That almost makes it worse." I sigh and lower my chin. "I think the two of us have grown to care for each other, yet we seem to not have a single conversation without getting angry with each other."

"Maybe it's how the two of you communicate, you know?"

"What, by sparring with words?"

"And with weapons." He waggles his eyebrows and I laugh.

"Yeah, I know, I can't believe I pulled a knife on him. Not to mention, you know—" I mime whacking someone on the forehead.

He winces, "That was quite an escape you made there, young lady."

"I ended up driving a wedge between Michael and Luca because of that, didn't I?"

"Luca did that all by himself, by betraying Mika."

I wince, "I played a role in it though. If I hadn't wanted to leave, Luca wouldn't have found the opportunity to do so."

"You just happened to be there. If it hadn't been you, it would have been something else. Luca was waiting to undermine Michael. It so happened that you came along first."

"Right." I blow out a breath, "Not sure if that makes me feel better at all."

"I know what will make you feel better."

"What?"

"Finding you a DJ."

"You know someone?"

He spreads his arms, "You're looking at one of the best DJs in Palermo."

"Which is not saying much, given the size of the city," I snicker.

"Hey," he thumps his chest, "you disparaging our fair city?"

"Not at all." I chuckle, "Besides, not like I have a choice."

"Jeez," he shakes his head, "you sure know how to trample all over a man's ego."

"I have been practicing." I tip up my chin, "Can you tell?"

"I can see why my brother likes to verbally spar with you."

"More like we can't stop fighting when we are in the same room."

"It's another way of showing how much you two care about each other."

"Oh, I am not sure about that."

"I am." He lowers his arms to his side, spears me with a look. "I have never seen Mika look at anyone the way he looks at you."

My heart begins to thud. My belly flip-flops. I push my hair over my shoulder, then pretend to study the pattern on the pile of fabric on the opposite side of the room. "You must be mistaken; it's really not like that."

He laughs, then throws back his head and laughs harder. "You can try to say otherwise, but you and I both know, you have Michael tied up in knots."

"Who's tied up in knots?"

I jerk my chin in the direction of the doorway.

34

Michael

She glances in my direction, and the expression on her face is laced with guilt. I prowl toward her and she tips up her chin. "Were you talking about me, Beauty?" I murmur and she huffs.

"My every conversation is not about you."

"What were you two talking about, then?"

"None of your business."

"Everything about you is my business," I pause in front of her, "and you'd do best not to forget that."

Xander clears his throat, and I shoot him a sideways glance.

"We were discussing the Christmas bash," he explains.

"Is that right?" I turn to her, "That what's got you tied up in knots, huh?"

"Exactly," she snickers, "*I* am the one tied up in knots." She exchanges a glance with Xander who chuckles.

"She's been worried about finding a DJ for the party. It's why I offered my services."

"You're going to DJ?" I scowl.

"Sure," he raises a shoulder, "it's no biggie. I did it at many of the parties during my university days."

"And here I thought you spent most of your time painting."

"Hey, we artists need to blow off some steam too, you know? Besides, music is a form of art, and DJing is simply a matter of arranging tunes into a pattern."

"Whoa, you a poet too?" she comments, her tone filled with admiration.

I scowl.

"I have been known to write a poem or two," Xander smirks.

I glower at him, "If you two have had enough of this mutual admiration society you've got going on here—"

Something brushes my leg. I glance down to find her kitten walking past me.

The beast heads over to Xander, who scoops him up. "Who do we have here? What's your name, little fella?" he croons as he tickles the kitten under his chin.

"His name's Andy," she replies with a big smile.

"Hello Andy, what a fine-looking kitty you are, too."

Andy purrs loudly, then rubs his head against the *stronzo*'s shirt. *Traitor.* Not only is my wife taken in with Xander, but her cat... The cat that *I* got for her seems to prefer his company to mine.

Good thing I trust Xander the most amongst all of my brothers; enough to not chew him out for spending time with her. Also, I can't exactly keep her hidden away forever, much as that would be my preference. If there is anyone other than me that I'd choose for her to spend time with, then it would be him.

So, I content myself with simply glaring at Xander, who smirks back at me.

"*Te ne devia fare in culo,*" I growl and he laughs. The bastard *laughs* as he rises to his feet. He pats the kitten once more, then hands Andy over to me. As he leaves, I pull the beast closer to me. The animal strains in my grasp, and glances over at her. It mewls pitifully, and I frown.

"Aww," she walks over to me and holds out her arms. The kitten promptly jumps onto her chest. She closes her arms about him, and he cuddles up against her breasts. I scowl at him, watch as he rubs his head up against the swell of her curves.

Only when her chin jerks up do I realize that I have growled aloud. *Porca miseria!* Apparently, I am jealous of a kitten?

I glare at the animal and she hugs him tighter to her chest. "Stop that," she orders, "you're scaring him."

"Scaring him, my ass! He's play-acting, just so he can get your sympathies."

"Play-acting?" She laughs, "Animals don't play-act. They are not like humans, who'll stoop to any level to get their way."

"Who are you talking about?"

"Who do you think?" she snaps

I fold my arms across my chest, "I have never play-acted."

"Haven't you?" She tosses her head, "You keep acting all tough and surly, but inside, you are as soft as…as that slushy thing which I had for breakfast.

"It's called a *granita*," I murmur, "and you must be mistaken. I don't play-act, and I am definitely not soft inside."

"Yes, you do, and yes, you are."

"Not." I harden my jaw

"Are." She juts out her chin.

And why can't I stop myself from rising to her bait, eh? I drag my fingers through my hair, "Look. Ever since I found out that you were pregnant... It's...ah... Confused me."

"Confused you?"

I nod, "When I think about your bringing my child into this world, it makes me feel like I am the most vulnerable person on this earth. What if my enemies got to either of you? If something were to happen to either of you, I'd... I don't think I'd be able to take it."

Her expression softens, "Nothing's going to happen to either of us."

"You're that confident, eh?"

"No, I am that confident that you will take care of us."

I stare into her features, that red-tinted hair that flows about her shoulders, those green eyes that sparkle at me, that tiny upturned nose, those beautiful pink lips that beg for me to lick them, thrust my tongue in between them and tangle with hers. The blood rushes to my groin and I am instantly hard. "You trust me to take care of you."

"I trust you." She holds my gaze, "I trust you to do what's right for the two of us. I trust that you'll never allow anything to harm us."

A hot sensation stabs at my chest. I close the distance between us, cup her cheek, "When you say things like that, it completely wrecks me, you know that?" I lower my face to hers, when there's an angry hiss from between us. Something sharp stabs at my chest... This time, for real. I wince, glance down to find the kitten has dug his claws into my shirt. He's grazed the same wound—now healed—that his mistress had bestowed on me not too long ago.

"Oh, sorry, Andy," she laughs. "Didn't mean to crush you there."

Wish I could say the same. I scowl down at the animal that glares back at me. Jesus, the cat has almost as much attitude as her. She reaches down, gently disentangles his claws from my shirt, then bends down to place him on the floor. He shakes his entire body, as if he's tossing off any residue of my touch, then struts off toward his basket in the corner of the room.

She straightens, then peers up at me from under her eyelashes. I hold her gaze and her cheeks pinken.

"Why are you looking at me like that?" she murmurs.

"Like what?"

She raises her shoulder, "Like you've never seen me before?"

"Maybe I haven't. Maybe I have underestimated you all along. Maybe, if I had known how you were going to turn my life upside down, I'd have run from you the first time I laid eyes on you."

She blinks, "Is that a compliment? Because I am not sure."

"It is," I push the hair off of her forehead, "a compliment. It takes a lot to surprise me, and I can safely say that you have done so at every turn, my Beauty."

"And you, my Capo," she goes up on her tip-toes and presses a kiss to the side of my neck, which is all she can reach, "constantly challenge me. You make me want to push myself to keep up with you. You make me want to reinvent myself so I can hold my own against you."

"Is that good or bad?"

"I am not sure," she says with a gleam in her eyes, then yelps when I pat her behind.

"What was that for?" She frowns.

"Couldn't help it. Your posterior is so beautifully rounded, that when I am near you, I have to squeeze it."

She reaches behind and grabs a hold of my butt, "Now we're even." She pouts, "Don't expect to cop a feel without—" She stutters as I grip her under her ass and hoist her up. She wraps her legs around my waist.

"Now we are even," I smirk.

She scowls, "That's not fair."

"Life's not fair, baby." I pivot, head for the door, and she peers up at me.

"Where are you taking me?"

"To dinner."

"Dinner, but—"

"Aren't you hungry?"

"It's not that. It's just..." She hesitates and I pause glance down at her.

"If we stay here, I am going to fuck you and that's not what I want."

"Why not?"

"I don't want to hurt you, not when you are in this condition."

"I am pregnant, not unwell."

"Exactly," I nod, "this early in the pregnancy, it's best to be safe."

"Is that what the doctor said?"

I hesitate and she huffs, "See? That's what I mean; I don't know where you got it into your head that just because I am pregnant, you can't make love to me."

"I'd rather wait until it's completely safe to do so."

"But the doctor never said any such thing."

"It's what I am saying."

"So, now you know better than the doctor?"

"Let's just say that when it comes to your well-being, I am taking no chances."

"This is ridiculous." She pouts. "I want you to fuck me and you are turning me down?"

"Oh, trust me. There's nothing I'd rather do more, but in this case, there's something more important than you and me at stake here."

She frowns, "You mean the baby?"

"Our baby." I nod, "I'd rather you feel better before I fuck you again."

She throws up her hands, "I've never heard anything crazier than that. I mean, are you hearing yourself? You're all worried for no reason."

"I'd rather be more careful than not."

She blows out a breath, "I am not changing your mind on this, am I?"

I shake my head.

"Fine, whatever," She folds her arms across her chest, stares straight ahead, as I head out of the door. I walk down the stairs and to the terrace on the first floor. I cross the breadth of it to a sheltered alcove and she draws in a breath, "What's this?"

35

Karma

"This is where we're having dinner," he murmurs as he lowers me into a chair. I take in the crisp white table cloth that covers a table that has been set with silverware for two. The alcove is sheltered from the breeze by a screen on one side. The view itself is undisturbed though, and I glance out at the sea that stretches out into the distance. A cool breeze tugs at my hair. I tuck the strands behind my ear, turn back to the table arrangement. There's a vase in the center of the table with one single perfectly formed black rose, the edges of the petals a blood red. It's a perfect bloom, unlike anything I have ever seen. He reaches for a blanket that has been placed on a stool by the side. He places it over my lap, then tucks it at the sides.

"How does that feel?"

"Good," I murmur.

"Not too cold? Not too warm?" He nods toward the patio heater, "Should I turn that off?"

"No," I pat the edge of the blanket, "I am comfortable, as is."

"Good." He reaches for a napkin, shakes it out, then places it on my lap over the blanket, before pushing my chair in, just so. Then he walks around to take his seat on the other side.

"What's all this about?"

"Can't I have dinner with my wife?"

"Hmm," I frown, "not that I don't appreciate it, but if you want to take me to dinner, why can't we go out?"

He tilts his head, and I scowl. "You don't want to take me out, is that it?"

He gazes at me steadily and I blow out a breath, "Since you found out I was pregnant you haven't let me out of the house. In fact, you've barely let me out of your sight, and it's really beginning to grate on my nerves."

He merely reaches for the jug of water and pours out a glass. "Drink," he orders, "you need to make sure that you are hydrated."

I open my mouth to refuse and he gives me a stern look. "Drink your water, baby," he winks at me, and bloody hell, when he calls me by that endearment, my heart seems to melt. I can't refuse him anything when he looks at me with that mix of dominance and lust and tenderness all entwined in the depths of those hypnotic blue eyes. I raise the glass of water, sip from it, and his gaze falls to my mouth. His pupils dilate and his nostrils flare. I lick my lips, scooping up a drop of water from the corner of my mouth, and his throat moves as he swallows. His chest rises and falls, he leans forward, reaches for me, when the sound of footsteps approaches.

Momentarily distracted, we look toward Cassandra, who makes her way over to us to place a basket of bread between us. "The chef will be along shortly with your main courses. Enjoy." She glances between us, then backs away without another word.

Steam rises from the bread. Whoa, have they been freshly baked? I mean, of course, they have to be freshly baked. Nothing but the best for Michael, after all. I reach for a roll, then gasp and pull back, "Ouch, it's too hot."

"Here, let me." He reaches for a roll, breaks off a piece. Steam rises from it as he offers me a bite-sized piece.

I glance at the piece of roll then back at him, "It may be too hot."

"It's not."

"What if it is?" I frown.

"And here I thought you trusted me, hmm?"

Well, he does have a point there. I open my mouth and he pops the piece of bread inside. I chew on it, and the strong, tangy, yeasty flavor of the freshly baked roll explodes on my palate. "Oh, yum!" I finish chewing, swallow the piece, then open my mouth again. He pops another piece of bread inside and I chew on that as well. "This is really good," I admit as I swallow it down as well.

He butters the remaining piece, offers it to me and I eat that too. The flavors only seem to multiply, thanks to the butter. "I have never tasted anything like it," I confess.

"The chef is the best in Europe," he confirms to me.

"It's not what's-her-name, Marissa, is it?"

"You mean Larissa?" He smirks.

I frown. "Don't flaunt your floozies in front of your wife," I snap.

He raises his hands. "*Scusa*," he murmurs, "*mi sono sbagliato*. I promise, I won't speak of her again."

"Or see her," I add, causing him to nod in agreement. *Wait a minute. What is he up to?* I stare, "You are being awfully conciliatory?"

"I admit my mistakes when I am wrong," he peers into my eyes, "but only for you, Beauty."

My stomach flip-flops; I clench my thighs. Gosh, can he be any hotter? Especially when he's being so nice to me? I push back my seat, rise to my feet, place my blanket and napkin on my chair, then walk around the table. His forehead quirks as I raise his arm then sink down in his lap.

His gaze heats as I twine my fingers with his, then reach up and brush his lips with mine. "This is nice, isn't it?" I murmur, and his breath catches. I press tiny kisses down the sharp edge of his jaw, to the hollow at the base of his throat. I lick the skin there and his hardness stabs into the side of my thigh. I bite down and a low growl ripples up his chest. He wraps his fingers around the back of my neck and tugs. I tip up my chin, stare into those blue eyes that blaze back at me.

He rakes his gaze down my features, to my lips, then back up to my eyes, "The answer, Beauty," he whispers, "is still no."

I scowl, "I didn't ask for anything."

"But you were going to."

"No, I wasn't,"

One side of his lips curls, "Still lying to me, darlin'?"

I try to pull away, but he tightens his grip. Goosebumps pop on my skin, my pussy trembles, and moisture laces my core. Shit. Why is it that when he begins to get rough with me, my body responds with such ardor?

"Let go of me," I say in a low voice and his grin only widens.

"That's not the message you were conveying a few moments ago, Beauty." He brings his hand up to cup my breast, and a moan bleeds from my lips. His gaze sharpens. "Your breasts are more tender, more sensitive than they used to be," he murmurs as he brushes his thumb across my nipple. Heat races down my spine and I shift in his lap. His thickness seems to lengthen against my thigh as he leans in closer, closer...

He brushes his nose against my throat and inhales deeply, "You smell of moonflowers, with a hint of something deeper, more complex." He sniffs me again, then glances up at me, "You smell the same, and yet, different." He peers into my features, "Like you are changing, even while, at heart, you are the same girl you once were."

"Wow," I swallow, "you can sense all that?"

A crease appears between his eyebrows. "Only with you, apparently."

He leans in, nuzzles my cheek, "You smell like you are mine."

My stomach flutters and my toes curl. Oh, my God, if anyone could bring me to orgasm just by his words, it would be this man. I turn my face toward him and our lips meet and... It's unlike any of our previous kisses. It's soft and tender, with just a hint of that unleashed dominance that is so very Mika; and yet, he's holding back the full force of his personality, which thrums in the background. And that only turns me on further.

I lean into the kiss, but he tightens his grip on my neck and holds me in place. He proceeds to leisurely nibble on my mouth, lick my lips, brush his mouth over mine again and again, until our breaths mingle and our chests rise and fall in unison, until the evidence of his arousal seems to grow so solid between us that I am sure his shaft is going to stab through his pants. My core clenches and moisture trickles down the inside of my thigh. I grind my butt into his thickness and a groan vibrates up his chest.

"Fuck," he murmurs, "you are killing me, Beauty."

"You are doing it to yourself, Capo," I bite down on his lower lip and he visibly jerks.

He pulls away, stares into my features, "You're tempting me to break my self-imposed abstinence."

"Why don't you?" I scowl at him, "This entire no-sex thing is ridiculous."

"You're cute when you are angry," he chuckles.

I open my mouth to tell him off, only he's already there. He kisses me. I part my lips and he sweeps in, thank god! He sucks on my tongue, sips from me, consumes me, devours me like he is hungry and I am his last meal. My head spins and my toes curl; he pulls away from me and I slump.

I hear footsteps behind me but don't turn.

"You okay?" he murmurs as he tucks a strand of hair behind my ear in a gesture that is becoming familiar to me.

I hear the sound of plates being placed on the table and the spicy scent of food tickles my nose. I turn to find two steaming dishes placed on the table.

"*Come va, principessa*?" a familiar voice asks.

"Paolo!" I cry in delight. "What a pleasure to see you here."

"And you." His rosy cheeks widen in a big smile.

"What are you doing here?"

"I was asked to come and cook my favorite dishes for you," he nods his chin toward the plates.

"So, you left your restaurant and came over to cook dinner for us?"

He jerks his chin toward Michael, "What the Capo wants, the Capo gets."

Of course, he does.

I shoot a sideways glance at Michael. "There was no need to have Paolo shut down his restaurant and come here to cook for us. We could have gone to him."

"And you know my thoughts on that already." Michael tilts his head. His gaze clashes with mine and those blue eyes of his—damn! It's like they can see my deepest thoughts, suss out my innermost fears. Like they are aware that underneath all the protests, I am secretly flattered that he did this for me. My cheeks heat and his smirk widens. Gah, can I not even glance at him without getting turned on?

I flip my hair over my shoulder, turn to Paolo, "Well, I, for one, don't take your coming here for granted. I hope the Capo, at least, compensated you for the lost business."

He laughs, "He did, and even if he hadn't, I promise you, it would have been my honor and my pleasure to cook for the both of you. Someone in your state needs to eat well, signora, and I have made sure that my dish is perfectly balanced, with all the nutrients you and your growing child need.

"Oh," heat sears my cheeks. Guess I am still not used to the fact that I am pregnant, especially not when someone else mentions it to me.

"I told him; I hope you don't mind?" Mika whispers. "He's like family."

"It's fine, "I murmur, then turn to Paolo again. "Thank you for coming out to cook for us." I hold out my hand and he takes it, then kisses it on the knuckles, before stepping back.

He glances at the food, then at Michael, "You need to eat the food before it grows cold."

"Oh, we will." Michael gestures to the plates, "Could you place her plate in front of me before you leave? I plan to feed her."

Paolo moves the plate over so it's front of us, then he retreats.

I turn to protest and Michael shakes his head. "Indulge me, Beauty," he implores in a soft voice and my heart stutters. It bloody stutters.

This man... All he has to do is glance at me with tenderness and I'll throw myself down at his feet and be ready to do his every bidding. Oh, who am I kidding? When he orders me, it turns me on even more. But there's something about Mika being so attentive to my wishes which is simply...completely...arousing, and which also makes me giddy with happiness.

My heart begins to thud in my chest and my pulse rate ratchets up. OMG, the way he's looking at me... It's as if he loves me, and like he's beginning to realize it himself.

"Beauty, I..." he searches my features, then hesitates, "I..."

"What is it?" I whisper, "Tell me, Mika, what do you want to say?"

He seems to get a hold of himself, then reaches past me for the fork. He twirls some of the pasta, then offers it to me, "I think you need to eat."

"But—"

"Later," he murmurs, "let's enjoy our food first, hmm?"

I want to push it, but something in his gaze warns me that it's time to give in. I nod, allowing him to feed me. The pasta is a simple dish made with vegetables and a sauce that is absolutely flavorful. Mika insists on feeding me, and I tell him he needs to eat as well. We compromise when he agrees that I can feed him too.

When both of our plates are empty, I lean into him with a sigh.

"Now what?" I murmur.

"Cassandra," he calls out, "make sure that we are not disturbed."

Cassandra pops her head through the doorway. She nods, then shuts the door on us.

I turn to him, "What's that all about?"

"That," he smirks, "means it's time for dessert."

36

Karma

"Dessert?" I blink rapidly. "Is Paolo going to serve us dessert?"

"He offered to make dolce for us, but I told him to wait. We'll have it after."

"After?" My cheeks heat, "After what?"

"After..." He lifts me up onto the table, then pushes my legs apart. The dress I'm wearing is pushed up to above my knees. He slides his fingers up my thighs, and I try to squeeze them together.

"Relax," he murmurs, "I am going to make this so good for you."

That's what I am afraid of.

I peer at him from between my eyelashes. "I thought you weren't going to shag me?"

"Doesn't mean I can't pleasure you," his eyes gleam, "while I feast on you."

A pulse flares to life between my legs. It mirrors the beat of my heart, the thud-thud-thud of the blood roaring in my ears as he rises to his feet. Without taking his gaze off of mine, he leans over and shoves the rest of the crockery aside. The dishes and remaining cutlery hit the ground with a crash that sweeps through me. I shudder, partly from lust, partly from the adrenaline that sweeps through me. Jesus, is that hot or what? And so damn erotic.

He eases me onto my back, then peers into my eyes as he slides his hand up my thigh. When he reaches my panties, he brushes my core through the drenched fabric and flickers of heat ladder up my spine. Oh, my god, he is going to torture me with his touch, his kisses, the way he cups my pussy as he brushes his lips over mine.

"Who does this belong to?" he whispers against my mouth. "Tell me, Beauty, who do you spread your legs for?"

"You, Capo," I murmur and he draws in a breath. He hooks his fingers in the delicate lace of the panties and tugs. The material snaps. Goosebumps pop on my skin. I gasp as cool air assails my heated core. He pulls off my panties, pockets them, then places his fingers on the pulse that gallops at the base of my throat.

"You're turned on, *amore mio*," he says in a low voice. "You like it when I surprise you like this?"

I nod, not trusting myself to speak. My ability to formulate sentences flees as he pulls his knife from where he carries it tucked into the waist-band at the small of his back. He holds it up. The blade gleams and I gulp. He slides it under the the neckline of my dress. I gulp. He tugs, the fabric tears down the center and I yelp.

The front falls open, exposing me to him. He sticks the blade of the knife into the wood of the table, then cups my breast. "Who does this belong to, *amore mio?*" he asks. "Tell me."

"You, Michael," I whisper. "It belongs to you."

He brushes his finger across my nipple, and my breast trembles. He brings his mouth down, sucks on my nipple, and a groan spills from my lips. I writhe under him as he curls his tongue around the pebbled bud, as he brings his other hand up to cup my other breast, as he bites down on the nipple gently, and oh, with so much care that my entire body seems to catch fire. I push my breast up and into his mouth. "Please, suck harder," I beg. "Please, Michael, please."

"I don't want to hurt you," he murmurs. "Your breasts feel heavier and your nipples are swollen. I want to make sure you enjoy this as much as possible."

"Oh." I blink as he tugs on my nipple, then blows on it. I shiver, arch my spine, chasing the suction I so crave, even as he drags his finger across my other nipple. I moan as he turns his attention to my other breast. He bites gently on the nipple, then lathes it with his tongue, before blowing on it. And my breasts are so tender that even that slight breeze sends ripples of sensations crawling down my spine. My core clenches and my toes curl as I raise my arms and throw them about his shoulders as he kisses his way down to my stomach.

He presses his lips to my belly as he grips my hips, then glances up at me, "Who does the child you carry in your womb belong to, *Tesoro Mio*?" He curls his tongue inside my belly button and I groan. "Tell me."

"You, Mi-kah," I gasp, "the child belongs to you."

He rewards me with a kiss, as he cups my swollen pussy. "Who does your cunt belong to, *Contessa*?" He whispers against my throbbing flesh, "Tell me."

"You, Mika." I push my hips forward, aching to feel him inside of me. "It belongs to you, only you."

He slips his finger inside my aching channel and I groan.

"More," I pant, "please, I want more."

I sense him smirk as he adds a second finger, then begins to work his fingers in and out of me, gently, oh so gently.

"Oh, my god," I moan. "Mika, please, fuck me with your tongue, please."

He pulls out his fingers, only to replace them with his tongue.

I writhe as he slurps his way up my pussy lips, and again, before he swirls his wicked tongue around my clit. And that's when I cry out. I dig my fingers into his hair and tug as he gently bites down on the engorged bud.

"Mika!" I yell as he grips my legs above the knees, wraps my legs about his neck. I lock my ankles, press my thighs into either side of his head and he laughs. The vibrations coil in my core, setting off a surge of heat that zings up my spine as I arch my back up and off the table.

"Ohgod, ohgod," I chant, "ohgod, please, Mika, please—" I scream as he thrusts his tongue inside my channel. In and out, he fucks me with his tongue just as I asked. He squeezes my butt, then slides a finger inside my backhole, working it in and out of me before adding another as he continues to plunge his tongue in and out of my pussy.

The vibrations scream out from my core, spreading to my extremities as my entire body bucks.

"Mika, I am going to—"

He pulls his tongue out of me, only to replace it with the fingers of his other hand as he leans over me and presses his lips to mine. "Come for me my Beauty, come right fucking now—" he growls and I shatter.

He closes his mouth over mine as he fucks my pussy and my ass with his fingers.

I scream but he swallows the sound. The climax pours over me, then fades away, leaving me shaking as I collapse against the table. The thud-thud-thud of his heartbeat against mine is reassuring, the heat of his body that envelops me is a beautiful reminder that I belong to him. I open my eyes, gazing into those blue eyes, as he licks my mouth. The sweet taste of my cum mixed with the darker taste of him fills my mouth as he holds my gaze.

"Mika," I bring my hand up and drag my fingers across his lips, "will you fuck me in the arse?"

"Eh?" He blinks, "Excuse me?"

"You told me you are not comfortable shagging me because you think it might hurt me or the baby." I raise a shoulder. "I figure this way you can shag me without worrying about any of that."

"You don't have to do that." He scowls, "I can go without sex for a little while, you know."

"I want to."

"You don't need to do this, Karma." His frown deepens, "I want you to be comfortable, and relaxed."

"And I can't be either of those when I am horny as hell."

"Woman, you just came." He arches an eyebrow, "Are you telling me that wasn't enough?"

"It wasn't enough."

"And you want me to take your ass because—"

"Because," I swallow, "I want you to own me completely, I want you to imprint your mark in every part of me, I want you to…possess me so absolutely that I can't think of anyone else but you."

37

Michael

This woman... The things she says... She never ceases to surprise me. I grip her shoulders to pull her up and she wraps her arms around my neck. "I mean it, Mika," she murmurs, "I want you inside me, one way or the other."

"I don't want to hurt you." I wrap a strand of her gorgeous hair around my fingers, "Right now, your comfort is more important than anything else to me."

"And I already told you that I want you."

I peer into her face, take in her flushed features, her gaze wide with anticipation; those green eyes stare back at me and in them is a look of feverish need. I wrap my fingers about the back of her nape and bring her forehead to mine, "Any other time, if you weren't pregnant, I'd not deny this to you, but right now, given your condition, it's not something I can give you."

"Michael," she pleads, "this is no time for an attack of conscience."

I laugh, "Trust me, if it were up to me, I'd be inside you so often you wouldn't be able to walk straight, but this is not just about you and me now, is it?"

She scowls.

"Think about the baby."

"I'd rather think about…" she places a hand on my crotch and squeezes her fingers around my already engorged cock, "this."

My groin hardens. I huff out a breath as she drags her fingers down my thick column. *"Gesù Cristo,"* I growl, "what are you doing to me, woman?"

"You said that you won't fuck me, but there's no rule against my going down on you, is there?" She pushes at my shoulders and I resist.

"Come on, Mika," she pleads. "Don't deny me this. At least, let me get off on getting you off."

I stare into her eyes.

"Please," she licks her lips, "please, Mika." She shoves at my shoulder and I sit back. She presses down and I sink back into my chair. She slides off the table and onto her feet and her already torn dress flutters down her arms. She shrugs it off, then slides down to her knees. She runs her hand up my thigh and my focus zeroes in on her. She holds my gaze as she outlines the length of my arousal. She rubs her fingers up and down the column and my balls harden. I part my thighs wider and she moves in closer. She brushes her fingers across my waistband and her fingertips graze my belly. My muscles jump, I roll my shoulders as I lower my chin.

"Take it out," I growl and a smile curves her lips.

"Oh, no, if we do this, we do it my way."

Che cazzo! How dare she try to direct the proceedings? "Is that right?" I reach down, curl my fingers around the nape of her neck. The column of her throat is so slender that my fingers meet around the front. "It doesn't work that way, Beauty."

She peers up at me from under half-closed lids, "Would you deny me this, Mika?"

I draw in a breath. Damn it. When she gazes at me with that beseeching look in her eyes, how can I deny her anything? I release my hold, lower my hand to my side.

Her smile widens as she unhooks my belt buckle. She lowers my zipper, then pulls down my boxers, and my cock springs free.

"Oh," she blinks, as she lowers her gaze to my throbbing shaft. She licks her lips and I swear I could come right then. She squeezes my shaft all the way up to the crown, then drags her fingers across the tip. Goosebumps pop on my skin.

Goddamn! "Your touch is killing me, Beauty," I growl and her smile widens. She lowers her head, licks the head of my shaft. Her pink tongue curls around the rim of the crown and the sight of it has my muscles tensing. I lean forward and she brings her hand up to cup my balls. She squeezes and a groan rumbles up my chest. She drags her other hand down to the base of my shaft, then up again.

"Oh, fuck," I swear as I curl my fingers into fists at my side. I glare down as she licks the tip of my cock again. I jerk my hips forward, chasing the suction I crave, and her eyes gleam. She massages my balls and I dig my heels into the ground. She licks her tongue down the length of my shaft and up again, and fuck if I don't almost come right then. "If you don't take me down your throat this instant, I'm going to—"

She closes her lips around the head of my cock. I grit my teeth as I watch my dick disappear inside her mouth. Fucking hell, if that isn't the ultimate description of erotic, I am not sure what is.

She peers up at me, holding my gaze as she pulls back, leaving a trail of wetness on my shaft. Only to dip her head and move forward, and this time, she does take me down her throat.

"F-u-c-k." I grab hold of the armrests as she proceeds to swallow. My groin tightens, my balls swell, and the tension at the base of my spine curls into a ball. She pulls back until my dick is poised at the edge of her lips, then she closes her mouth around me again. Heat flushes my skin as she drags her teeth across the underside of my shaft. My muscles tense and the ball of tension at the base of my spine explodes out. "By the *Santa Maria*," I snap, "I am going to come all over your face, Beauty."

I pull out and grab my dick and position it as the climax grips me. The heat vibrates out, my cock jerks and I come, shooting a stream. I paint her face, her hair, position my cock to eject across her creamy breasts. By the time I am done, streaks of white crisscross her hair, her features, curve across her nipples.

I shove my fingers through her hair, grip the nape of her neck, haul her up, and fasten my lips on hers. I swipe my tongue across her teeth, tangle my tongue with hers as I grab her hip with my other hand. I squeeze and she moans into my mouth. And fuck, if that doesn't send the blood emptying to my groin again.

I reach between her legs and the wetness welcomes me. I slide my fingers inside her melting pussy, as I kiss her and finger fuck her, and she trembles, and writhes under me, but I don't stop. I shove four fingers inside her and she gasps. I continue to kiss her as I move my fingers in and out of her, in and out. I press my thumb into her clit and her entire body bucks. She grips my shoulders, holding on as I continue to finger fuck her. I tilt my mouth, suck on her tongue, bend her back as I curl my fingers inside her. Her body jolts and a trembling grips her. A moan bleeds from her and I swallow it down. Her body shudders, her pussy clamps down on my finger and I know she is going to— I tear my mouth from hers. "Come," I order, and she shatters.

Karma

We didn't get to the dessert, after all.

After I came, he'd taken off his shirt and made me wear it over my torn dress. Then he'd scooped me up into his arms and carried me to his bedroom. We hadn't encountered anyone on the way. Not Cassandra, not Paolo. Apparently, his staff knows when to make themselves scarce. And, yep, he broke his own rule for us to have separate bedrooms. Score!

I had fallen asleep promptly. When I woke up, he was gone. I had spent the rest of that day working on my dress, with Andy for company. Oh, also I'd moved my things into his room, and he hadn't said anything.

It might be because I didn't see Michael all that day, or for that matter, on any of the days that followed our reconciliation. Cassandra mentioned to me that he has been deep in negotiations with rival clans to restore some semblance of peace in the country.

This means that the security around the house has been tripled… Or so she tells me. Not that I can tell the difference. For all practical purposes, I am still a prisoner of sorts in the house.

At least, I have the preparations for the upcoming party to keep me distracted. At some point though, I know I have to pick up the phone and call Summer. At some point, she is not going to be happy with just the text messages that I send her.

She has promptly replied to all of them, and by all indications, she seems deliriously happy in her marriage to Sinclair Sterling… So that lessens the guilt somewhat.

Still, I suppose I'll have to tell her the truth of my condition at some point. Just not yet. Maybe after the party...? Maybe once I've gotten to know my husband a little better? Okay, so they are excuses, but once the party is over, I'll have time to think and decide what I want to tell her, you know?

I sit back, taking in the creation I have been working on, then stretch. Just one more week to go. It will be touch-and-go, but hopefully, I'll be able to complete it.

The morning sickness has abated somewhat, and I am finally getting my taste back. So, I can actually taste what I am eating, which is a relief. There's a knock on the door, and I turn to find a familiar figure at the entrance.

"Oh, my gosh!" I jump up, "Aurora, is that really you? How did you get here? Are you okay?"

She nods, then smiles uncertainly, "Can I come in?"

"Of course," I admonish her, "you don't need to ask me that."

She walks over to me, her doctor's satchel in her hand. I meet her half way, hug her, and she feels thinner, frailer than before. I step back, take in her pale features.

"You've lost weight," I murmur. "What did they do to you? They didn't mistreat you or anything, did they?"

She shakes her head. "They didn't do anything to me. Actually, that's the problem."

"Huh?" I step back, "What do you mean? I was so worried about you. When I realized that Michael knew about your part in helping me escape, I was so worried. I know it's not something that he would forgive easily, and he refused to tell me what had happened to you." I peer into her features, "You are okay, aren't you?"

She nods, a ghost of a smile on her lips, "Physically I am okay." She swallows, "But emotionally, mentally... I... I am in a kind of limbo."

"Tell me everything." I lead her to a chair and she sits down, places her bag on the floor.

"They have me put up in a safe house, not far from the city. I can't leave, can't see anyone else. This is the first time I have been out since I went to the Capo and told him that you were pregnant."

I lean back in my seat. "What I don't understand is why you didn't tell me."

"I wasn't sure how you would react. And," she glances away, "I didn't want you to do anything rash and hurt yourself or anything, you know?"

"As if." I huff, "I have more sense than that."

"Well, you were in an emotionally vulnerable state, and I guess, I wanted to protect you."

"So, Michael was telling the truth," I murmur.

She jolts and I explain, "That's what he told me, as well." I frown, "Which still doesn't answer the question of what you are doing here."

"I was told that I am going to be your doctor until the birth of the child."

"You are?" I murmur. Apparently, Mika agreed to my demand, after all. I lean forward, taking her hand in mine, "I am so pleased about that."

"So am I." She smiles, and this time, her eyes light up with genuine pleasure. "And not only because it means I'll be allowed out of the house, but because I do actually like you."

I laugh, "I like you too." I rub her slightly chilled hand between mine, "When was the last time you ate? Why don't I get you something? I—"

There's a knock and Cassandra shoulders open the door. In her hands, she carries a tray piled with plates of food. "I thought the two of you could do with some refreshments.

"You're a mind reader," I exclaim, "and the food is most welcome."

She walks in, places the tray on the table, then removes the covers. Delicious smells fill the room and my stomach growls. She steps back, "Enjoy." She smiles and turns to leave.

"Cassandra," I call out, "why don't you join us?"

She turns and glances between us, "Oh, no, I couldn't."

"Oh, please," I wave a hand in the air, "there's no one else in the house—"

"Except Christian," Aurora corrects me.

"Christian?"

Aurora nods, "He picked me up and dropped me off at the door. He'll wait for me to finish and accompany me back."

"Wow, so they really are making sure that you don't escape."

"I have no intention of even trying," she mutters. "If I did, the Capo would not spare my family."

I bite the insides of my cheeks. She's talking about Michael, my Capo. The father of my child... The man who has pleasured my body and brought me to orgasm countless times. The man who is so concerned about the wellbeing of my child that he refuses to have sex with me. The man who puts my needs before his. The same man who, I know, is also capable of killing if the need arises.

Yeah, Michael wouldn't spare her family. He won't take betrayal of any kind lying down. That, I know, first-hand. I blow out a breath. "Well, I am glad he allowed you to come see me."

Aurora glances at the food and her stomach rumbles loudly.

I chuckle.

She laughs, "Oops, sorry. Not that they are not feeding me. Actually, I've been quite comfortable where I am, except for the fact that I can't leave the place or see anyone."

"I know how that feels," I murmur as I reach for a plate and offer it to her. "Please, help yourself." I turn to Cassandra, who's still standing, "You are joining us, aren't you?"

"Um," she shuffles her feet, "I—"

"Please," Aurora glances up at her, "it will be so nice to listen to the voices of others instead of those in my head."

Cassandra laughs at that. "Fine, but just until lunch is over."

"And then, I still have to examine you." Aurora looks me up and down, "Not that you don't look good. In fact, you are positively glowing, but I need to make sure that you are completely okay."

"There'll be time after we eat."

Just then, Andy slips through the half open door and patters over to me, purring loudly. He brushes his body against my leg and I laugh, "You just ate, and this food isn't good for cats, I promise."

He tosses his head, and walks away toward his bed.

"The life of a cat," Aurora muses. "If only we could all be as single-minded about our needs."

"Speaking of," I turn to the food, "I know what I am going to be single-minded about for the next little while." I reach for a plate and pile mine high with helpings of *Arancini* (creamy risotto rice), *Caponata* (fried eggplant filled with celery, onion and tomatoes, and flavored with capers, pine nuts and raisins), and *Busiate al pesto Trapanese* (a fusilli-like pasta with pesto). I reach for another pasta dish and pause, "What's this?"

"Pasta a la *Norma*," Cassandra explains. "It's one of Sicily's most famous pasta dishes. It's made with local tomatoes, eggplants, garlic, basil and *ricotta salata*, or salted ricotta cheese. It's called *Norma* after the nineteenth century opera of the same name. Both the dish and the music are regarded as true masterpieces."

"You really like to cook, don't you?" I observe.

She laughs as she places minuscule portions of the food on her plate, "It's the one thing that I can rely on. Food. It can't hurt you or break a promise to you..." Her words trail off. She blinks rapidly, then smiles a little too brightly, "I love cooking, and I love feeding people. It fills something inside of me to see them enjoy what I make. After all, we are what we eat, right?"

"Right," I murmur, exchanging glances with Aurora, who shakes her head. Yeah, she's right. This is not the time to delve into those cryptic comments. "So," I train my gaze on her, "did you always know that you wanted to become a doctor?"

Aurora tilts her head, "Actually, yes."

"You did?" Cassandra's gaze widens, "Like when? I mean, how did you know that was your calling?"

Aurora glances down at her plate, then at us, "My mother was sick a lot when I was growing up. I accompanied her on her hospital visits, saw how the doctors helped her. In the end, they couldn't save her, but I knew then, one day I was going to do my best to help other people too."

"I am so sorry for your loss," I reach for her hand and squeeze it, "I lost my mother when I was very young too."

"I lost a husband," Cassandra murmurs, then bites her lips. She turns back to the food and I glance at her shuttered face. Yeah, there is a lot of grief hidden under there, all right.

"Do you want to talk about it?" I venture, and she shakes her head.

"What about you?" she asks, "Fashion designing is obviously your passion."

"Yes, it is," I nod. "I became a fashion designer because it feels like a link to my mother."

"Was she a designer too?" Aurora asks.

"Not professionally, but from what my sister tells me, she loved experimenting with colors and patterns and styles. She stitched all of her own clothes, and my sister's clothes. I never really knew her, but when I'm creating a design, when I am lost in the palettes and textures and immersed in images of what the finished product is going to look like, that's when I am truly happy. That's when I feel closest to her."

"You miss her?" Cassandra's voice is soft.

"I never knew her," I glance down at my food, "but there was always a mom-shaped hole in my life; always will be."

"The pain never goes away." Aurora draws in a breath, "It just becomes a shadow that settles in your heart, one which you are not really conscious of, but which is always there when you look inside."

"And how does it feel now that you are going to become a mother, yourself?" Cassandra tilts her head at me, "Does it fill the hole in your heart somewhat?"

I start, shoot her a glance, but see only genuine curiosity on her features. Her choice of words though... It reminds me of the one secret that I am keeping from all of them...including myself. A secret which I hope I never have to acknowledge. Maybe if I ignore it long enough, it'll stop being real. At least, I can hope.

"You okay?" Aurora puts down her plate of food, then reaches over to take my hand, "Maybe we should carry out that examination now?"

"Let's finish our food first." I nod at her plate, "Please, I am completely okay, and I really want us to do justice to this tasty food that Cassandra has made for us."

"Speaking of," I frown, "it is you who cooked this food, right?"

She shoots me a curious glance, "Who else would cook?"

"Not that Larissa woman, who I met on the island, and who Michael introduced as his chef, I hope."

"He let go of her, shortly after," she replies.

"He did?" I blink.

"Yep, told her to pack her bags and leave the very next day."

"Oh, wow!" Another thing he'd done... For me? Because he knew I couldn't stand the sight of her? I bite the inside of my cheek. Had I judged him that harshly? And this was even before I had become pregnant... Had he actually already begun to develop feelings for me then? I shake my head. Either way, it's clear that he wants to make up for how things started between us. It's why he's allowed Aurora to resume her duties as my doctor. Something for which I am very grateful. Something which I hadn't thought he'd do in a million years. He actually compromised on some of his beliefs for this... And that is huge. And I want to show him how much I appreciate it, in my own way. I turn to the both of them, "You are both coming to my Christmas party, obviously."

"We are?" Aurora frowns.

"We are?" Cassandra gapes.

"Of course, you are," I tell Aurora. "And you," I scowl at Cassandra, "you'd better be there, no excuses.

38

Michael

"I hear your wife's throwing a Christmas party?" JJ Kane, the head of *The Kane Company*, tilts his head, "That's the thing with women. They have to make their presence felt, don't they?"

I curl my fingers into fists at my sides. How dare he talk about her? And how the hell does he know about the Christmas Party? Invitations had only been extended to my brothers, my father and my Nonna. And yeah, Beauty had insisted that Cassandra and Aurora be included.

Initially, I had refused her and she had pleaded with me. She had batted those big, green eyes at me and I had been a goner. Of course, I had agreed. Cassandra is loyal, no question. And Aurora? She knows better than to open her mouth about anything she sees and hears. There's no way either of them would have spoken to anyone about the event. My brothers wouldn't have breathed a word to anyone... Nor would Nonna. As for the Don... Well, much as I don't trust him, given he knows that Karma is pregnant with his grandchild, not even he would endanger her life...

I hadn't wanted to invite him but Nonna had insisted. He's family. And family sticks together. We look out for each other, no matter what.

Within the four walls of our home, we may turn on each other... Like my father had on my mother. Nonna's reasoning is flawed, and yet, it makes sense. It helps us put up a unified front against our enemies. Like the Kane Company, the leader of whom graces my dinner table. I had invited him and Nikolai Solonik, the head of the Bratva for a three-way talk.

If you had asked me a few weeks ago if I'd ever think of negotiating a truce with my rival clans I'd have laughed. Yet that's exactly what I am doing. That's what having a baby on the way does to you, apparently. You have to try to make the world he or she is arriving into a better place. It's the least you can do, really. If I manage to take away any possible motives for my most dangerous enemies to come after my family, I reason, I am, at least, buying us some peace...some level of safety, during which time I can devote myself to being a husband and father, spend time with my wife and child, and bond with my new family as we find ourselves?

Besides, if, indeed, it was JJ who was behind her kidnapping, that's all the more reason to keep him close, until I find a way to kill him... Without drawing attention to myself. I'd sworn to hunt down whoever was behind the kidnapping and kill him... But the fact that I am going to be a father has put things in perspective. Don't get me wrong; I still want my revenge. Only, I want it in a way that it doesn't leave my child without a father.

"Michael?" JJ's voice interrupts my thoughts, "are you inviting us to this Christmas party too?"

"It's family only," I train my gaze on him. Besides, I don't trust the guy. The only reason I have him here is because it's easier to keep an eye on him when I know what he's up to. It's why I am proposing an alliance with JJ and Nikolai... On the face of it, at least, it's a business deal, but really, it's so I can understand JJ's...and Nikolai's weaknesses. The only way a man survives in my cutthroat world is to keep one step ahead of his rivals.

"And here I thought you consider us to be as close as your blood relations?" Nikolai drawls. "Not that I'd want to be there. It's bad enough that I have to spend Christmas with my entire extended family, of which there are way too many people."

I turn to him, accepting the diversion in the conversation. I owe Nikolai for getting the bastard JJ's attention away from the topic of the Christmas party. *My wife's* Christmas party. If he thinks I am going to invite him to be anywhere within a mile of her, he has another think coming.

"Are you returning to Russia for Christmas?" I ask Nikolai.

"I'm going home," he nods.

"To Russia?"

"To Los Angeles," He scowls at me.

I raise my hands. "Apologies, when you said home, I just assumed —"

"Yeah," he snorts, "of course, the man with the foreign sounding surname has to be from an exotic land, eh?"

I redden. "An honest mistake," I murmur.

"You can make up for it by giving me control of the gun smuggling routes through Latin America."

"No chance," I smirk. "I am sorry, but not that sorry."

"What about the cybercrime syndicate you control?" JJ growls. "That's something we are —"

"Nope."

JJ frowns, "So, what's in it for me? Why should I agree to any kind of peace treaty?"

"Because it's the only way for you to grow your reach in the rest of Europe. I am the key to your expanding outside the UK, and you know it."

JJ's features harden, but he doesn't deny what I said outright. He can't, because I have pointed out his weakness. The reason that has brought him here to the negotiating table, in the back office of Paolo's restaurant. We, each of us, have left our men and teams behind. It's just the three of us at this table, and the talks so far have been interesting, to say the least.

"So," JJ leans back in his chair, "I repeat, what's in it for me?"

"Money, power —"

"What are you specifically offering me, Michael?"

I raise an eyebrow at his usage of my name. He's testing me by not using my title, calling me by my name and implying a familiarity which we don't share currently, nor at any point in the future, if I have my way.

"Real estate scams."

"Excuse me?" He blinks.

"Real estate," I murmur, "it's where there's lot of money to be made in Europe."

"You're kidding me, right?" He leans forward, his hard British accent growing more pronounced, "If this is why you called me all the way to a back office behind a smelly restaurant then—"

"Cryptocurrency," I throw out and he blinks again.

"Cryptocurrency?" he says slowly.

I nod, "The two of you…" I glance between the two clan leaders. "Partner with us in the deals we have going there. Nikolai, you bring the cyber experience. We bring the contacts of those at the highest echelons in the top 100 investment firms in Europe. JJ, you bring the contacts of those in the UK and together, we'll all be able to walk away much, much richer."

"Hmm," JJ strokes his chin, "how much richer?"

"Molto più ricco."

He frowns, "I'd prefer you be specific."

"Take a number, triple it, and I guarantee, the three of us will come into enough money to increase our sphere of influence on a global scale."

JJ's eyes gleam. His right eyelid twitches. He taps his fingers on the table, before he stops… And bingo, the guy is interested, all right. I turn to watch Nikolai surveying me with a shrewd look in his eyes.

"It's going to be a challenge," Niko murmurs. "No one knows exactly how cryptocurrency reacts to worldwide influences. Hell, we know far less about it than we know about the weather or the stock market. It's a big risk."

"The higher the risk…" I raise a shoulder.

"You getting cold feet, Solonik?" JJ smirks, "You can opt out of the deal. More for the two of us."

Nikolai's gaze narrows. He tilts his head, a question in his eyes, one he's not going to voice because he's not going to give away his hand. He's smart. I respect that. And he abides by the same kinds of laws that we do. Family first and last, and above all, keep your enemies close at hand. It's why he's sitting here at the negotiating table.

"Perhaps it's you who's getting cold feet at the thought of keeping pace with the both of us?" Niko murmurs.

JJ's features harden and a nerve throbs at his temple. "That's enough of pleasantries," he growls, then turns to me. "The money we make is split three ways."

"Sixty, twenty, twenty, is more what I had in mind—"

He opens his mouth to protest.

"But I can work with fifty, twenty-five, twenty-five," I add.

"Split three ways evenly," JJ snaps "and not a penny less."

"You think the same way, Nikolai?" I turn to him, "A three-way split, I presume."

Nikolai drums his fingers on his chest, "You know what they say about three being a crowd."

"Are you saying you are not interested?"

"I am..." he glances from me to JJ, then back at me, "interested."

"Well then," I knock my knuckles on the table, "gentlemen, let's drink to our new business partnership, shall we?"

The door opens and a woman walks in with a bottle of Macallans whiskey and three glasses. She retreats, but not before JJ has looked her up and down. "Part of your crew?" he asks, "Is she—"

"No," I pour out a shot of whiskey into each of the glasses before sliding one over to Nikolai. "She's part of my clan and off limits to anyone except her fiancé."

"Take care of your own, eh?"

I raise my glass, "Always."

JJ glances down, spies the glass still on the tray. He leans over and picks it up. "Now, that's not being very polite," he arches an eyebrow, "but to each their own." He raises his glass.

"I don't like this," Christian mutters.

After the two other men leave, the rest of my crew walks in. They hadn't been in favor of this meeting. Definitely not that I go in unarmed and without any of them as back up. But it was something that had to be done, and by me.

"What guarantee do we have that they don't renege on their agreement?" He scowls.

"What guarantee do we have that we are all going to be alive tomorrow?" I widen my stance from the position at the head of the table. I had opted to stand, too keyed-up from the earlier meeting. Normally, I wouldn't tolerate this kind of post-meeting analysis of my actions, but if the alliance with the rival clans is going to work, then I need my crew behind me... And currently, they, clearly, are not.

"That's a rhetorical question, and you know that." Christian runs a finger around the collar of his shirt. "Forming an alliance with the enemy is only going to come to bite you in the ass if we're not careful."

"Much as it pains me to admit it, in this instance, I agree with Christian." Seb glowers. "Nikolai, maybe, I understand. Not that I'd trust the

Bratva, but at least, they'd come at you from the front. With the Kane Company? Those asshole Brits are going to stab you in the back, make no mistake."

I roll my shoulders, glare at the faces around the table.

"You know I don't give a toss about your alliances," Massimo murmurs, "but in this case, I have to admit, I don't quite understand the reasoning behind this move. It reeks of desperation, Michael." He leans forward in his chair, "And that's not like you. You always plan each and every move. You strategize for months, sometimes years, before you decide to act. This time, you're just jumping in, without any due diligence." He drums his fingers on the table, "It's not like you, Michael."

"You're right," Xander drawls from where he's sprawled out in a chair in a far corner of the room.

"I am?" Massimo turns to him. "So, you agree that this is Michael acting out of character?"

"It is." He rises to his feet and prowls over to us. "This is not the Michael we know anymore."

I glare at Xander as he comes to a halt at the table.

"It's not?" Christian stares at his twin, "What the hell are you talking about?"

Seb curls his fingers into a fist, "Do you know something you haven't shared with us yet?"

"Maybe."

"This is not the time for one of your artistic jokes," Seb growls. "Not that I could ever understand them, but if you have to say something, then now is the time."

"Back off, Seb," Adrian says mildly. "Have you ever known Michael to do anything that could jeopardize our future?"

"I am afraid this time he has," Xander comes to a halt at the table.

I draw in a sharp breath, glance at him. "What are you trying to say, Alessandro?" I say in a soft voice.

"Just that you are no longer Michael, the Capo of the Cosa Nostra."

"I'm not?" I frown.

He nods, "You are a husband and a father-to-be, too... Roles which you, clearly, place a lot more importance on than just being the leader of our clan."

I blink, "If you mean I am neglecting my duties as the head of the clan—"

"I mean that you are taking a bigger picture into view. You are looking to the future, and for the first time, you are planning with peace in mind, rather than a short-sighed chance to gain the upper hand."

I rub the back of my neck, "Is that a backhanded compliment? If so—"

"It's not a compliment. It's a fact." He folds his arms across his chest. "You want to ensure that you neutralize any possible threats against your family. It's understandable. It's why you went ahead and met with two of our fiercest rivals. It's why you didn't breathe a word about it to anyone before-hand. You were going to do it anyway; nothing would have deterred you. And you know this is also for the good of all of us... Even though there is a very good chance that this tactic could backfire on all of us."

I lower my hands to my sides.

"So yes, you did put us all in jeopardy, but not without reason. And I, for one, support you in this tactic."

There's silence around the table. The rest of the guys turn to me. Seb and Christian wear twin expressions of surprise. Xander's lips stretch in a smile. Massimo looks like he is taking it all in. Adrian rises to his feet and walks over to me. "I am also with you. It's time to give peace a chance. If we can grow our business and do it without bloodshed, I am totally behind you."

"You are?"

"You bet." He holds up his hand and I fist bump him. "It couldn't have been an easy decision to make, Capo. It took guts to go through with it. Courage that you have. And while it could just as easily come back to haunt us, I am willing to give this tactic a chance."

Adrian backs away a few steps and stands behind me. He's the quiet one, but his loyalty is unshakeable. I admit, I have taken him for granted sometimes, but it's clear that when I need someone in my corner, Adrian will always be there.

Xander's face splits in a smile, "I am glad that Karma came along." He plants his palms on his hips, "You've been a changed man since you met her. Hell, sometimes I can't even recognize you anymore, and in a good way."

I scowl, "Now, *that* is definitely not a compliment, though I appreciate your sticking up for me, *fratellino*." I glance around at the rest of them, "You all do realize I don't need approval from any of you to go ahead with this alliance. But given a choice, I'd rather you be behind me, than not."

Christian rises to his feet. He rounds the table and grips my shoulder, "I can't claim to understand how it feels to know that you are about to have a child, but I get the rationale behind what you did. And in all honesty, I can say that I am for it."

Massimo raps his knuckles on the table, "Count me in, *fratellone,* I trust you to keep all of our interests at heart, with whatever action you take."

"And you, Seb?" I glance toward the man at the foot of the table. "As my possible successor what do you think?"

"I still wish there was another way out." He folds his arms across his chest, "I can't, in all fairness, say that I agree with this alliance, but," he raises a shoulder, "I understand why you did it. And I hope, for all our sakes, that it works out."

So, do I. I tilt my head, "Fair enough, Seb." I narrow my gaze on him, "You still owe me information."

"Luca," he exhales a breath.

I nod, "Your time is running out to track him down."

"He's being more elusive than I gave him credit for." Seb rubs the back of his neck. "Give me until Christmas to track him down, Capo."

"That's—"

"A week away," he murmurs.

"Seven more days," I look down at him, "and not a minute more."

39

Karma

It's six days to the Christmas party, and I am almost done with the projects I have undertaken. My dress is done. So is the other outfit I have been working on. My morning sickness is also almost gone. And if I have to stay another day cooped up in here, I am going to go stark, raving mad. Argh! Andy saunters over to me. He winds his way around my legs and purrs loudly. I scoop him up, pet him, but he glances the other way. He's one demanding cat. As demanding as the other man in my life... That is, he used to be demanding...and mean...and growly... And now? He's just grouchy.

Clearly, the lack of sex is getting to him. Since our tryst on the terrace, I have not seen him at all. If he does sleep at night... It, clearly, isn't in the bed next to me, as his side of the bed remains untouched when I awake in the mornings. He hasn't been in the room, as far as I can tell. Which means he is sleeping somewhere else. Likely, in his office at *Venom*. Is he also sleeping *with* someone else there? But he said that he wasn't fucking anyone else. That he wouldn't fuck anyone else. He wouldn't lie to me, would he? I tighten my fingers and Andy yowls in protest.

He flicks out his baby claws and I yelp as he scratches me. I release him and he jumps down to the floor, then walks away with his tail high in the air. I glance down at the streak of blood across the back of my palm. Shit! I walk over to the bathroom, and hold my hand under the running water at the sink. Then raise my hand to check the scratch. Blood begins to drip out again. Oh, damn. I reach for a tissue when, "What are you doing?" His voice interrupts me.

I yelp, lose my grip on the tissue which flutters to the ground. "You scared me," I mumble.

He prowls into the bathroom, wearing his well-fitted suit—all black, of course. With a tie that's blue enough to bring out the blue in his eyes. His jaw is clean-shaven, and when he leans in close, his dark, spicy scent envelops me. My nipples pebble and my belly flutters as he extends his hand. I draw in a breath, freeze, and he switches off the tap.

Jerk.

His lips curl in a smirk, then he glances down at the still-bleeding scratch on the back of my hand. His eyebrows draw down. "You're hurt?"

"It's only a scratch," I reply, "Andy… I may have scared him."

"If I had known that the cat was going to wound you—"

"Seriously, he barely broke the skin," I glare about, spot the tissue on the floor and go to pick it up.

"Leave it," he orders as he snatches up a fresh one. Then circles my wrist with his fingers and presses the tissue to the scratch. He presses down and I hiss out a breath. "Did that hurt?" He scowls at me.

"No," I lie.

He shoots me a glance and I redden, "Just a little, but it's nothing."

"Let me be the judge of that." He grabs another tissue, holds it over the previous one, then brings my other hand down on it, before lifting both to my chest. "Hold it there, above your heart, and apply pressure," he commands.

Before I can protest, he turns away. He reaches up to pull open a door near the sink, then pulls out a first-aid kit. He pulls out cotton balls, antiseptic, and bandages, lays them out near the sink, then turns to me. He throws away the bloodied tissues, then proceeds to dab the antiseptic onto the scratch. I wince and he blows on it to cool down the injured skin. Then he places a band-aid over it. "There," he steps back, " all done."

I glance down at the neatly bandaged wound. "Thanks," I murmur as he puts away the first-aid kit.

"Where have you been all these days?" I burst out when he straightens. "I haven't seen you at all."

"Did you miss me?" He smirks, and a ripple of heat runs down my spine. Man, that smirk of his... It's sooo hot. Even when he's being a jerk, it turns me on. Clearly, I am fighting a losing battle against his charm.

"Of course, not." I toss my head, "It's just colder at night when you are not in bed with me."

His grin widens, "So, I am just a substitute for an electric blanket, huh?"

"Yep," I nod, "that's all you are. A warm body to keep my toes from getting cold at night."

"And here I thought you had other uses for me."

"If you mean as a sperm donor, well, that ship has already sailed."

I scowl, and he chuckles. "You always have been able to match me word for word, wife."

Wife. Hell, I still can't get used to him calling me that. And he's been so tender to me, taking care of me. Tears prick the backs of my eyes. Oh, hell, and now these stupid pregnancy hormones have my insides all twisted up.

I turn my head away, but he catches my chin. "Hey," he murmurs, his voice soft, "what's this all about?"

"Nothing." I sniffle, "Everything. It all just seems too much."

"The party?" He frowns, "We can call it off."

"No, not the party," I respond. "I am looking forward to it. It's the one time I'll get to visit with other people, other than you or Cassandra or the occasional visit from Xander."

"Xander's been coming by, eh?" He scowls, "He hasn't been troubling you, has he?"

"Oh, please." I roll my eyes. "At least, he keeps me company, unlike his oldest brother who's, clearly, been avoiding me."

"I haven't been avoiding you."

"Oh?" I shoot him a look from under my eyelashes, "So you haven't been keeping away from me over the last week."

He has the grace to flush. "M-a-y-b-e." He shuffles his feet.

"See?" I point my finger at him, "I knew it." I pivot away from him and walk toward the door.

"Beauty?" he calls out and I ignore him. I reach the doorway of the bathroom and step out, then cross the floor.

"Stop," he commands.

"Oh, F' off," I hold my middle finger up, above my shoulder, head for the door to the room.

"Karma!" He commands, "Stop."

I freeze. Damn, I want to disobey him, but of course, my body responds to his orders. It's as if he has a direct line of communication to the most primal part of me that will bend to his every will. Damn it. And soon, I'll have a child and he won't need me anymore. Then what? Will he keep me imprisoned here for the rest of my life? Hidden away for fear of his enemies getting to me? Despite the fact that he, clearly, has feelings for me, he hasn't even been able to tell me that he loves me. And damn it, I hate these histrionics. I am used to fending for myself, to finding my way out of tough spots. But the very fact that he is there for me, has weakened me. He's coddled me, and turned me into this blubbering mess who I don't recognize anymore, frankly.

More tears squeeze out from the corners of my eyes as I hear his footsteps approach. "Hey," he steps around, and notches his knuckles under my chin. "Don't cry, *Bellezza*," he murmurs. "Please don't. When I see your tears, I swear, it hurts me so fucking much."

"Does it?" I sniff.

"You bet." He drags his thumb across my lower lip, "I'd kill anyone who caused you pain, my Beauty. I'd change anything to see you smile again."

"Would you?" I peer up at him.

"No doubt about it."

"A car."

"What?"

"I want a car and I want lessons to learn to drive it, so I can drive myself around the city."

"No way." He lowers his hand and steps away. "No fucking way, am I allowing you out on your own."

"I'll be in a car, Mika," I snap. "Surely, that would be safe. Besides, I don't know how to drive yet—"

"You don't know how to drive?"

I shake my head.

"How do you not know how to drive?"

"Because I grew up in a city with good transport links so I never needed to learn how to drive. Also," I scowl, "I didn't exactly have an overabundance of money so I could buy a car, you know?"

"So why do you want a car, if you don't know how to drive?"

"So I can learn how to drive?"

He shakes his head, "Your logic, as always, is irrefutable."

"Thank you," I mutter. "So can I get a car?"

He seems like he is about to refuse.

"Please, Mika, please," I wheedle. "It would, at least, give me an illusion of being in control, and I'd love to have some semblance of freedom."

"Hmm." He scowls.

"Also, surely, being stuck in here is not good for my mental health. And I do need to stay happy if I want the kid to be born healthy, right?"

He blows out a breath, "Fine."

"Yay!" I throw my arms about his neck, and rise up on tip-toe to kiss him.

"On one condition."

I pause before my lips touch his, "What?" I scowl, "What is it?"

"I'll teach you how to drive."

"You are too busy," I roll my eyes. "I mean, I'd love for you to teach me, but seriously, when have you been able to tear yourself away from your work to spend time with me?"

"You're more important than any job," he retorts.

"Really?"

"Have I ever given you reason to doubt that?"

"Umm, yeah?" I scoff. "I mean, if I'm more important, wouldn't you have spent more time with me over the last month?"

"That was only so I could keep distance between us so I wasn't tempted to—"

"I know," I say hastily, "Still, you have to admit, from where I am, it seems that your work takes priority."

"Well, I am going to prove to you that it doesn't." He grips my cheek, "Tomorrow, after lunch, be ready."

40

Karma

At least, last night, he had come to bed at midnight, and I had woken up enough to wrap myself around my husband and fall asleep. He'd kissed me tenderly, had run his hands down my body, aroused me to fever pitch, only to slip my nightgown and my panties aside and slide his fingers into me. He'd slid down my body, eaten me out, then he'd risen over me and pinched my clit as he'd commanded me to come. And I had. I had shattered right there, and then, promptly fallen asleep, sated.

It was almost noon when I woke up to find a letter on his pillow, asking me to peek out of the window. I had, and had cried out when I had seen a car... Not just any car, a Maserati. A twin of his...but in black, with a red line running across its side, and wrapped up in a bow. It's my car. My car! OMG! I had showered, changed, eaten a late breakfast, then rushed down to examine my new toy.

It is beautiful, with sleek lines that remind me of him, a color dark enough to hint at his growly personality, and a motor under the hood that is powerful enough to outpace any other car on the road. A bit like him, really... And also, like me, if I am being honest. It's a twin of his car, and he sees me as his equal enough to gift it to me.

Now, I stand staring at it when my phone rings. I glance at the screen then answer it, "Hey," I say softly.

"Hey, yourself." His deep voice sends shivers down my back. "What do you think?"

"What do I think of what?"

"You know what," he laughs, "do you like it?"

"I… I love it," I blubber as a tear streaks down my cheek. "When are you coming to teach me how to drive it?"

"About that, ah," he sighs, "something came up."

"Knew it," I hunch my shoulders. "So, you can't come?"

"I can't, but Xander will."

"But I wanted to have the first lesson with you."

"I know, baby," he murmurs. "I am so sorry, but I'll make it up to you."

I hang up, and am about to turn away, when a Ferrari drives up. A red Ferrari that screeches to a halt right behind the Maserati. Xander pushes open the door and steps out. He swaggers over to me and I burst out laughing. "Oh, my god, you sure do know how to make an entrance."

"Nice wheels, eh?" He flicks a satisfied glance over his shoulder, "Not that yours isn't almost as good..."

"Almost, eh?" I chortle as he runs his finger down the lines of the Maserati. "Nice one, what say we inaugurate this baby, eh?"

I laugh, "Well, why not?" The last thing I want to do is go back inside and hide myself away, moping. Not when I really, really do want to drive this car. And I do want to learn how to drive. That is one more step toward leading some kind of a normal life… Or as normal as it can be, being the wife of a Capo.

I step forward, grab hold of the ribbon that's stretched across the car, and pull at it. It falls away and I walk around to the driver's seat. I step in and Xander slides in from the other side.

"Ready?" He turns to me, "First, let's adjust the seat so you are able to reach for the accelerator and the brake with ease." He helps me do so, then sets about pointing out the pedals for the accelerator and the brake, as well as the various buttons on the dash all of which seems like an exact twin to the one I had seen in Mika's car. But really, when you have to operate it, it becomes an entirely new ball game. "This is an automatic car, so it's really very easy."

He shows me how to adjust the mirrors, then points out the additional buttons on the console for the headlights, the wipers on the windshield, the taillights, the buttons to be used to signal that I am going to turn, etcetera.

He makes me run through the entire routine twice. Then, when he is satisfied that I know my way around the console, he leans back. "Well, that was the first lesson."

"What?" I stare, "It's over already?"

"Yep."

"But I want to take the car out."

"You never do that on the first lesson."

"But I want to," I scowl and he laughs.

"Just kidding, let's do it."

"Ass." I swipe at his shoulder. Xander is every bit the brother I never had.

I reach for the ignition button when a movement catches my attention from the corner of my gaze. I look up to find my husband's Maserati screeching to a halt in front of us. He shoves open the door and jumps out. Michael isn't wearing his suit jacket and his tie is askew. He races toward us.

"What is he doing here?" Xander scowls.

Michael raises his arm. I see his mouth move. I am not sure what he's trying to say, but I want to show him how much I love this car, and how I am already able to drive it.

Xander turns to me, his face pale. "Don't do it," he yells, but I've already touched the ignition button. For a second nothing happens, then the entire car seems to erupt.

I glance up, see Michael's face, as if from a distance, then everything goes dark.

To find out what happens next read Mafia War HERE

Read an excerpt from Summer & Sinclair's story in The Billionaire's Fake Wife

Summer

"Slap, slap, kiss, kiss."

"Huh?" I stare up at the bartender.

"Aka, there's a thin line between love and hate." He shakes out the crimson liquid into my glass.

"Nah." I snort. "Why would she allow him to control her, and after he insulted her?"

"It's the chemistry between them." He lowers his head, "You have to admit that when the man is arrogant and the woman resists, it's a challenge to both of them, to see who blinks first, huh?"

"Why?" I wave my hand in the air, "Because they hate each other?"

"Because," he chuckles, "the girl in school whose braids I pulled and teased mercilessly, is the one who I —"

"Proposed to?" I huff.

His face lights up. "You get it now?"

Yeah. No. A headache begins to pound at my temples. This crash course in pop psychology is not why I came to my favorite bar in Islington, to meet my best friend, who is — I glance at the face of my phone — thirty minutes late.

I inhale the drink, and his eyebrows rise.

"What?" I glower up at the bartender. "I can barely taste the alcohol. Besides, it's free drinks at happy hour for women, right?"

"Which ends in precisely" he holds up five fingers, "minutes."

"Oh! Yay!" I mock fist pump. "Time enough for one more, at least."

A hiccough swells my throat and I swallow it back, nod.

One has to do what one has to do… when everything else in the world is going to shit.

A hot sensation stabs behind my eyes; my chest tightens. Is this what people call growing up?

The bartender tips his mixing flask, strains out a fresh batch of the ruby red liquid onto the glass in front of me.

"Salut." I nod my thanks, then toss it back. It hits my stomach and tendrils of fire crawl up my spine, I cough.

My head spins. Warmth sears my chest, spreads to my extremities. I can't feel my fingers or toes. Good. Almost there. "Top me up."

"You sure?"

"Yes." I square my shoulders and reach for the drink.

"No. She's had enough."

"What the —?" I pivot on the bar stool.

Indigo eyes bore into me.

Fathomless. Black at the bottom, the intensity in their depths grips me. He swoops out his arm, grabs the glass and holds it up. Thick fingers dwarf the glass. Tapered at the edges. The nails short and buff. *All the better to grab you with.* I gulp.

"Like what you see?"

I flush, peer up into his face.

Hard cheekbones, hollows under them, and a tiny scar that slashes at his left eyebrow. *How did he get that?* Not that I care. My gaze slides to his mouth. Thin upper lip, a lower lip that is full and cushioned. Pouty with a hint of bad boy. *Oh!* My toes curl. My thighs clench.

The corner of his mouth kicks up. *Asshole.*

Bet he thinks life is one big smug-fest. I glower, reach for my glass, and he holds it up and out of my reach.

I scowl, "Gimme that."

He shakes his head.

"That's my drink."

"Not anymore." He shoves my glass at the bartender. "Water for her. Get me a whiskey, neat."

I splutter, then reach for my drink again. The barstool tips, in his direction. This is when I fall against him, and my breasts slam into his hard chest, sculpted planes with layers upon layers of muscle that ripple and writhe as he turns aside, flattens himself against the bar. The floor rises up to meet me.

What the actual hell?

I twist my torso at the last second and my butt connects with the surface. *Ow!*

The breath rushes out of me. My hair swirls around my face. I scrabble for purchase, and my knee connects with his leg.

"Watch it." He steps around, stands in front of me.

"You stepped aside?" I splutter. "You let me fall?"

"Hmph."

I tilt my chin back, all the way back, look up the expanse of muscled thigh that stretches the silken material of his suit. *What is he wearing? Could any suit fit a man with such precision?* Hand crafted on Saville Row, no doubt. I glance at the bulge that tents the fabric between his legs. *Oh!* I blink.

Look away, look away. I hold out my arm. He'll help me up at least, won't he?

He glances at my palm, then turns away. *No, he didn't do that, no way.*

A glass of amber liquid appears in front of him. He lifts the tumbler to his sculpted mouth.

His throat moves, strong tendons flexing. He tilts his head back, and the column of his neck moves as he swallows. Dark hair covers his chin —it's a discordant chord in that clean-cut profile, I shiver. He would scrape that rough skin down my core. He'd mark my inner thigh, lick my core, thrust his tongue inside my melting channel and drink from my pussy. *Oh! God.* Goosebumps rise on my skin.

No one has the right to look this beautiful, this achingly gorgeous. Too magnificent for his own good. Anger coils in my chest.

"Arrogant wanker."

"I'll take that under advisement."

"You're a jerk, you know that?"

He presses his lips together. The grooves on either side of his mouth deepen. Jesus, clearly the man has never laughed a single day in his life. Bet that stick up his arse is uncomfortable. I chuckle.

He runs his gaze down my features, my chest, down to my toes, then yawns.

The hell! I will not let him provoke me. Will not. "Like what you see?" I jut out my chin.

"Sorry, you're not my type." He slides a hand into the pocket of those perfectly cut pants, stretching it across that heavy bulge.

Heat curls low in my belly.

Not fair, that he could afford a wardrobe that clearly shouts his status and what amounts to the economy of a small third-world country. A hot feeling stabs in my chest.

He reeks of privilege, of taking his status in life for granted.

While I've had to fight every inch of the way. Hell, I am still battling to hold onto the last of my equilibrium.

"Last chance —" I wiggle my fingers, from where I am sprawled out on the floor at his feet, "—to redeem yourself..."

"You have me there." He places the glass on the counter, then bends and holds out his hand. The hint of discolored steel at his wrist catches my attention. Huh?

He wears a cheap-ass watch?

That's got to bring down the net worth of his presence by more than 1000% percent. Weird.

I reach up and he straightens.

I lurch back.

"Oops, I changed my mind." His lips curl.

A hot burning sensation claws at my stomach. I am not a violent person, honestly. But Smirky Pants here, he needs to be taught a lesson.

I swipe out my legs, kicking his out from under him.

Sinclair

My knees give way, and I hurtle toward the ground.

What the—? I twist around, thrust out my arms. My palms hit the floor. The impact jostles up my elbows. I firm my biceps and come to a halt planked above her.

A huffing sound fills my ear.

I turn to find my whippet, Max, panting with his mouth open. I scowl and he flattens his ears.

All of my businesses are dog-friendly. Before you draw conclusions about me being the caring sort or some such shit—it attracts footfall.

Max scrutinizes the girl, then glances at me. *Huh?* He hates women, but not her, apparently.

I straighten and my nose grazes hers.

My arms are on either side of her head. Her chest heaves. The fabric of her dress stretches across her gorgeous breasts. My fingers tingle; my palms ache to cup those tits, squeeze those hard nipples outlined against the—hold on, what is she wearing? A tunic shirt in a sparkly pink... and are those shoulder pads she has on?

I glance up, and a squeak escapes her lips.

Pink hair surrounds her face. *Pink? Who dyes their hair that color past the age of eighteen?*

I stare at her face. *How old is she?* Un-furrowed forehead, dark eyelashes that flutter against pale cheeks. Tiny nose, and that mouth—luscious, tempting. A whiff of her scent, cherries and caramel, assails my senses. My mouth waters. *What the hell?*

She opens her eyes and our eyelashes brush. Her gaze widens. Green, like the leaves of the evergreens, flickers of gold sparkling in their depths. "What?" She glowers. "You're demonstrating the plank position?"

"Actually," I lower my weight onto her, the ridge of my hardness thrusting into the softness between her legs, "I was thinking of something else, altogether."

She gulps and her pupils dilate. *Ah, so she feels it, too?*

I drop my head toward her, closer, closer.

Color floods the creamy expanse of her neck. Her eyelids flutter down. She tilts her chin up.

I push up and off of her.

"That… Sweetheart, is an emphatic 'no thank you' to whatever you are offering."

Her eyelids spring open and pink stains her cheeks. Adorable. Such a range of emotions across those gorgeous features in a few seconds? What else is hidden under that exquisite exterior of hers?

She scrambles up, eyes blazing.

Ah! The little bird is trying to spread her wings? My dick twitches. My groin hardens, *Why does her anger turn me on so, huh?*

She steps forward, thrusts a finger in my chest.

My heart begins to thud.

She peers up from under those hooded eyelashes. "Wake up and taste the wasabi, asshole."

"What does that even mean?"

She makes a sound deep in her throat. My dick twitches. My pulse speeds up.

She pivots, grabs a half-full beer mug sitting on the bar counter.

I growl, "Oh, no, you don't."

She turns, swings it at me. The smell of hops envelops the space.

I stare down at the beer-splattered shirt, the lapels of my camel colored jacket deepening to a dull brown. Anger squeezes my guts.

I fist my fingers at my side, broaden my stance.

She snickers.

I tip my chin up. "You're going to regret that."

The smile fades from her face. "Umm." She places the now empty mug on the bar.

I take a step forward and she skitters back. "It's only clothes." She gulps, "They'll wash."

I glare at her and she swallows, wiggles her fingers in the air, "I should have known that you wouldn't have a sense of humor."

I thrust out my jaw, "That's a ten-thousand-pound suit you destroyed."

She blanches, then straightens her shoulders, "Must have been some hot date you were trying to impress, huh?"

"Actually," I flick some of the offending liquid from my lapels, "it's you I was after."

"Me?" She frowns.

"We need to speak."

She glances toward the bartender who's on the other side of the bar. "I don't know you." She chews on her lower lip, biting off some of the hot pink. How would she look, with that pouty mouth fastened on my cock?

The blood rushes to my groin so quickly that my head spins. My pulse rate ratchets up. Focus, focus on the task you came here for.

"This will take only a few seconds." I take a step forward.

She moves aside.

I frown, "You want to hear this, I promise."

"Go to hell." She pivots and darts forward.

I let her go, a step, another, because... I can? Besides it's fun to create the illusion of freedom first; makes the hunt so much more entertaining, huh?

I swoop forward, loop an arm around her waist, and yank her toward me.

She yelps. "Release me."

Good thing the bar is not yet full. It's too early for the usual office-goers to stop by. And the staff...? Well they are well aware of who cuts their paychecks.

I spin her around and against the bar, then release her. "You will listen to me."

She swallows; she glances left to right.

Not letting you go yet, little Bird. I move into her space, crowd her.

She tips her chin up. "Whatever you're selling, I'm not interested."

I allow my lips to curl, "You don't fool me."

A flush steals up her throat, sears her cheeks. So tiny, so innocent. Such a good little liar. I narrow my gaze, "Every action has its consequences."

"Are you daft?" She blinks.

"This pretense of yours?" I thrust my face into hers, "It's not working."

She blinks, then color suffuses her cheeks, "You're certifiably mad—"

"Getting tired of your insults."

"It's true, everything I said." She scrapes back the hair from her face.

Her fingernails are painted... You guessed it, pink.

"And here's something else. You are a selfish, egotistical jackass."

I smirk. "You're beginning to repeat your insults and I haven't even kissed you yet."

"Don't you dare." She gulps.

I tilt my head, "Is that a challenge?"

"It's a..." she scans the crowded space, then turns to me. Her lips firm, "...a warning. You're delusional, you jackass." She inhales a deep breath, "Your ego is bigger than the size of a black hole." She snickers, "Bet it's to compensate for your lack of balls."

A-n-d, that's it. I've had enough of her mouth that threatens to never stop spewing words. How many insults can one tiny woman hurl my way? Answer: too many to count.

"You—"

I lower my chin, touch my lips to hers.

Heat, sweetness, the honey of her essence explodes on my palate. My dick twitches. I tilt my head, deepen the kiss, reaching for that something more... more... of whatever scent she's wearing on her skin, infused with that breath of hers that crowds my senses, rushes down my spine. My groin hardens; my cock lengthens. I thrust my tongue between those infuriating lips.

She makes a sound deep in her throat and my heart begins to pound.

So innocent, yet so crafty. Beautiful and feisty. The kind of complication I don't need in my life.

I prefer the straight and narrow. Gray and black, that's how I choose to define my world. She, with her flashes of color—pink hair and lips that threaten to drive me to the edge of distraction—is exactly what I hate.

Give me a female who has her priorities set in life. To pleasure me, get me off, then walk away before her emotions engage. Yeah. That's what I prefer.

Not this... this bundle of craziness who flings her arms around my shoulders, thrusts her breasts up and into my chest, tips up her chin, opens her mouth, and invites me to take and take.

Does she have no self-preservation? Does she think I am going to fall for her wide-eyed appeal? She has another thing coming.

I tear my mouth away and she protests.

She twines her leg with mine, pushes up her hips, so that melting softness between her thighs cradles my aching hardness.

I glare into her face and she holds my gaze.

Trains her green eyes on me. Her cheeks flush a bright red. Her lips fall open and a moan bleeds into the air. The blood rushes to my dick, which instantly thickens. *Fuck.*

Time to put distance between myself and the situation.

It's how I prefer to manage things. Stay in control, always. Cut out anything that threatens to impinge on my equilibrium. Shut it down or buy them off. Reduce it to a transaction. That I understand.

The power of money, to be able to buy and sell—numbers, logic. That's what's worked for me so far.

"How much?"

Her forehead furrows.

"Whatever it is, I can afford it."

Her jaw slackens. "You think… you—"

"A million?"

"What?"

"Pounds, dollars… You name the currency, and it will be in your account."

Her jaw slackens, "You're offering me money?"

"For your time, and for you to fall in line with my plan."

She reddens, "You think I am for sale?"

"Everyone is."

"Not me."

Here we go again. "Is that a challenge?"

Color fades from her face, "Get away from me."

"Are you shy, is that what this is?" I frown. "You can write your price down on a piece of paper if you prefer," I glance up, notice the bartender watching us. I jerk my chin toward the napkins. He grabs one, then offers it to her.

She glowers at him, "Did you buy him too?"

"What do you think?"

She glances around, "I think everyone here is ignoring us."

"It's what I'd expect."

"Why is that?"

I wave the tissue in front of her face, "Why do you think?"

"You own the place?"

"As I am going to own you."

She sets her jaw, "Let me leave and you won't regret this."

A chuckle bubbles up. I swallow it away. This is no laughing matter.

I never smile during a transaction. Especially not when I am negotiating a new acquisition. And that's all she is. The final piece in the puzzle I am building.

"No one threatens me."

"You're right."

"Huh?"

"I'd rather act on my instinct."

Her lips twist, her gaze narrows. All of my senses scream a warning.

No, she wouldn't, no way—pain slices through my middle and sparks explode behind my eyes.

To find out what happens next get The Billionaire's Fake Wife HERE

Read about the seven in the Big bad Billionaires series

US

UK

Other countries

Join L. Steele's Newsletter for news on her newest releases

Claim your FREE copy of Mafia Heir the prequel to Mafia King

Claim your FREE billionaire romance

Claim your free paranormal romance

Follow L. Steele on AMAZON

Follow L. Steele on BookBub

Follow L. Steele on Goodreads

Follow L. Steele on Facebook

Follow L. Steele on Instagram

Join L. Steele's secret Facebook Reader Group

More books by L. Steele HERE

FREE BOOKS

CLAIM YOUR FREE COPY OF MAFIA HEIR THE PREQUEL TO MAFIA KING
CLAIM YOUR FREE BILLIONAIRE ROMANCE
CLAIM YOUR FREE PARANORMAL ROMANCE BOOK HERE
MORE BOOKS BY L. STEELE
MORE BOOKS BY LAXMI

Made in the USA
Monee, IL
26 April 2024

57556016R00134